Theodore R. McCormick

Post Mortem Blues

Darker Intentions Press

Published by
DARKER INTENTIONS PRESS
POB 569
Freehold Township, New Jersey 07728-0569

Printed in the United States of America

ISBN:0-9769612-0

For more information on Darker Intentions Press, please visit us on the Web at: www.darkerintentionspress.com Or contact jzdakota@hotmail.com

Morgue Photography
by Scott Bowlin of Steelcoast Creative
www.steelcoast.com

"Elderly Eyes" Photo by Anita of Tartumaa, Estonia

ACKNOWLEDGMENTS

I would like to thank Dr. Tien Lau, M.D. of Johns Hopkins for his assistance on the medical aspects of this story. I would also like to thank my dear friend, former prosecutor Marilyn Goceliak Zbobinski, Esquire for her invaluable assistance and experience in the criminal aspects of the case. Finally, I would also like to thank fellow author J. Reccoppa and my friend, M. Narayanan who help keep the inspiration going.

"Either that guy is dead or else my watch has stopped."

Groucho Marx

Chapter 1

APRIL FOOL'S DAY, 1988
PARAMUS, NEW JERSEY
7:45 A.M.

"Morty? Did you turn off the Mister Coffee?" An impatient woman with spongy pink hair rollers yelled to her husband as he stood in the hallway.

"Yeah, Roz, I did."

"Mort are you sure? I smell coffee. Burnt coffee."

"Aw Roz, cut me a break."

Ignoring his wife's demands, Mortimer Hopmyer grabbed his New York Post, and trotted off to the bathroom. What a fine morning it was! No grandkids around. His wife hadn't given him a "Honeydo list." It was a perfect moment to have eye sex with the Post's sports page as his cotton boxers dangled around his ankles. Morty wouldn't have to yell, "I'm in here!" or "Be out in a minute!" Total bathroom privacy — the operative word of Morty's day. As he made his way to the downstairs bathroom, he would greet his "other family."

His lawn, second only to his children and cheap beer, was his true love. When his intestinal alarm clock rang every morning at eight, the retired dentist passed through his living room and gazed at his manicured landscape, organized in a way only Martha Stewart could appreciate. From a window, he saluted the maroon colored Japanese maples, the arborvitae, and the flower beds, before entering the Kingdom of the American Standard with its soft padded throne.

Furthest from his mind was the coffee pot, its syrupy dregs cooking away on a burner. His seventy year old bowels commanded priority. But as Morty looked out the window, his eyes focused on something else.

"What the hell — " he screamed.

At the edge of Willow Court's cul-de-sac, Morty saw a Mercedes Sedan moving backwards in circles. Each time the car closed in on the Hopmyer property, the rear tire slammed up the curb, recklessly cutting across a sliver of his lawn. He watched in abject horror as the front tire bumped back down onto the macadam, circling the street again and again. Tread marks flattened his single blade, weed-free Kentucky fescue, sending the retiree into a tailspin. His little green babies were being systematically slaughtered, their tiny chemically cultivated lives squashed flat. It was more than the old man could take.

"You lousy bastard! Sonavabitch! Get off my lawn!" He screamed from inside the house. Throwing down his newspaper, Morty bolted out the front door and ran to the street. He barely missed being run down by the car.

"Shut down your lousy stinkin' car and get off my grass!" Morty shook his fist again at the arrogant driver, unaware that the driver was in no condition to respond. The car crashed up the curb for another assault on Morty's lawn. With a raised middle finger, he bent down to get a better look at the lawn killer who ignored him. When he saw the driver, he yelled to his wife.

"Holy God! Roz, Roz! Get my gun! Quick! Get my gun!" Roz Hopmyer appeared at the door in her robe and hair curlers. Irritated, she wanted to see why her husband stood in the middle of their front yard in his underwear. On her way out, Roz shut off the Mister Coffee.

"Dammit, Morty, you burnt another coffee pot!"

"Forget the goddamn coffee pot!"

"What's going on?"

"Just get my gun!"

"For what do you need your gun for? Morty, have you lost your mind?" She joined her husband. Despite her arthritis, Roz bent over to get a better look inside the car. The couple saw a man – or what was left of him.

"Oh my God, Morty! Look!"

Each time the car passed the stunned couple, they were able to see a little more. The first pass showed limp, dangling arms and a torso slumped over the steering wheel. In the second pass, Morty and Roz caught a glimpse of a three quarter head – the entire rear quarter was missing. The third view displayed a sad set of dead eyes.

A bloody corpse piloted the automobile.

"Outta my way Roz! This is man's work!"

While his wife stared in shock, Morty ran back into house. Seconds later, he returned with a loaded revolver.

"My God Morty, what are you going to do? Shoot that poor man *again*?"

"Do you think he cares? He's dead for Pete's sake!" He cocked the revolver. "Watch this, Rozzie. I will disable the car with just one shot, just like in the movies." He aimed the loaded revolver at the tires of circumambulating Mercedes. Closing one eye, he squeezed the trigger, proudly pumping an entire round of bullets into the tires.

Nothing. Less than nothing. Morty only succeeded in deflating the rear left wheel. He hadn't planned on steel belted radials.

"Roz, get me more bullets!" he barked.

"I won't. I'm calling the police!"

She didn't have to. Within seconds a police cruiser screamed around the corner with an ambulance tailgating it. The uniforms jumped out of their cars and raised their service revolvers at the knobby-kneed old man.

"You in the underwear! Drop the gun and put your hands in the air!"

"Morty, you knucklehead! They're going to think you did this!" Roz shrieked.

"Officer! I am a citizen merely trying to protect my family. I tried to shoot out the tires. There's a dead guy driving the car! Don't you people keep track of the dead?"

No one noticed the unmarked police vehicle trailing the ambulance. Morty was just about to launch into the "where's a cop when you need one" speech, when another man did what Mort Hopmyer couldn't do, even at the age of twenty.

Mo Rodriguez, a detective from the Bergen County Homicide Unit, took control of the situation before someone got hurt.

For five foot eight, Moraimo Rodriguez was cat foot light on his feet. The muscular, sandy haired detective dove on the roof of the moving vehicle. Punching in the window on the passenger's side, he dumped all one hundred ninety pounds of him through the window and into the car. Just as the Mercedes was about to slam over the grass again, Mo yanked on the handbrake, forcing the car to a screeching halt. The sudden break in momentum caused the slumping corpse to jolt upward right before it lurched over the police officer. Draping its arms across Mo, he found himself in a dead man's bloody embrace.

"*Tu Madre*! Get off me!" He pushed the body back into the driver's seat. Quickly, Mo's eyes scanned the inside of the car. The lamb's wool seat cover beneath the corpse acted like a giant sponge, absorbing a lot of blood. A skull fragment, bits of gray matter, and a piece of bloody tissue, lay on the back seat. Blood splatters were everywhere. Mo went eye-to-eye with the dead man.

BAM! A close contact shot right between the corpse's eyes made the man look like a Cyclops.

"Aw, shit." Mo Rodriguez shook his head. "It's going to be a long morning." He opened the car door and gestured to a friend.

"Lieutenant Miller, come over here. You got to see this." Ever so gently he turned off the engine and stepped out of the car. "Eighteen years on the job. I ain't never seen a self propelled stiff." Disgustedly, he pointed to the new blood stain on his overcoat. "See this? This just came back from the cleaners from the last homicide. I can't win." The cop smiled back.

Feeling safe because of a police presence, people emerged from their homes to see the morning's oddity: an old gunslinger in his Fruit of the Looms and a man driving *post mortem*.

"What should I do with Wyatt Earp over here?" Miller asked, pointing to the old man.

"Take a statement from him and get the other people back in their houses. This isn't a good time for a parade."

"Is the medical examiner here, yet?" Mo asked looking through the small crowd.

A uniform standing nearby yawned. "Excuse me, Detective. It's not the company. Double shift. Ah, look. Here comes Dr. Handsome now."

Enter Dr. Thomas Clarefield, the Bergen County Medical Examiner with his criminalist team. From the look on his face, he wasn't happy. The homicide call probably cut short a perfectly good lovemaking session with a former charge nurse. Removing his sunglasses, he stepped into the circle of cops and announced his own arrival.

"So guys, what's up? Do we know who the dead guy is?" The flamboyant medical examiner turned around. "Hello Moraimo. Good to see you."

"Yeah. Hope we didn't disturb your tanning session." Mo Rodriguez actually *liked* Thomas Clarefield, but he never lost the opportunity to show his disdain for the nouveau riche. Having grown up in New Jersey's finest public housing disguised as a garden apartment, it was the *riche* part of people that always annoyed him.

"I wasn't getting tanned. I was engaged in lewd acts when you beeped me." He put on his latex examining gloves with a surgeon's panache, as he brushed back his dark mane. "Here. Take these." He tossed the detective a pair of gloves. Mo and Doc Clarefield started walking toward the Mercedes.

"You know, it's weird, Tommy. As many times as we've done this dance, I always feel angst when I first see the corpse."

"Angst? You sure it's not gas?

"Very funny."

"Talk to me, Mo."

"Weird scene. Gunshot. Apparently, the car was going backwards in circles. The old rodeo cowboy over there tried to shoot out the tires. When I got here, I did one of my Starsky and Hutch routines, jumped inside Benz and pulled

4

up the emergency brake."

"Jumping on the hoods of moving vehicles. Stunt man stuff. Impressive. You can still move like an adolescent jackrabbit even at forty."

"Aw, shut up."

A uniform met them half way over to the car. "Hey Mo. We got some i.d. from the glove compartment. You're never going to believe this."

"Try me. Who is he?"

He opened the wallet and pulled out a Bergen County Bar Association membership card and a driver's license. "He's a lawyer, Terence McShand, Esq. Lives in Upper Saddle River."

"A dead lawyer? Why is that such a surprise? People hate lawyers."

The uniform ignored the remark and continued probing the wallet. He handed Mo a driver's license. "Born in '41, makes him about forty seven. President of the Real Estate section of the New Jersey Bar Association. Looks like he's married. Pictures of kids in his wallet."

"Was married. Doc, you want to take him down the road?"

"Do I have a choice? Don't notify the family until I've examined him in the morgue." Clarefield ordered.

The medical examiner took a few steps back to take in the whole scene. When they reached the car, the body was still propped behind the steering wheel. While cops yelled at curious onlookers, someone covered the door of the Mercedes with an opaque blue plastic sheet, providing a last bit of privacy for Terence McShand before the medical examiner dissected him like a lab rat.

Nonchalantly, Clarefield peeled backed the blue covering. As he poked around the body, he dictated run-on sentences into a tape recorder. A young coroner-in-training stood by his side, taking copious notes.

"Let's see, we have Mr. Terence McShand, a lawyer, quite dead, shot at point blank range through the forehead, the projectile appears to have entered through the frontal lobe expelling massive amounts of brain tissue through the occipital lobe. Can we get a temperature on the body, please? Thank you. Looks like we have some flash powder burns around the forehead, and I will —". The medical examiner's eyes widened a bit.

"Hell-o. What's this? Mo, come here a minute." Dr. Clarefield and Mo leaned over the body. Gently, the doctor's fingers pulled back the collar of the dead lawyer's shirt. A thin blue-black line comprised of broken blood vessels with tiny, tree-like branches circled Terence McShand's neck like a macabre necklace. Dr. Clarefield gently ran his fingers around the corpse's neck to see where it both began and ended. Then he pinched the corpse's nose as he opened its mouth.

"Look here. He's missing a piece of his tongue. Oh, wait. I think I found something." The doctor opened a small specimen container and picked up a small piece of flesh. "Okay, I found the tongue tip, I think. Now check this out. There's two bruises, probably knuckle impressions, toward the back of the neck. A garrote, Spanish Inquisition style minus the iron collar. I've seen enough here. Let's get him down to the morgue."

#

"Yes, that's him."

An attractive, petite green eyed blond with a head full of frosted highlights stood behind a glass window. Mo nodded as Doc Clarefield shut the blind on the morgue window. Mrs. Inez McShand grabbed the detective's hand, jamming her nails into his palm.

"Why? Who would do this? He was a good man. He was a good father." Mo shook his head and gently released her grip.

"Mrs. McShand, I don't know. I'm sorry. Take it easy."

"You said he was strangled first?"

"Well, that's what we believe. We also found something on him that was kinda strange. Would you mind taking a look at this necklace we found on your husband's body?"

Mrs. McShand nodded. Clasping her hands over her mouth, she squinted several times suppressing the tears about to pour out of her eyes. Using latex gloves, he pulled the object out of a bag, and showed it to the distraught widow.

"I'll have to ask you not to touch it. Have you ever seen this before?"

He showed her a silver, man-in-the-moon medallion suspended on a black satin cord. The moon's face had a long ski slope nose and a curious half grin, obviously a moon that kept secrets. On the reverse side, was a pentagram and a series of stick lines resembling strange lettering.

The woman started sobbing. "No I haven't. Wh-what is this thing? We're Christian, this looks like devil worship."

"Mrs. McShand, I don't mean to pry, but was your husband involved in the occult?"

"No, no never." She placed her hands on her stomach.   "P l e a s e take this away. I feel sick."

"Would you like sit down?"

"Thank you."

Mo knew the woman was in pain, but he prodded one more time. He had to ask the hard questions. "Is there any reason your husband would be in Paramus at quarter to eight in the morning?"

She dried her eyes, trying to hide her grief. "He wasn't in New Jersey."

"What?"

"Terry wasn't in town. He called last night and said he was meeting a client in Manhattan. He said the meeting would be running really late, so he'd just stay in New York like he usually does, then go straight to his office in the morning. He does that once, twice a month sometimes."

"Did you know where he was staying?"

"The Broadway Marriott." Tears streamed down her face as she sobbed. "I don't know what to tell my children." Inez McShand's composure disintegrated before his eyes.

"Thank you, Ma'am. If I have anymore questions, I'll be in touch. Lieutenant Miller will see you out."

#

After finishing a rather putrefactive autopsy on a homeless man who died of multiple stab wounds, it was time for a coffee break. Dr. Clarefield shamelessly cranked up his favorite Frank Sinatra tape, while preparing a latte with his new cappuccino maker. Just as he was about to froth some milk, Mo appeared in the doorway.

"What's up, Doc?"

"Like a bad penny you turn up again."

"Whew! Smells like rotten potatoes in here. Worse in here than usual. How the hell do you stand the stink?" Mo waved his hand in front of his face.

"What stinks?" He put down a tiny metal carafe and drew back the morgue sheet over another homeless man. "Let me show you something. This poor fellow met an untimely end in an alley three days ago. He's slightly odoriferous because of gas gangrene in the leg. Incredible how you can hear the skin crackle. Want to have a look-see?"

"Nah, I'll pass." Mo chuckled. "Forget the smelly guy for a minute. You got anything on the dead lawyer? Has the press been down here yet?"

"One problem at a time, Detective, one problem at a time. Oh sure, the press paid me a visit. But I gave them my standard line of bullshit. 'No comment', 'go see the Chief of Police', etc."

"So what do you make of this whole thing?"

"Well, he didn't croak from the gunshot wound. Like a belated birthday card, it was an *afterthought*."

"Really?"

"C'mon, let me show you what I mean."

The two men walked over to the corpse. As the medical examiner rolled back the sheet, Mo looked at the grey-hued mass on the steel examining table. Only a few days ago, the corpse probably got out of bed, drank coffee and kissed his wife before going to work. But dead is dead no matter who Terence McShand was when he was alive. And this kind of dead was the worse kind. McShand didn't just drop dead of a heart attack at the office. Somebody executed him.

Through the corpse's ashen color, Mo saw the pronounced blue line around the man's neck.

"Look at the ligature marks. A nice deep groove. His larynx was crushed." Clarefield lifted up the dead man's eyelids. "See these small red dots? Petechial hemorrhages. But now for the really interesting part." He opened McShand's mouth. "Part of his tongue is gone. Not such a clean cut either. Whoever did this, used a serrated knife. I matched the piece of flesh I found in the backseat of the car with McShand's tongue. It's a perfect fit."

Raising his arms for a dramatic denouement, the Doc continued. "I'd bet my bottom dollar that someone came up from behind with a wire and started doing this." He made several twisting motions with an invisible garotte. "Then when the perp finished strangling him, out came the knife and off came the tongue like this." He grabbed an invisible tongue and brought an invisible knife down. "Chop, chop, chop." He picked up a small container with the piece of tongue floating in formaldehyde and held it toward the light. "Yes, it's a perfect fit, all right."

Mo winced. "You do have a flair for the dramatic. What about the gunshot wound?"

"Oh, that. Whoever shot him between the eyes did it just for entertainment, pure unadulterated haha's. He died because somebody choked him, Mo. Asphyxiation. I recovered one bullet fragment, possibly a .22 caliber. But remember everything I'm telling you is preliminary. I'll have the final report sometime next week."

Just when he had finished the sentence, Frank Sinatra crooned in the background, "It's witchcraft, nothing but witchcraft..."

Clarefield grinned. "God, I love that tune. What did you make of that funky necklace with the star? Was he into some strange Puerto Rican cult or something? C'mon now. I'm waiting for a sharp retort."

"I thought that he was a Jewish lawyer with that star thing going on."

"The Star of David has six points, my friend, not five. And really, Mo. A name like McShand?"

"So may be he changed his name to sound like a W.A.S.P." Mo chided. "The way you changed yours."

"But you forget. I *am* half W.A.S.P."

Both men laughed. They enjoyed each other's morbid sense of humor and ethnic slurs. No offense was ever taken, but today the humor wasn't going to last too long.

"Moraimo, you have your hands full with this one, I'm afraid." The medical examiner walked over and turned the cappuccino maker on.

"Thanks for reminding me."

"That necklace is part of another necklace. That funky looking moon interlocks with another piece, another half crescent moon."

Despite his outward calm, Mo was nervous. "Really. That's interesting. So I guess I need the other half of the necklace." Mo glanced over at the body on the morgue slab again. He sighed. "I caught this case and I got no suspects right now. All I know is that he was in New York the night he was killed, sleeping at the Broadway Marriott." As he complained, Frank Sinatra continued crooning in the background. "Well Doc, guess what? Maybe Frankie is trying to tell me something. I'm gonna have to go out and find me a witch," he said, rubbing the stubble on his chin and stretching his back.

"Long night, Detective?"

He gave him a salacious grin. "Very long. Yes. I did things that you only see animals do in those National Geographic TV specials."

"With who? The Swedish hairdresser or the Cuban librarian?"

"Librarian." He pushed back a lock of blond hair that fell across his face. "She's great. And more than about stacking books. But she wants a commitment already."

"To what? Marriage or dumping the hairdresser."

"Both," he laughed.

"By the way, would you like a cappuccino?"

He stared at his coroner friend. Clarefield held a stainless steel frothing carafe in one hand, and a bloody scalpel in the other as he stood over the corpse of the rotting homeless guy.

"Nah, Doc. I'll pass."

Chapter 2

Each day as G.P. Scalisi opened the door to The Aura Quest, he felt more powerful. His supply store was a small but terrible empire in the world of white light sending, incense burning, crystal kissing New Agers. Today, a special sale on money spell candles would force the desperate and the destitute to flock to his storefront. G.P. wouldn't just smell incense today. In a few hours he'd bask in the wonderful aroma of dead presidents.

He reached down to grab the doorknob, then yanked his hand back. Horrified, he noticed several smudge marks, a tell-tale sign that dirty human hands had been there. Thank the Gracious Goddess he caught himself! G.P. removed one of the pre-packaged iodine cleanser wipes he kept in his wallet in case of emergencies. And right now, *this* was an emergency. In times of AIDS, Ebola, and Lyme Disease, you could never be too careful. Who knows what microbes, tiny transmitters of death, lurked on that knob? He rubbed furiously with the iodine wipe until the marks were gone.

Now that the knob was properly sterilized, he entered his safe haven, the Aura Quest. And what a haven it was! Two years ago, the store was a gift from his Uncle Hugo, and it was to Hugo that he owed his life — in the literal sense of the word. He wouldn't be in business if it weren't for his family patriarch. He never forgot the night he inherited the shop.

#

WAREHOUSE DISTRICT
WEST STREET
NEW YORK, NEW YORK
NOVEMBER, 1986

It was 1:00 a.m. and the warehouses and lofts on West Street were dark. The art galleries, nearby restaurants and coffee shops were closed. A ghostly haze hovered over the street lamps, and the night sky was so blue, it was almost black. If Manhattan is the "City that Never Sleeps" for some eerie reason, tonight it quietly dozed.

Time stopped for a solitary man walking down the street. A wind wrapped itself around Gino Patrick Scalisi like an icy sheet, cutting through his leather coat. He pulled the coat around him tighter and tighter, yet he felt no warmth. Bleary eyed, the thirty five year old man reached for a crumpled paper stuffed in his breast pocket. Tears fell from his eyes onto the paper smudging the ink, making the address illegible. Now he would never find his Uncle's warehouse. He thought the address was 749 West Street, but he wasn't sure. When he found a door with some numbers, he decided to take a chance, and knocked politely.

"Hello? Any one home?" No one answered. Not a good sign. Finally, he couldn't stand the cold anymore. "Open up! Dammit, I'm freezing out here!"

He pounded on the door, until he heard a buzzer. The door popped open. A nervous G.P. entered the building.

"Hello? Helloo-o-o?" he asked. He peered around a corner looking for assassins before he proceeded down the hallway.

He sighed. Tonight was his reckoning. Time to meet his Maker. How would he die? A gunman's bullet from a dark corner, ripping into his back severing his spinal cord? A knife in the chest, then dumped in an alley way, left to choke on his own blood? Maybe this whole little lure to the warehouse "meeting" was a ploy, and he would be dropped by a rooftop sniper after he left the building.

His life was over. He would be taking the dirt nap very soon.

Once inside the building, an open elevator waited for him at the end of a hallway. With the stealth of a frightened sewer rat, he entered. The dirty metal cage clanged shut behind him and he pushed a greasy button marked "ten."

"Oh God, what did I do! It's filthy!" he shrieked. Panicking, he ripped open the pre-moistened iodine towelette he kept in his pocket for these kind of emergencies. G.P.'s hands rose into a strange orange lather, and he dried his fingers off one by one with a handkerchief he kept in a plastic baggie.

"Must avoid infection." he panted. "No way to die. Don't want to die from infection. Yeah. Die because someone shoots you in the head. Anything but disease."

Filth, dirt, and germs sickened him. He wanted to wipe away the insidious bacteria that festered on that red plastic button with an alcohol swab, but he had none with him. He recalled a cornerstone on the building, which had "1900 A.D." embossed in Gothic lettering. That meant eighty six years of filthy human hands tweaking that elevator button. Vomit rose in the back of his throat.

Haemophiles influenza, salmonella, pinworm. Crazy things to think about right before you die. His last memories of life would be a joke. A dirty elevator button, and the realization that he'd lost the battle against filth he'd fought all his life. He'd soon be buried under that which he feared the most: mounds and mounds of dirt.

After interment, there's the rotting process. First, come the blow flies, then their eggs, and young larvae feasting away at his liver, cleaning away flesh from bone. He gagged at the thought of his own decomposition.

Ashes to ashes, dust to dust. My miserable existence will be over soon enough. Maybe there was still time to leave my body to science. Why didn't I sign that damn organ donor card?

Too late. He hoped that his mother, Virginia Scalisi, would at least honor his memory with a proper monument. He closed his eyes and envisioned the granite tombstone.

Here lies my son, a man who waged war against filth...and lost.

The elevator came to an abrupt stop on the tenth floor. The metal cage slammed open. G.P. poked his head out, caught a whiff of cigar smoke, and started sneezing. The hallway extended itself in two opposite directions. He wasn't sure which way to go, until he heard a charming voice.

"Hey asshole. Down here."

A broad shouldered shadow outlined in moonlight leaned against a wall at the hallway's end. Cigar smoke surrounded Lino De Simone, one of his uncle's best marksman and business associate. A former green beret, he could drop G.P. with one shot.

"Lino, how's it going, my friend? You look great. Must have a picture aging in an attic somewhere."

"What the hell does that have to do with anything?"

"You know. Oscar Wilde? Dorian Grey? The story about the guy who stays young but his picture gets old and decrepit?"

Unimpressed by the compliment, G.P. realized that the Dorian Grey reference was far above the comprehension of a man who thought duck hunting with an Uzi was funny. Lino looked at him like a stray dog who'd announced his arrival home by puking on the new carpet.

"Yeah, who cares. Your uncle is waiting for you. Follow me."

"Are you going to kill me there?"

"If I had my choice, I would have blown your head off outside. But why bloody up new cement?"

G.P.'s stomach grumbled audibly as he followed Lino. At the end of a dark hallway, Lino opened a door.

From out of the darkness emerged light. In the back offices of Orion Imports, the sun never sets. Drenched in permanent fluorescent daylight, the office was incredibly well lit. The beige stippled walls were compli-mented with genuine art deco fixtures. The reception area, usually filled with fresh Birds of Paradise and a chirpy, buxom receptionist, had one of his Uncle's mustachioed gunmen behind the desk instead.

Hmm, must be a new hire. G.P. thought quietly. *Why do all these killers look alike?*

The doomed man heard his Uncle's voice boom from a back office. "G.P., get your ass in here. We have to talk."

With De Simone breathing down his back, G.P. entered in his uncle's office and looked into his eyes. He both feared and admired him.

Hugo Scalisi was seventy one years old if he was a day, but looked much younger. Fortune had favored Hugo. An occasional murder, lucrative "pump and dump" penny stocks, and a successful trucking operation, made life quite comfortable for a man whose criminal career spanned four decades. Money he had. Power in the Scalisi crime family he had. And unfortunately he had G.P., an ever present thorn in the old lion's paw.

As G.P. sat down, he saw that his Uncle Hugo could barely contain himself. Stone faced, he finger drummed on the mahogany desk, while G.P. began pleading.

"Look Uncle Hugo, I know you are upset. But would my father want to see me..."

"Do not dishonor the memory of my brother with moronic ranting. And that's what you *are* G.P., a moron."

"I am?"

"Yes."

Lino walked up behind G.P. and jammed the barrel of his .38 special into the back of G.P.'s head. "It would be an honor to kill him for you, Mr. Scalisi. It would save you *agita*, Sir."

The old man sighed in disgust. "Sit down, Lino. You ain't killin' nobody tonight."

"Whatever you say, Boss." Lino backed off. "But that's a cryin shame." He spat on the ground next to G.P.'s foot. The gunman's saliva bounced onto the tip of G.P.'s shoe. Unnerved by the germ infested spittle, G.P.'s heart raced. He began to perspire. A drop of sweat stung his eye as he sputtered, "I'm-mm so-sorry Unc-c-le Hugo."

The old man's face went beet red. "Sorry?" He slammed a clenched fist on his desk. "You stupid fuckin' idiot! I coulda sent a monkey to do the job. It was simple. Three trucks pull in. One has Pennsylvania plates, one has New York plates. A man pulls up with Jersey plates. All you had to do was tell the Pennsy and Jersey trucks to unload their stuff into the empty New York truck. What was so complicated about that? Instead, a truck with Tennessee plates pulls in, and now I got a report from my people down South that there's a bunch of red necks sportin' my Armani suits!"

"But Uncle Hugo, let me explain. You see, when the first truck pulled into the loading dock—"

"Shut up! I ain't done speakin' yet. I got you a job down at the track. I gave you some stuff to jack up a couple of my trotters so I'd have a winner or two. What do you do? You over inject the nags, and the two bastids drop dead at the starting gate. Two hundred thousand dollars worth of race horses down the crapper!"

"In all fairness Uncle, a stable is no place for a man who fears he can be mortally wounded by filth. I never meant to harm those poor horses. That manure all over the place terrified me."

"You and your fear of dirt! You aren't a mental case, you're just an asshole."

G.P. looked down at his feet. Inadvertently he'd worn two different socks, one blue, one black. That just about summed up his life. A failure, a man obsessed with germs, wearing two different colored socks with brown shoes.

He truly was an *asshole.*

"I've given it careful thought. I've very generously provided you with every option this family has to offer, import-export business, racing business, junk bonds. You have completely screwed up everything this family has given you. Anything you touch turns to crap. You could fuck up a one car funeral! And now what do you do? You clean up in a hospital for six bucks an hour, dealing with the very thing you hate—other people's germs. You're a disgrace." Hugo threw a paper towel at him. "Here take this. Your sweat's drippin' on my clean floor."

G.P. wiped his face. "Well, at least it's an honest living."

"You're too stupid to make a dishonest living, G.P.!" the old man raged. "You're an embarrassment to the Scalisi family. As I see it, I got two choices. Either I kill you or get you involved with another business where you won't hurt nobody. It is only because you are the only son of my older brother that

I have decided to spare your miserable life."

Lino bent over, hissing a demonic cacophony into his ear. "You should kiss Mr. Scalisi's ass, you useless piece of shit."

As G.P. sat through this verbal massacre, for a split second, he wondered if he wouldn't have been better off taking a bullet in the first place. At least he'd be dead by now. This tongue lashing was just too painful.

"So listen. I bought you another business to get you out of my hair," Hugo declared as he threw a business card across the table. "Here's the address. It will provide you with a living, I hope. I'll bank roll you for one year. If you get the shop off the ground, you won't owe me a thing, but you sign away any interest you have in our other family businesses. Remember how you used to read the cards when you was a kid? Nonna Scalisi always said you had the 'eye,' that you could see into the future. Right now, I'm seein' *your* future. Good luck and good bye." G.P. watched as his uncle stood up.

"Uncle Hugo wait! You want me to run a fortune telling parlor? Like some kind of a crazy gypsy? I can't do that. It's…it's embarrassing."

Hugo ignored his whining and pulled out a series of contracts. "My lawyer, Billy Callis, drew these up. Sign here. After you do, I never want to see you again. You will not show up to my house on Christmas Eve, Easter, Thanksgiving or even fucking Ground Hog Day. In fact, you will never speak to me again. I disown you. Take my offer."

"Can I sleep on it, Uncle Hugo? I always like to get a good eight hours before I make a major life decision."

Hugo winked at Lino. G.P. jumped as Lino plugged his .38 special back into his neck again. With chattering teeth, G.P. picked up the contracts.

"Which line do I sign on?"

#

So that was G.P.'s entrance into the world of metaphysics, an unceremonious ouster from his mob family. But at least he was alive, so every morning he gave silent thanks to his Uncle Hugo and the gullible public that needed his bogus magic.

The Aura Quest was located on Halsey Street in Newark, wedged between a tattoo parlor and an Italian restaurant. G.P. knew that Hugo stuck him in Newark for a reason. He'd be far enough away from Scalisi family activities in Manhattan, but if G.P. did anything asinine, his Uncle would hear about it and kill him immediately. If he kept a low profile, he could earn a living and not die in the process. And working at the Aura Quest wasn't entirely unpleasant, even though on any given day, the air in the shop smelled of bleach, Lysol with a hint of eggplant parmigiana, and Sandalwood incense.

Like any new business, the Aura Quest struggled at first. He didn't know the difference between Love Oil or St. John the Conqueror root. Within six months, the 5"4', coarse haired man, with the large probocis and horn rimmed glasses, wore a white cotton robe eight hours a day. He created love spell kits, did Tarot card readings, and advised people on financial investments based on phases of the moon. Holding himself out as the premier local authority on witchcraft, Santeria, and ceremonial magic, he knew it was all bullshit, but so what? G.P. had it for sale; the public bought. And for the first time in his life, Gino Patrick Scalisi found that he was actually good at something, even if it was only scamming people by selling them their dreams for $14.95 a bottle.

As G.P. heard the <u>Jersey Daily Journal</u> being shoved through the mail slot, he grabbed it before it hit the floor to avoid the paper's exposure to any additional germs. He read the headlines, and the words disturbed him. "Prominent Bergen County Lawyer Murdered—Terence McShand Found Shot to Death In Car."

Immediately, G.P. reached for more hand sanitizer. He forced himself to get a grip on reality. A line of eager customers were waiting for him to open the store.

"Poor Terence, must get over it, " he gasped. "Must forget him. Can't keep my public waiting They need spell kits. First of the month, Social Security and welfare checks are in. No time to worry about dead lawyers." The makeshift witch felt an uncomfortable chill come over him. He wondered who killed his lover, the real estate lawyer.

Chapter 3

O'BRIEN'S FUNERAL HOME
RIDGEWOOD, NJ
APRIL 10, 1988

The parking lot of O'Brien's packed in more cars than Macy's on a 50 percent off sale day. Mo invited himself to the funereal festivities, eagerly looking for potential murder suspects. A valet smiled in his direction as he pulled up. Mo opened his wallet.

There was nothing in it but air and a receipt for the dry cleaners. With no money for a tip and a crappy Toyota Corolla with a rag for a gas cap, he sped away and parked his car in a dark corner. Mo didn't realize the valet followed him. As Mo stepped out of the Toyota, he barely locked the door when he smacked right into the smiling parking attendant.

"It's okay my friend. I parked my car out of the way."

The little man said nothing, and kept smiling. Mo looked at him again. "It's okay man, I parked my own car." Blocking his way, the valet didn't move.

"You don't understand a word I'm saying, do you?" The man simply kept grinning. Finally, Mo spoke.

"La noche agradable para un funeral, no?"

The parking attendant's eyes widened with surprise at the sound of Spanish. *"O si, señor, si. Hace buen tiempo. Esta bien?"*

"Si."

The valet stepped back to let him pass. Mo muttered out loud. "Right buddy, nice night for a funeral."

He sighed. Mo wasn't in mourning; McShand's wake was a professional obligation. Tonight he had better things to do than attend some dead lawyer's wake. He missed a televised Yankee game, and a return phone call from a woman he really wanted to sleep with. But he knew some killers like to go back and admire their handiwork. A wake is the most innocuous place for a murderer to do that. Mix in with the mourners, feign some sympathy, and no one knows the difference. Surveillance, that's why he was there. As he crossed the parking lot, he jotted down a few license plates on the back of an envelope. Tomorrow, he would run the plates and get the names of the car's registered owners.

When he made it to the doorway of O'Brien's, two men in dark suits stationed at the door stopped Mo in his tracks. The larger of the two gorillas stepped in front of him.

"May I help you?"

"Yeah. I'm here to pay my respects to Mr. McShand."

"I'm sorry. The family has restricted visitors. Are you on the list?"

Mo gave him an effusive grin. Reaching into his pocket, he whipped out his badge.

"Yeah. Here's my invitation. Bergen County Homicide Unit. Now can I come to your party? Ple-e-ease?"

Somewhat annoyed, gorilla number one stepped aside to let him pass. Out of the corner of his eye, Mo saw both men give him dirty looks. He was about as welcome to the McShand wake as a ham sandwich at a Kosher picnic, but he could give a rat's ass. Wading through the crowds of people in the main viewing room, he looked around. For who? He wasn't sure. But he had that annoying feeling in the pit of his stomach, that the killer was present.

#

McShand's wake was a fountain, a wellspring of prominent local lawyers, politicians, doctors and judges. Some faces he knew from the court house, some he didn't, and some he hated. As Mo took a panoramic approach to the scene, he jumped when someone came up from behind and tapped him on the shoulder.

"Yeah?" he said turning around.

"Hello, Detective Rodriguez. Fancy meeting you in a place like this."

"Holy shit, Jack. I can't believe it's you."

The man was an aged but bronze god. The years on the street as a beat cop hadn't taken its toll on Jack Halloran. With the help of hair dye and a tanning salon, the sixty-year old man kept his ruddy Irish good looks and the twinkle in his eyes. And Jack's twinkling eyes, even at his age, always meant trouble — for someone else.

"So, buddy, how's retirement? You have the look of a native Floridian."

"Florida in the winter and fall, Jersey in the spring and summer. Right now this here," he said, pointing to his skin, "is just the local tanning salon. Great look for me, right? Who cares if the rays are giving me melanomas? At least, I look healthy, right? Mo, you oughta go with me one night, where the girls are young and willing." He laughed heartily.

"You joker! How's the insurance fraud business, Jack? They need any help? Like maybe a burned out homicide detective?"

"You sound disgusted, my friend. You're too young to be disgusted. Only rock n' roll old farts like me get disgusted."

"What's the matter with you, Jumpin' Jack Flash? Can't get no satisfaction?"

"Bullshit. I get lots of satisfaction. Why I'm even engaged."

"Again? What does this make it? Third marriage?"

"No, Mosey. It's actually my fourth."

"Really?"

"But she's thirty eight with nice tits, so whose counting? Four's a charm. And you know what? She's just mad about me." He ran his fingers down his tie as though he played a saxophone. "See this tie? My sweetie, gave me this tie. Ralph Lauren, I think. Designer tie. Nice pattern, right?"

In response, Mo grabbed the tie and pretended to blow his nose into it. "Now it has a nice pattern to it."

"You jealous little bastard." Jack yanked the tie out of his hands as he laughed. Both men turned their heads toward the entrance of the viewing room. A crowd formed. Someone important arrived.

"Hey Jack, look what the wind blew in."

" 'Tis an ill wind at that, son. It's old Arabella. Nasty, miserable Arabella."

Mo watched Judge Arabella Esel walked into room. She looked around, demanding the attention that rightfully belonged to the corpse. He grimaced. The woman was as round as she was tall. She wore outdated Foster Grant sunglasses that were way too large for her face trying to imitate the look of a movie star traveling incognito.

"Get a load of those sunglasses. Halloran, I don't see any sun in here, do you?"

"Remember, there's a shiny crucifix on McShand's coffin. She's a vampire, Mo. Without wearing those specs, the reflection could kill her."

With a down turned mouth, Judge Arabella Esel had the strange appearance of an angry owl yet lawyers, young and old, flocked to her anyway. Watching her greet them, Mo nudged Jack with his elbow.

"Listen. You can hear the kissy-kissy sounds from here," he stated. "That's some major sucking up going down in that corner over there."

"Ah, but Mosey, you know lawyers are the masters of the proverbial suck up. You can't blame them. They've all had surgery." Jack rubbed his chin contemplatively with his hand.

"What kind of surgery?"

"The surgical implantation of the nose up the right ass. Mandatory when they pass the bar exam, particularly if they plan on practicing in Bergen County."

"Give me a break. Just look at her, the old witch."

"Now Mo, calm down. The last time you got pissed off at her, I bailed you out of jail."

"Yeah, unfortunately I remember."

How could he forget her? Esel dismissed his rape case. He never recovered from it.

In 1982, the "Madonna look" was common among teens and preteens, and some men couldn't tell the difference between the teenagers and the twenty somethings. Some men didn't care.

A sixteen year old girl had been raped by her stepfather. She walked around in leopard spandex, six inch heels, and a bustier, trying to pass as a twenty five year old fashion model. The stepfather couldn't keep his hands out of the cookie jar. There wasn't a hell of a lot of physical evidence, and in the early eighties DNA evidence was in its infancy. But it was more than just a case of 'he said, she said.' The stepfather had tossed the girl's bloody clothing in a dumpster near the apartment where they lived. And when apprehended, the stepfather confessed, explaining how the girl enticed him by her dress.

"She wanted me. She lured me. It's better I break her in than some stranger. She was ahead of the game, anyway." he complained.

She *was* only sixteen. However, Judge Esel had her own opinion, after suppressing the State's evidence.

"I don't like the State's search, I don't like the amount of time they interrogated this poor man without a lawyer and I don't like the victim's manner of dress. This young woman clearly drove this poor man beyond the pale. She needs a lesson in modesty. She brought this on herself. I see no rape here. He admitted they had a close relationship. She should have known better. Given the totality of the circumstances, I see no sexual assault. Case dismissed."

The victim didn't have the stomach to go through an appeal. Mo freaked out in the courtroom, and threw a microphone, barely missing Judge Esel's head. She held him in contempt. An hour later, the cop found himself cooling his heels in a holding cell. He pissed her off, she made him pay for it. But Mo wasn't the only person to suffer from the wrath of Nasty Arabella.

A mean spirited person, her demeanor was unpredictable. Yelling and screaming from the bench during trial call was expected. Among local attorneys, Monday trial calls in Room 9302 were nicknamed "The Crazy 'A' Show." Prosecutors found their evidence in solid cases suppressed on a regular basis because she favored a defense attorney who flirted with her. If a litigant switched firms, she thought nothing of making inquiry as to why the litigant left the firm of the partner who happened to be her golfing buddy. Queen of the *ex parte* conversation, she played favorites openly and shamelessly. Throwing lawyers and clients out of her court room for no apparent reason other than a mood swing, was a regular occurrence, along with appeals from her off-the-wall judicial opinions based on what she ate for breakfast that morning.

As her time on the bench increased, so did her arrogance. The ethics rules didn't apply to Arabella Esel. She was just a long playing bulldozer who thought she could do what she wanted with anyone because she was one of the anointed. She wore the black robe.

Finally, she met her comeuppance. She took on the wrong prosecutor, humiliating him in front of the entire courtroom. Phone calls were made and the good judge suddenly found her 250 pound self presiding over small claims court in Camden County for nine months. But after her punishment, she was back in Bergen County.

Seeing her at the McShand's wake was an unpleasant surprise. "Look at her smiling. The lady of the manor," he spat.

"Yeah, with none of the charm. But I'm testifying before her next week, so I'm gonna be a good boy, hold my nose, and go over there." Jack adjusted his tie and smiled at his ex-partner. "Time to pucker up."

"You'll be alright, my friend. I hear she loves insurance companies." Mo shook his head. "Hey, did you know she used to date a detective downtown?"

"I heard that, I heard that. Then he dumped her, and the old biddy's been pissed off ever since."

"So *that's* why she takes it out on the rest of us, sonavabitch. May be all she needs is a nice big *chorizo* to grab onto and she'd be human again. So buddy, what brings you here?"

His eyes widened slightly. "To McShand's wake?"

Mo looked around and opened his arms. "Where else?"

For once, the ever smooth Jack Halloran was at a complete loss for words. "Mo, I've been hired by Inez McShand to conduct an independent investigation into her husband's death."

"What? You've got to be kidding. What the hell does she think? I'm some sort of incompetent? This is bullshit."

"Look, Mo. I fully intend to stay out of your way. In fact, I'm even willing to share information."

"I don't need your help, Jack."

Jack reached out and put his hand on Mo's shoulder. "I know you don't. You're a damn good murder policeman. But don't take it out on me. I don't even think Inez McShand really wanted this."

"So why are you here?"

"I'm not really sure. My firm was retained and I caught the case."

"So now I'm a little confused. The wife didn't really want to hire you, but you're hired. So, like, who's paying you?"

Jack's face clouded over. "I can't discuss who pays our bills. Firm policy."

"Firm policy. We've known each other since I was twenty six, and you have the balls to pull that 'firm policy' crap. That sucks, Jack. Excuse me, but I got work to do."

Just as Mo started walking away, Judge Esel came up to Jack Halloran with her usual unabashed aplomb, completely ignoring Mo's existence.

"Well, hello there, Detective Sergeant Halloran." she cooed. "Fancy meeting you in a place like this. I didn't know you knew Terry McShand."

Gritting his teeth, Mo eeked out the words, "Good evening, Your Honor."

With icy hazel eyes, she lowered her head and peered over the top of her sunglasses. "Hello Detective." She turned her back on him and focused her attention on Jack.

Mo's brain vapor locked, as his mind filled with horrible fantasies. The things he would do to her if murder were legal!

Dangle her by the heels from the Empire State building, let her drop, then place the squashed remains on a stick in a Secaucus landfill where hungry seagulls could peck at her eyes. His favorite vision? Tie her up with bailing wire onto the hood of a remote controlled Lamborghini Countache. He would let the race car complete its first lap at the Indianapolis 500 and smash it into a wall. Arabella, Splatterbella.

Or maybe he would just hang her from the ceiling in her bedroom, and call it suicide: the same fate met by the rape victim after the good judge dismissed her case.

Mo walked away from Judge Esel before he found himself back in jail again. Besides, he had work to do.

#

The closed coffin of Terence McShand, Esquire was a fine piece of funerary furniture, a deep rich bronze, the color of an old penny. The dead lawyer left this world in a king's sepulcher, with several 8 x 10 inch framed photos propped on the coffin lid.

The first picture showed a young, athletic McShand jogging along the Jersey shore, tanned and muscular. Another photo showed him shaking hands with the New Jersey Attorney General, while another showed him fishing at his Sanibel Island hideaway with his wife and children. McShand's family wanted the public to remember him as a lawyer, a family man and a statesman, not some strangled, shot-in-the-head freak. Mo worked his way through the crowds to reach McShand's widow.

Inez McShand was the quintessential, standard issue, wealthy suburban housewife, with all the appropriate accouterments: perfect hair, figure and jewelry. Mo watched as she tearfully greeted people, sometimes speaking with platitudes and occasionally shedding real tears. The looks, the moves, the talk— the pretty widow had social politics down to a science, even in the face of tragedy. Amidst the embraces and handshakes of the politicians, Inez saw Mo patiently waiting in line.

"Oh Detective Rodriguez, thank you for coming." She grabbed his hand.

"I know this mustn't be easy for you." He pointed to a set of four year old twin girls. "Are these your children?"

"Yes. Irene, Marilyn, please come over here."

Two identical little girls ran over, latching onto their mother, peeking out from behind her legs periodically. Inez McShand smiled sadly.

"This has been the hardest part. I tell them that Daddy's gone to heaven."

"So when is he coming back, Mommy?" Irene asked innocently. Mo watched the widow's eyes fill up.

"Sweetie, why don't you and Marilyn go see Grandma Sheila for a minute." She shooed the little ones away and whispered in Mo's ear.

"If there is anything you need Detective Rodriguez, let me know. Find out who did this. Find the bastard who killed my husband."

"Would you have any objection if I attend the funeral service tomorrow?"

"None whatsoever."

"Mrs. McShand, this is probably a bad time to bring this up, but I understand you have a private detective working on the case."

She hesitated. Then her face clouded over. "Yes, but this is not the time and place to discuss that."

He caught the arctic chill in her voice, so he backed off. "Sorry, Mrs. McShand. We can talk later."

"Indeed. Won't you excuse me? More members of the judiciary just arrived and, well, you know how that goes."

"Sure. I understand. Thank you for your time." Mo walked away from the receiving line, and looked for a seat in the back of the funeral parlor. Not a single chair was empty. Mo observed an elderly woman leaning forward on her cane, pushing herself to her feet, struggling to stand up. He rushed over and placed his arm beneath hers, lifting her to her feet.

A sweet-faced old lady with cheerful eyes looked up. Her grey hair was tied up in a bun, and she had tiny pearl drop earrings. When Mo looked at her, he noticed that she painted a set of Cupid's bow lips on her face with a bright pink lipstick. As she spoke, her dentures flopped. She had one of those charming wrinkled, Granny faces. "Thank you, my dear. I'm actually going to the ladies' room, but you can have this seat for a minute, if you like."

"Why that is very kind of you, Ma'am."

The old woman slowly ambled in the direction of the vestibule.

The room buzzed. Mo quietly watched people, family members and visitors, talking to each other. He noticed that Judge Esel never made it anywhere near the coffin or Mrs. McShand. Far too busy, she held court in back of the funeral parlor with a bunch of young male lawyers. His pal, the ever circulating Private Investigator Halloran, worked his way through the room like a lonely hooker on a naval base, meeting and greeting. He finally circulated back in Mo's direction.

"You again?"

"C'mon Mo. You ain't mad at me are you?" Jack winked.

"Nah, not really."

"You know, Mo. You shouldn't kill yourself with this case. Just ain't worth it."

"Gotta do my job, buddy. You know that."

"If I can help you, you know I will." Excusing himself, Jack wandered across the room to kiss an ex-girlfriend.

Mo shook his head. Schmoozing women was always one of Jack's strong points.

"Time's up, Sonny." The old lady returned. "So get your young self up, and let an old gal sit down, will you?"

He chuckled and stood up. "Sad about Mr. McShand, isn't it?"

She brushed a silver wisp of hair from her face before she answered. "No. All rats meet fitting ends in the garbage dump of humanity."

"Whoa-a! That was kinda cold."

"No colder than the dead man lying in that twenty thousand dollar box. Who are you? Can't be relative."

"Nah, just a friend."

"Friend? I didn't know Terence McShand had any *real* friends, and besides," she sniffed, "you don't look like you'd swim in his circles. Look at your clothes. You're not rich enough." The old lady pointed to several Brooks Brothers suits clustered in a corner, then glanced at the watch around her neck. "Oh well, it's late and I've got to go. You can have the seat back, dearie. So long."

"Wait! Can I ask you why you're here tonight if you don't really like the guy?

The old lady hoisted herself up again with difficulty. "Damn arthritis. So, you want to know why I'm here? I'll tell you. My wish came true. Terence McShand is dead and I wanted to see his rotten corpse for myself. It's a shame, too. Closed casket and they're only waking the bastard tonight. I planned on gloating for two full nights."

"Did he say something to offend you, Ma'am?"

"Stop calling me 'Ma'am'. Ma'am is what I called my grandmother and I'm not *that* old."

"Oh yes, you are." He laughed.

"Well, may be. The name's Brinkworth, Mrs. Sophiah Brinkworth. To answer your question, knowing that I lived in the same county as McShand offends me. But I'm happy now. He's dead." She cackled gleefully.

"I'm Detective Moraimo Rodriguez and I'm investigating Mr. McShand's death. Can I talk to you about the dead lawyer sometime?"

"Sure. Why don't you help me to the door? The stench of all these law-yers in one room is killing my sinuses."

He wanted to laugh, but Mo kept his outward calm as he escorted the old lady to the funeral home's exit. The two-suit wearing gorillas gave the couple nasty looks. Sophiah caught their expressions and returned the looks with an equally hostile glare.

"Look at those men, Detective," She whispered. "Just look at them. Like you, they're wearing cheap suits. I know if they could, they'd kill me."

"Aside from the suit insult, you've intrigued me. Why would those men want to kill you? Tell me about it. How did you get in here? I thought this party was by invitation only."

"I used to date Danny O'Brien Senior, the funeral director, when I was a young pup like you. Here. I want to give you something."

Sophiah's hands were gnarled arthritic knots. Mo could see that looking for something in her purse was an effort. After rummaging around, she handed him a business card. "See you soon, Detective. Oh by the way, you must be Spanish with a name like Rodriguez?"

"Puerto Rican."

"With blonde hair and green eyes? How unusual. Puerto Ricans are usu-ally dark."

He hated when people made statements like that. He could pass for any-thing, even Eastern European. When he told people he was Puerto Rican, he saw the immediate disappointment in their faces – like they'd just noticed he was covered in dirt or something. That pissed him off with people his own age, and he got into more bar fights because of it. But Mo more or less ac-cepted the ignorance of older white people as a cultural thing. And he didn't want to get defensive, because defensive cops never get information.

"Surprise, but yes, I am Puerto Rican."

"You ought meet my granddaughter. She just loves Spanish boys."

"Well, if she's as pretty as you…"

"Stop blowing smoke, Detective. I'm just an old bag. But do give me a call sometime. Would love to chat with you. Good night, Detective." With that Mrs. Brinkworth gently hobbled away into the night. Mo read the card in his hand. It said "Sophiah Elizabeth Brinkworth, Certified Genealogist, and Historian."

Mo wondered is she had anything to do with the McShand's murder. He looked at his watch and noticed that the crowds were thinning. Time to leave. He had enough death for one night.

#

Violating the local speed limits, Mo drove home. He owned a small Cape Cod, a cracker box palace, on Summit Lane on the outskirts of Hackensack and Maywood. It was the smallest home on a street of elegant oversized homes. As he pulled into the driveway, he saw his Jack Russell terrier, Salsa, pressing his paws and nose against the new Davenport window. Mo yelled from inside the car.

"Dammit dog! Get down from there!" He punched his car horn. "You're gonna scratch up my new window! Get Down!"

Salsa was the only dog who owned a man and a house. His last dog had been a Great Dane, who lived with him and his girlfriend in a tiny apartment. After the girlfriend left, the apartment became comfortable with just the detective and the big dog. When the Great Dane died of old age, Mo replaced him with Salsa, only to find out his place wasn't big enough for the small, free wheeling energy ball. He needed a yard and an extra bedroom – for the dog.

After calling a rubbery frozen pizza dinner, he tossed the burnt crusts to Salsa. The terrier sniffed them contemptuously, as though he'd been thrown a rubber sink washer for dinner.

"Don't look at me like that, dog. Charcoal's good for your teeth." The dog growled then began gnawing the crusts.

By the time dinner was over, it was after eleven. Mo gave his teeth a lick and a promise then flung himself across his big brass bed, buck naked. He rolled the night's events around in his head over and over again. He recalled several faces, the old genealogist, the gorillas at the gate, and the nasty judge. What a cast of characters! Anyone of them could have killed McShand. He had so much to learn.

After the funeral, the fun would really begin.

#

The sky was a perfect shade of turquoise and the sun was blinding mis-shapen orb set way up high. It was a perfect day to bury a lawyer.

Mo's and his partner, Lindell Teishia Wheeler, drove together to McShand's funeral mass at Immaculate Conception Church in a unmarked squad car.

"Where they planting him?" she asked matter- of-fact.

"Hackensack City Cemetery."

"Not St. Joseph's? I thought he was Catholic."

"He was. But St. Joseph's is filled to capacity. He's going to move in with his Protestant brothers. Hey, where were you last night? I was hoping to see you at McShand's wake."

"Kids had basketball practice. That takes precedence over some dead law-yer. And besides, this was a family only, Irish wake. You can pass. I'm black. Who's side of the family am I supposed to be on? If you say black-Irish, I'll slap you."

He smiled. "That's cool. Whatever. Hey listen, I ate some bad frozen pizza last night, and I kept dreaming about McShand."

"All this homicide stuff's been buggin' you, ain't it? You need to be buyin' one of them stress relievin', squeezy balls or those midget zen gardens for your office. You know, about a foot long, comes with sand and little rake, then you can play with the sand, arrange the little rocks and shit. You need one 'cause you look depressed."

"Thanks Dr. Feelgood. I'll remember to buy one." Mo frowned as Teishia kept laughing.

"Oh, by the way some of the forensic stuff came back from the lab. All they have are a few fibers unrelated to McShand. Clarefield says he's still looking."

"In other words, we have dick on his killer so far."

"Yep."

"Great. What about that star necklace?"

"Five pointed stars are called pentagrams. I called a buddy of mine over in Essex County who claims he knows a cop who's an expert on occult crimes. His name is Fulchess. I made us an appointment to speak to him."

"We're here. I'm pulling along side of that roadway."

"Do it."

The two detectives parked inconspicuously on a cemetery roadway, and stood outside their car. In the distance, they saw McShand's new place of residence, a large triangular plot of land set apart from the rest of the dead landed gentry. A crowd of people spilled out from under a small funerary

27

tent. Tei and Mo stood far away to get a wider field of vision.

With a small set of hand-held binoculars, Mo panned the faces. He recognized many of them from the night before, including Sophiah Brinkworth who leaned on her cane toward the rear of the crowd. He was thoroughly sure that she received some mundane satisfaction knowing Terence McShand would begin pushing up daisies.

"Let me have a look with those." Tei ordered as she pulled them out of his hands. "There is a single old lady standing way in back of the crowd. She has a big smile on her face like she just hit the lottery or something."

"Yeah. Sophiah Brinkworth. She was at the wake last night. She snuck in somehow. Wasn't sorry to see McShand die. Very vocal about it, too."

"So you like her for this kill?"

"Nah. Look at her, Tei. Looks like she can barely get up from a toilet."

"Okay, not her. But that group might be suspect. Look who else is here to mourn."

A tall, gaunt man with hawk-like features and a full head of salt and pepper hair stood next to two men in dark suits. Dignified yet sinister, he had the same frightening presence found in sociopathic dictators or medieval inquisitors. Total control, total agenda, total purpose. Once you met John Wilkinson Cane, you never forgot him.

"Tei, see that big guy off to the left? The black suit?"

"Yeah."

"He was at the funeral home last night. Had to push my way past him. Now he's Cane's body guard. Why does a millionaire need to attend a funeral surrounded by bodyguards?"

" 'Cause he's rich and so people like you don't kill him."

"I guess."

Mo had tangled with the man and his lawyers on a homicide case once before and lost. John Wilkinson Cane had been indicted three years ago for murdering his wife. It seems the poor woman met an untimely death, after a vintage Philco transistor radio plugged into a wall outlet, made its own way into her evening bath. Considering transistor radio popularity ended in the late sixties, it was a Hitchcockian way to die in the eighties.

Arabella Esel had presided over the murder trial. She overruled every single objection by the prosecution, resulting from the histrionics of a zealous defense lawyer. Cane's lawyer did such a good job twisting the facts, the jury wouldn't convict. After all, Laura Cane had a psychiatric history. Maybe she killed herself. Or maybe the pissed off ex-housekeeper did it. Or the gardener she was sleeping with. J.W. Cane, low income housing developer, philanthropist, kill another human being? Perish the thought.

Despite the fact that Cane was the only person in the house at the time of her death, the jury bought the unknown burglar entering the house theory. TV cameras showed a tearful husband carrying his wife's body out of the house to the morgue wagon, completely compromising the crime scene. The jury came to one conclusion: a pillar of the community and an overwrought husband would never drop an old radio into a bathtub to electrocute his wife. Next to the rape case, it was the second trial Mo lost with Judge Esel presiding.

"I can't believe that sonovabitch is here."

"Believe it. He might be worth talking to."

"You talk to that scumbag, Tei. Last time I talked to him, it nearly cost me my job."

Tei cocked her head and looked down at her hip. "Wait a minute. My beeper."

She read the message. "Shit Mo, we've got a situation down at the courthouse."

#

Once their squad car was a comfortable distance away from the cemetery, they sped away. Minutes later, they walked toward the Bergen County Courthouse.

"Damn. Looks like they evacuated the whole place, Mo."

Judges, lawyers, courthouse staff, and members of the public stood in small circles. Some spoke in hushed whispers, others laughed and talked. The detectives walked up to a Sheriff's officer standing guard at the entrance to the building. The officer recognized them immediately.

"Rodriguez, Wheeler, homicide, right? Sheriff Freddie Peters." He extended a short stubby hand. "My men secured the scene and evacuated the third and fourth floors."

"Why the hell did you evacuate two floors?"

Underneath a large, bushy, unkempt moustache, Mo saw corners of an upturned mouth. "Too many well wishers." The Sheriff's Officer winked. "Wait 'til you see who's dead."

Tei's impatience showed. "Well, c'mon now. Don't keep me in suspense. Who's dead?"

"A secretary found Judge Esel dead in her office this morning."

Mo didn't bother hiding his feelings. "So what made you think it's homicide? She's a big, fat slob. Maybe she just keeled over after stuffing her gut with one too many Philly cheese steaks. Remember Mama Cass and the ham sandwich? Happens like that with fat people sometimes."

"Mo, that story ain't even true and it ain't funny," Tei said.

The Sheriff guffawed. "I hear what you're sayin,' Rodriguez, but I think you need to see the body, if you know what I mean."

"I can hardly wait." Mo said flatly.

The footsteps of the trio echoed down the long narrow hallway of the third floor. Several local Hackensack police officers stood outside of her chambers.

"Where'd they find her, Sheriff?" Tei asked.

"In her chair." He turned to Mo and Tei. "You know, you guys shoulda brought the stake and the silver bullets. Want to make sure she stays dead." Mo doubled over laughing, but his partner was less than amused.

"You two ought to be ashamed of yourself! That is *total* disrespect for the dead."

"Like she ever had any respect for the living. " Mo retorted.

The burly Sheriff chimed in. "Oh man, when the Medical Examiner hauls her dead ass outta here, he's gonna need a truss."

"What truss? Hope he paid his last insurance premium. The poor bastard's gonna need hernia surgery." Mo howled, wiping the tears from his eyes.

"Both of you! Shut up! We got a dead judge on our hands. It's more than we can handle right now."

"Well, look you two, love to stay around and chat but I got things to do. Happy hunting." Sheriff Freddie walked away chuckling.

The detectives donned latex gloves. Breaking the crime scene tape, the cops entered her chambers. There sat Judge Arabella Esel in all her glory. Dead glory, of course.

She was dressed in the uniform she was renowned for throughout the courthouse, navy blue skirt, and starched white high-necked cotton blouse with Victorian brooch. Her bright orange colored hair was lacquered in place by hair spray in a curious Gibson Girl fashion. She was still wearing round, oversized sunglasses.

The dead judge sat propped up. Her head hung slightly over the back of the chair. At first glance, she could have been dozing. Except that her eyes were frozen open and her mouth was packed with dirt. As Tei and Mo examined the crime scene, Dr. Clarefield waltzed in.

"Well, Doctor Frankenschteen is here." Mo announced.

"Now I *know* Detective Wheeler would never make such a caustic remark." He rewound the cassette inside his pocket recorder. "Mo, how did you get so lucky? Two prominent dead legal eagles in almost a week." He took a look at the corpse's dirt filled mouth. "H-mmm-m. I wonder what this is all about. Oh by the way, new hairstyle, Detective Wheeler? I like your braids and beads. Very attractive. Very African."

"Oh thank you," she cooed. "I always try to do something a little different."

"Would you two like to be alone? Here Doc." He flung a pair of examining gloves at the medical examiner. "Have a set of gloves on me."

Tei looked around the room. "Pretty bizarre, right? Looks like nothing's been touched. Let's face it. If you struggle to kill a woman this size, the room shoulda been tossed."

"An excellent observation Detective Wheeler." Dr. Clarefield looked thoughtfully at the body for a minute. "The room does looks untouched."

Grabbing a tiny spoon, he poked around at the dirt packed in her mouth. "How strange." He placed his voice activated tape recorder on the desk and pulled a small container from his morgue kit. He removed some dirt samples from Judge Esel's mouth and placed them in a sterile container. Not one to miss the opportunity for a joke, he pointed to the corpse's mouth. "A judge with a filthy mouth? Who says it never happens?"

Mo snickered, but after looking at Tei's face, he realized the Esel jokes were starting to get old.

"Well kids," Clarefield continued, "from the looks of the dear girl and body temperature, I believe she's been dead only a few hours. We don't have too much lividity yet, but most of it will be in her buttocks anyway. She's cool but not cold. I need a liver temperature."

As Clarefield launched into his death investigation litany, a uniform entered the room. "Mo, the word is out about Esel. The press is swarming the place."

"Great. We gotta get out the back door without the corpse making tomorrow's front page. I have to notify the family first."

"Right."

"Who found the body?"

"The judge's secretary. Came in early and found her dead in the chair."

"Where is she?"

"She's outside."

While Tei and Dr. Clarefield continued their investigation, Mo left the judge's chambers. He entered an adjoining room where, Sarah Hunter, a small frail blue haired lady sat, looking like a deer caught in headlights. He gently extended his hand.

"Hello. Are you Mrs. Hunter, the judge's personal secretary?"

"Yes." Her eyes filled up. "She wasn't a nice person, but she didn't deserve to die like this."

"Now that's an understatement. She was a holy bitch," Mo thought to himself. "I'm sorry, Mrs. Hunter. I know this can't be easy for you. You worked for Judge Esel for how many years?"

"Seven."

"Can you tell me what happened?"

"If I could tell you what happened, I'd be the detective and you'd be the judge's secretary, right?"

"Okay."

"I'm sorry. I'm just upset."

"No problem."

"I get to my office everyday around eight. We don't get started until nine, but I like to get in early and set up my day."

"Who's we?"

"The Sheriff's Officer and Court clerk. But both have been on vacation for the past two weeks."

"What about a law clerk?"

She inhaled and sighed heavily. "Judge couldn't seem to keep one. They all quit on her. Judge Esel was very demanding of them."

She probably abused the piss out of them the way she does everyone else. He thought.

"When did the last one quit?"

"Early on. She barely lasted a month." Mrs. Hunter paused for a minute. "You don't think she..."

"I don't think anything, Ma'am. Right now, I'm just looking for some information, that's all."

"I see."

"Besides you, who usually comes here in the morning?"

"Well, the building is cleaned by a group called The Joyous Workers. They're mentally handicapped people." She barely finished her sentence, when a cheerful man in a lime green coat bounded through the door. Sewn on the sleeve of his coat was a big embroidered patch reading 'Joyous Workers of New Jersey.'

"Is there garbage in here?" he asked.

Mrs. Hunter got up. "Good morning, Al. Everything is fine today."

"But I got to get the Judge's garbage." He started to head into the crime scene area until Mo blocked his way. When he went face to face with Al, he saw the man's mongoloid eyes.

"Sorry big guy. But my people are working in there."

"But Judge Esel gets really mad at me, if I don't get her garbage first. She says that she'll tell my boss to go and get some real help and I like my job collecting garbage."

"Listen Big Al, I appreciate your concern, but I don't think you'll have to worry about that ever happening."

Al peered over Mo's shoulder. Mo noticed that the green coat made a strange face when he saw the judge seated in her chair with Tei and Doctor Clarefield moving around her.

"Oh. Is the Judge sick?"

"Yeah, yeah. That's right. She's sick."

"So her garbage is okay then. Well, I'll just pick up Mrs. Hunter's garbage."

"No, my friend. Leave everything as is."

"Uh. Okay." Whistling a monotone, he cheerfully lumbered away.

Mrs. Hunter continued. "The Joyous Workers would be the only people, besides the regular maintenance people hanging around the building early in the morning. The public can't get in, unless they pass through metal detectors. I'm sorry. I got a little sidetracked. When I came in I noticed Judge Esel's office was dark which isn't unusual, since she doesn't arrive here until nine thirty each day."

"So then what happened?"

"Well, the Judge gave us specific instructions. We are never to pick up her private line, and we are not to go into her office for any reason when she isn't there. But a lawyer called this morning to ask if an order had been signed. He's a really nice local fellow and well, I wanted to help him." Her voice cracked. "So I broke the cardinal rule. I opened up her office door and that's when I saw her. Right away I called 911."

"How long did you stay in the room?"

"Seconds once I saw her." She removed a tissue from a tissue box and dabbed the tears from her eyes. "You know, I was due to retire the end of next year, but I'm eligible right now. I'm going to put my papers in early."

He stood up and placed a hand on her shoulder. "So why not? If I could retire myself right now, I would." Little did the secretary know that he meant it. He didn't feel like being a homicide detective at that moment.

Tei entered the room. "Detective, can I talk to you for a minute?"

"Sure. Mrs. Hunter, if I need anything I'll call you."

"Thank you." The old secretary left.

He turned to his partner. "What's up?"

"Nothing good. Come over here and take a look at this."

Mo went back into the room. The ever vigilant Dr. Clarefield dictated furiously into the tape recorder and stopped when Mo entered the room. He pointed to the empty garbage container.

"I see Doc. Well, I'll be damned. Someone emptied the judge's garbage."

The phone sitting on the late Judge's desk rang on the inside line. Tei answered. "Judge Esel's chambers. Hello? Hello?" She turned to Mo. "Whoever it was, hung up."

#

Tei wanted to drive today. Mo gave in knowing that driving with Miss Tei

33

wasn't an easy chore. The Statue of Liberty she kept on the dashboard usually wound up under the floor mat before the ride was over. He chided her about Lady Liberty diving for cover. Tei watched in amusement as Mo's right foot smashed down on an invisible passenger's side brake.

"Get the hell outta my way!" She yelled to an old man in the left lane. "Old men wearing hats are the worst." She hit the sirens, passed him up, cut *him* off, and glared at him as she zoomed by. "Hey Rodriguez, hand me my sun glasses, baby. The sun's blinding me."

"I wish I was blind so I don't have to see us crash into that pole. Slow down, dammit!"

"Calm down, wussboy. You behind the wheel with Teishia."

"That's what I was afraid of."

Driving aside, he thought his partner was a remarkable woman. Like Mo, she'd grown up in the same town, and understood the hierarchy of the Hackensack hill. If you grew up on top of the hill on Summit Avenue, you were a wealthy doctor, lawyer or businessman. If you lived down the hill on Railroad Avenue, you were poor.

Lindell Teishia Dellwood grew up in single family home on Railroad. Oldest and the largest of three girls, Tei was raised by her mother and grandmother. Mary Dellwood, a widow, owned a small restaurant off Railroad Avenue called the Dellwood Inn. From this tiny bastion of barbeque, Mrs. Dellwood paid off the mortgages on the inn and saved for her children's college education. Mrs. Dellwood's children would live at the top of the hill, even if she couldn't.

When she was about to enter a local community college, Tei found herself pregnant. She married her high school sweetheart, Elford Wheeler. Three babies later, she completed her college education with a degree in sociology and a minor in art history. Her real love was art, much to the disdain of her chronically unemployed husband, who refused to let her take any kind of an art related job. Hell, how could knowing about the life of Rembrandt help support him?

But she was always practical. Tei sat for the civil service exam for both police officer and fireman. As it turned out, her calling was blue. A decade later she moved up from beat cop to homicide detective. During that process, she divorced her husband. It was a cheerless but necessary farewell, lest she shoot him with her service revolver. Battle scars from taking a couple of bullets on the street are bad, but the scars from an abusive marriage were worse. She couldn't get rid of Elford Wheeler fast enough, and when the ink finally dried on the divorce decree, she felt a great sense of relief.

The sun burned brightly overhead as Tei ripped down Route 21 to the Essex County Prosecutor's Office in Newark. After pushing through downtown Newark traffic, Tei pulled into a Visitors Only lot. She parked in the first illegal space outside of the yellow lines.

"Tei, move this piece of shit over. You're sittin' on the yellow line."

"So what? We're here, ain't we?"

"Your driving stinks."

"So do you, but I haven't said a word." She huffed.

Once inside the Essex County Prosecutor's Office, a civilian assistant led them through a government gerbil maze, a series of corridors and soft walled cubicles which ultimately took them to a solitary, one man squad room buried in the very back of the Prosecutor's Office.

Before walking away, the young woman pointed to the door left ajar. The top of it was opaque white glass and the bottom was a dark hardwood. Mo touched the door gently, pushing it open with his fingertips. He peered around the door's edge, and saw a large stout man, sitting behind his desk, chin resting upon hand, and eyes shut. He resembled a grizzly bear in a state of repose. Mo turned to Tei and grinned.

"Watch this."

WHAM! WHAM! WHAM! Mo pounded on the opaque glass.

The startled man's eyes popped open and he jumped to his feet. "Jesus H. Christ, who are you people?"

Tei stepped forward. "I'm Detective Tei Wheeler and this is my partner, Detective Mo Rodriguez. You and I spoke on the phone regarding the McShand murder."

"Oh yeah, yeah, that's right. Don't mind me. I was having a mystical moment doing some investigative case management. Ronnie Fulchess." Tei shook his hand and handed the heavy faced man a manila envelope.

"I understand that you are an expert in the occult."

He puffed up his chest. "As a matter of fact, I am."

"Can you help us out with this, Ronnie? Me and Rodriguez here are at a loss with this occult stuff."

"Well, I don't like to brag, but you know I am a high priest of the Celtic tradition by birth."

Tei observed him carefully. "Really? How impressive."

"So, are you like some kind of witch?" Mo asked casually.

Fulchess ignored his sarcastic tone. "Well, if you must know, my grandmother in Ireland was a pagan, and her grandmother before her."

Mo's observation was sharp and quick. He gestured to a tourist photograph of Fulchess in front of the Vatican as the Pope blessed the masses. "So does His Eminence know that you fly around on a broomstick at night?"

"Is he always so cheerful?"

"Ronnie, ignore him. Today is actually one of his better days. What can you tell me about this?" She held up the necklace. "This medallion was found draped around the dead lawyer's neck. It had some kind of a star on it. A

35

pentagram?"

"Well, that isn't a symbol of devil worship like *some* people think." He glared at Mo. "Was the point on the star up or down?"

"On the medallion?"

"Amulet, my dear. It is called an amulet."

"Of course. Well, I think the point was up, wasn't it Mo?"

What a bunch of bullshit all this is, he thought. "Yeah, the point was up."

"That's a very good sign." Ronnie nodded.

"Not for the dead guy." Mo replied dryly.

"What I meant was that the pentagram is a pagan holy symbol with one point up. It symbolizes the elements of earth, fire, water, and air bound by spirit. Point down? A sign of chaos and imbalance. That is a symbol of Satanism. And besides, the devil was a creation of the Christians not the Pagans."

"Forget all the religious rhetoric for a minute. Let me ask you this. Why would a prominent lawyer be found dead with that thing around his neck? What does this pentacle —"

"Pentagram." Fulchess interrupted. "A pentacle is different."

"Whatever. Does it have to do with human sacrifice? Does that mean that this guy was involved some kind of a cult or something?"

"No, no, nothing like that." Ronnie Fulchess shrugged. "Pagans are peaceful people and don't bother anyone. But I'd hazard a guess to say that this was some kind of a perverse message."

"So do these people like to do things like sacrifice babies to obtain power?"

"You *really* don't listen do you? I already told you. These people are harmless. I'll introduce you to a few. One of my favorites in fact."

#

Twenty minutes later, Ronnie Fulchess pulled up in front of a Newark storefront with Tei and Mo behind him in separate cars. An entire window pane had been replaced by a thin plywood plank. As the trio walked through the door, they saw a solitary black candle burning behind the plywood where the glass pane should have been. Fulchess didn't seem suprised. He looked at Tei and Mo. "The reason for the candle? Trying to ward off bad psychic energy from criminal activity."

Mo looked at the sign above his head. "Blessed Be. Welcome to The Aura Quest?" He turned to look at Tei. "You've got to be kidding."

"Why would I be kidding?" Fulchess retorted. "You know if you ever intend to catch this killer you had better take this stuff seriously."

Tei tried to smooth Fulchess' ruffled feathers. "Forgive him, Ronnie. I love him 'cause he's my partner, but the man's a spiritual zero."

"Thanks Wheeler. Thanks a lot." said Mo.

Upon entering the Aura Quest, Ronnie went to the back office, trying to locate the store's proprietor. Left to their own devices, Tei and Mo wandered around.

Mo was impressed how clean the little store was. The whole place smelled of bleach, Lysol and incense. Looking around, he sensed that the owner had a remarkable sense of order. Each section was carefully alphabetized. Books were in completely separate sections sorted by topic then alphabetized by author. One part of the store was dedicated solely to oils, another to incense, and other strange concoctions. Statuary covered an entire wall. Some pieces were huge and belonged in outdoor landscaping, while others were only a few inches tall. Row upon row of incense sticks with peculiar names such as "Lord of the Midnight Wood," "Madre's Blessing," and "Hopi Vision" covered another area. Mo picked up 'Lord of the Midnight Wood' incense.

"Midnight wood? Hey Tei, I've always been Lord of the Morning Wood myself."

Mo yelped when she pinched his arm. "Listen these people take themselves very seriously. Don't make fun. Especially if we need his help." Tei pointed in the direction of a man wearing a neatly pressed white robe with a huge pentagram around his neck. The robe studied the detectives for a minute.

"H-mm-m. Yes." He raised his thumb and index finger to his head. "An energy field surrounds you. Yes, yes. I feel it. An Orisha. The Lady Oya." G.P. walked over to a little statue and handed it to him. "She calls to you. She seeks you. Only twelve dollars."

Mo put the statue back. "No thanks. I have an aunt in Puerto Rico who believes in all that crap."

G.P. jumped. "It is not crap, Detective. I'd watch your mouth. You can offend the Ancients Ones."

"Let me jump in here. Hi. I'm Detective Wheeler."

"G.P. Scalisi, proprietor."

"Detective Rodriguez."

Droplets of perspiration formed on G.P.'s forehead when he looked at the cop's extended hand. "Excuse me while I get some tissues." G.P. wouldn't touch him but he politely nodded and began walking in the other direction.

"Wait a minute. What happened to your window, G.P.?"

"Run-of-the-mill teenage vandals, I suppose. So I hear you're on a mission. Detective Fulchess tells me you may need some help interpreting something you found. An amulet. You want to understand its mystical meaning."

"Forget mystical. I want to know where they come from, and who makes them. Do you?" The detective looked intently at the shop owner with the quavering upper lip. G.P. turned to Fulchess expecting him to provide the answer.

Hesitating, G.P. drew a breath. "Excuse me, Detective. I must check on something in the basement. I'm melting some paraffin to make money spell candles." He left the room with Fulchess trailing him.

"Money spell candles? Yeah, right." He looked at Tei. "Catch that little interaction?"

"Yup. What was that about?"

"Don't know. But looks like we got something going on over there."

Three teenage girls unobtrusively entered the store while everyone was talking. The detectives watched the three giggling teenagers pick up a series of candles in different colors. When they were done, the tight jeaned, crop top teens moved over to the oils. Mo noticed that one of the girls looked around cautiously. Delicate fingers took a tiny bottle of Aura Quest Love Oil and stuffed it her jacket pocket.

"See that, Tei?"

"I'm on it." Tei marched over to the hormonally challenged, gaggle of girls. "Excuse me!" She ripped an oil bottle from the hand of another girl who was about to shove it into her purse. "Didn't your mamas teach you that it's not right to steal?" She flashed her tin at the trio. "Now get your asses outta here."

"C'mon, let's go," whispered the thieving ringleader. The girls took off, dropping items other items as they ran out the front door. Tei bent over and started picking them up just as G.P. and Fulchess returned.

"Thank you. Those girls are in here every week and I always manage to find a few things missing after they leave. Here, I have something to show you. I usually buy them in bulk." G.P. cautiously handed the detectives several necklaces, then picked up a rag and started wiping off the objects handled by the teens and Tei.

Mo toyed with the necklaces. "I need to know where they're made and if you have sold any recently."

Ronnie Fulchess grew impatient. "Not for nothing, Detective, but I think that your focus should be more on the meaning of the amulet."

"I'm more interested in where they were made, how they got here, and why one wound up on the neck of a dead man. Don't tell me how to conduct an investigation."

"Suit yourself, Rodriguez. May be that's why the jury didn't believe your testimony in the Cane murder trial. Your focus was all wrong. Don't think we don't read the papers here in Essex County."

"Shove it up your ass, Fulchess. If you're so great, why are you buried in the back of Prosecutor's Office taking morning naps?"

"I don't think I like your tone."

"I don't give a damn what you like!"

Mo wanted to push his bulbous nose so far into his face, that it would pop out the back of his head. "Tei, may be we're just wasting our time with this jerk off."

"Look boys, enough already." She turned to G.P. "Can we come back another time? I was wondering if you had any receipts for necklaces you might have sold within the past month."

"I'd have to look. Can I have a few days?" G.P. said nervously.

"I'm done here." Mo left the room slamming the door to the Aura Quest.

Tei turned to Fulchess. "Ronnie, I'm sorry if Mo was a little nasty. He's working another homicide beside McShand's. He caught the Esel case. Stress is his watchword right about now. I apologize if he was rude."

The old cop bristled. "Maybe he'd be under less stress, if he took the counsel of older wiser cops. I been working murder cases when he was still trying to learn how to pee standing up." Fulchess softened a little bit when he looked at Tei. " But on the other hand you, my dear, have been delightful. If there's anything I can do, by all means let me know." Fulchess grabbed her hand and kissed it lightly. He turned to G.P. "Help her, anyway you can."

"Okay." G.P. drew back. A swell of queasiness passed over him. The hand kissing scene made him sick. The thought of kissing the hand of she, whose hand shook hundreds of hands, that shuffled stacks of confessions signed by dirty, filthy criminals, alarmed him. All G.P. could do was muster a friendly, weak wave at Detective Wheeler as she walked out the door. When the door closed, Fulchess lit into the unsuspecting shop keeper.

"What kind of moron are you, G.P.?"

"What are you talking about? Now what did I do?"

"You don't want the law poking around this place do you? Don't be so eager to help the next time. Your Uncle Hugo would not appreciate it."

"What do *you* know about my Uncle Hugo? I don't care what my dear Uncle thinks. I've been estranged from him. He doesn't speak to me any-more. Besides you just told me to help her."

"Well, you wouldn't want to get blamed for Terence McShand's death would you?" The look on Fulchess' face had an evil quality to it. "I mean let's face it. We both know that you are the only place that makes and sells those moon pentagram necklaces. Who knows what kinds of stories people could concoct?"

"I don't understand." The look in Fulchess' eyes frightened G.P. He felt uncomfortable, as though Fulchess had the one big secret that could ruin his life in a New York minute, and wasn't telling. G.P.'s bowels twisted from the inside out. "I don't know what you mean, Ron."

"Well, let's just say, my little pagan friend, if something were to go wrong, I may not be able to protect you. I have go back to the office. Have a nice day

G.P." With that last warning, a whistling police detective exited the Aura Quest.

I'm screwed, so screwed. G.P. thought.

G.P. had no idea where Fulchess was going with all this. He hadn't seen his Uncle Hugo since the night he had disowned him. Even the few times his mother saw Hugo, the conversation was friendly, but G.P.'s name was never mentioned. And now this cop, who came in once in a blue moon to buy candles, threatens him.

So why would one of Essex County's finest try to pin the McShand murder on him? He was no more capable of killing a man than using a public toilet. G.P. Scalisi was just a harmless con man. Fulchess knew that. But somehow he had this terrible feeling that the crafty old cop was up to something, and he would become a pawn.

Chapter 4

75 MAIN STREET
HACKENSACK, NJ

It was a pleasant day for a walk downtown.

McShand's former office was located on lower Main Street, two blocks from the Bergen County Courthouse in an old building.

Most of Bergen County's prominent lawyers were housed in the New Court's Plaza building. McShand's office was almost invisible, identified only by a single plastic shingle taped to the inside of a beveled glass door adjacent to a convenience store. Mo thought it odd that McShand's office was located in such a decrepit place. He tried the door handle. It was locked. Just as he was about to walk into the convenience store, the store owner approached him.

"Can I help you? Are you looking for someone?"

"Yeah, I'm Detective Rodriguez. I'm investigating the murder of Mr. McShand. I need to get into that office upstairs. And you are?"

"Krishna Desai. I'm the landlord. We were all very troubled to hear of Mr. McShand's death. Nice man, good tenant, too. Paid the rent on time or in advance. I'd be happy to let you in."

The shop keeper ran back inside and retrieved a large set of keys. Mo listened as the chatty landlord spoke of the virtues of Terence McShand. The two proceeded up a long beat up staircase.

"What kind of rent was Mr. McShand paying?"

"Well, the condition of the building is not perfect. As you can see, I am still renovating. Walls are only half painted and the like. But he only paid 700 hundred a month. On Main Street that's cheap rent. This area is quite popular, you know."

"Sure is. How long was his office here?"

"Mr. McShand was my tenant since 1980. Ah, here we are Detective. Let me open the door for you."

Mo was a little more than surprised when the door opened. He was shocked. It was a one man office, and it reminded him of his cousin Alberto's solo practice office in Jersey City.

Alberto Rodriguez renovated an old Italian bakery and turned it into a law office. As a new practicing lawyer, he made ends meet—barely. His name was written in soap writing on a glass store front, right above the phrase, "*Se habla Espanol*" and "*Notario Publico Aqui*." Alberto also ran a small insurance company out of the back office of his law office, and a numbers racket when no one was looking.

Terence McShand's office was no different than his cousin Alberto's. It wasn't the office of a lawyer playing in the big leagues. There were no armies of secretaries and support staff, no mahogany paneled law library with oil paintings of the firm's partners. He saw a single rotary phone on an old desk. The office was disorganized; newspapers were everywhere. Seventy Five Main Street shouldn't be the office of a successful real estate lawyer. On top of all this, another situation bothered him.

The room was covered in black fingerprint dust. One name came to him without a second thought: Jack Halloran. Jack beat him to McShand's office.

"That S.O.B." he muttered. "Do you mind if I stay here and look around for awhile?"

"No, of course not. You know someone from your office was here already. He took the fingerprints, as you can see."

"Did you get his name?"

"No Sir, but he had a badge like yours. I'm sorry. If there is anything I can do, please do not hesitate to ask. If you are a friend of Mr. McShand, I will give you a great deal on the rent. A great deal. Cheapest rent in all of Hackensack."

"Yeah, thanks. Will do, Mr. Desai."

Desai turned to leave but he had one final thing to tell Mo. "Detective, did you know that this building has a peculiar history? It used to be a Spiritualist Church run by a Princess White Cloud in the seventies. Isn't that strange? A Spiritualist Church now a law office, and now the lawyer is dead and returns to the spirit. Life and death come full circle. Strange, yes?"

Mo didn't really care about the philosophical connection Desai tried to make. "If I see McShand's ghost hanging around, I'll let you know. Thanks for the info."

"Yes, yes, very good. Just lock the door, on your way out." Desai continued yattering about McShand until Mo ushered him into the hallway and closed the door behind him. He was relieved to get away from Desai.

Mo donned plastic gloves right away then checked to see if McShand's telephones were still working. He heard a dial tone and called Thomas Clarefield at home. He was lucky. The doctor was in.

"Tom? You busy?"

Holding the phone in left hand, the medical examiner looked at his right hand, which strategically cupped the protuberous breast of a pretty young woman laying next to him.

He was smack in the middle of what could only be described as an amateur breast exam. Now *this* was annoying. He looked back at the telephone.

"Well, I was just puttering around the house, if you must know. *Now* whose dead? Another lawyer or judge? I can't take many more dead legal eagles. Mo, you're wearing me out."

"Look, can you come down here to 75 Main Street. A coupla blocks away from the court house."

"Do I have a choice? There's no body there, right? Do I have to go or could I send my assistant?"

"This is the McShand murder, Thomas. Do me a favor. Show up with an assistant and a fingerprint kit."

"If you insist."

"I owe you one."

"You most certainly do."

#

In his usual flamboyant style, Tom Clarefield arrived at McShand's Office with a crime scene technician. He looked around at the cramped office.

"This is the office of the millionaire real estate lawyer? What a shithole. He probably died of embarrassment. "

"Tom, whoever did this fingerprinting did a half assed job." A voice commented. Mo looked over at the man tried to retrieve latent prints from various surfaces.

"Who the hell is that?"

"The voice from the Peanut gallery? Mo meet Peanut. Peanut meet Mo. My criminalist."

The two men exchanged friendly nods." "Is that your name?"

"Nah," the criminalist answered. "It's Penotuccio. Peanut is just easier."

"I got here and found the place already dusted." Mo continued.

43

"Well, since there isn't a dead body up here, why did you call me?" The medical examiner asked.

"I need a fresh set of eyes, Doc." Mo paused. "Thanks for coming out."

"Okay. Sure. Go ahead. Take my eyes. Ruin my sex life. Talk to me."

"I was going through McShand's files. This guy had quite a business." He picked up an open red robe file labeled The Shamrock Properties. "Here. He owned a strip mall out on Route 17 a couple of years ago. Owned it under Shamrock Management Ltd. Sold it for 750 grand then turned around, and keeps a property management contract for 300 grand per year. He was also the lawyer for Shamrock, and paid himself a 100 thousand dollar retainer. One real estate deal and this asshole makes over a million dollars. There's not a lot of files here, but with a few like this, how many clients does he need, right?"

"Right. And why would someone dust his office for prints? Any evidence that he was killed here?"

Peanut piped up from the background. "Don't know yet, but it's possible. Someone wanted prints really bad, but it seems like they weren't looking in any specific areas. Mostly on the file cabinets. They missed a lot of finger-prints. The dust was applied, but apparently lifters weren't used correctly to pick them up. They did a real shitty job. Watch this."

His dexterous fingers twirled the Zephyr brush ever so lightly over the print. Peanut sprayed compressed air over the area, removing excess dust. He worked the lifter tape in a circular motion over the area to remove static. Placing the center of the tape over the developed print, he smiled. Gently, he lifted the tape from the surface of the cabinet and placed it on a medium. "Gotcha."

Mo noticed two index cards sloppily taped on the cabinet. The cards read Wildegrenn, Inc., W.C. Land Development, and The CrestCane Properties. He opened the door of the cabinet. "Bedtime reading kiddies. Let's see what's in these files." His face fell. "Dammit, the folders are empty. All the paper-work is missing for W.C. Land Developement. I've heard that before. Wait, didn't that deal catch a lot of heat in the press because of the —"

"Dead bodies. During an excavation to lay a foundation for one of Cane's architectural monstrosities, the work crew came across an old Potter's Field. Cane was supposed to follow state regulations and remove the bodies. Rumor has it that he either didn't, or did a bad job of disinterment. A lot of litigation over that piece of land. The whole thing really pissed J.W. Cane off. But as usual, Cane got his way."

The Peanut gallery chimed in. "That's right. The case made headlines in the Bergen Record for weeks then just died. Yep, W.C. Land Development. That was the project."

"So what happened?"

"Seems like some old lady sued Cane, his development company, and the city for failing to do the right thing with the bodies. And the case was dismissed."

"Well, if you want my two cents, maybe McShand had something to do with that lawsuit, and someone's trying to get even with him. Let's face it. The W.C. Land Development folder is missing. All the other folders remain in place correct?"

"Most are, yeah."

"So am I dismissed? I have an appointment." The medical examiner quickly tired of the whole thing. Mo knew that his thoughts were no doubt elsewhere, probably back in bed next to some twenty something woman.

"For now."

"Mo, Peanut will stay and finish up. You should thank him for coming out, too."

"Thanks. I appreciate it, Peanut."

The criminalist smiled. "No problem. Gets me out of the lab. See you back at the office." He slammed the door on the way out.

After Clarefield left, Mo stood in McShand's office staring out a dirty window facing the street. At that moment, he remembered the old arthritic woman hobbling around Terence McShand's funeral, gloating over his untimely death.

High time to talk to my new girlfriend, Sophiah Brinkworth, he thought to himself.

Chapter 5

BERGEN COUNTY PROSECUTOR'S OFFICE
HACKENSACK, NJ

Tei Wheeler couldn't swallow anymore of the courthouse cafeteria's coffee. Most days it was bearable, but today the brew was awful. Drinking a sulfuric acid cocktail would have been a better option than the decaf. As she sipped the bitter coffee, she looked up. Captain Edgar Baldwin propped himself directly on her desk.

It was hard to believe this man was a master of manipulation. His frame was small and wiry, with a well cultivated beer belly. Looking at the top of his head, his male pattern baldness, stretched from ear to ear making him look like Friar Tuck. If she closed her eyes, she could easily picture him making a Trappist port wine jelly, or baking bread in a long, brown woolen robe.

But Edgar Baldwin wasn't a monk and a long way from humility. The two had a tenuous employer-employee relationship. A formidable enemy or fair weather friend, Tei Wheeler tolerated him because she had to. She didn't trust him, and he didn't like her, but at least he respected her police work.

"How's the Esel case going, Wheeler? Is the autopsy finished? Someone better pick her body up immediately, or else I'm charging Clarefield rent."

Tei laughed. "Captain, it's a problem. Despite all the publicity, no one has claimed the body. "

"So what have you done to expedite the process?"

"I started shakin' the family tree, if you know what I mean, to see if anyone's interested in burying her."

"Any luck?"

"None. No immediate family member wants to bury her."

Baldwin looked somewhat puzzled. "She had family, right? Her sister, the assemblyman's wife? What about her?"

"Yep, Maybelle Esel Smithfield, Assemblyman Smithfield's wife, and the judge's younger sister." Tei carefully opened her spiral note pad. "Let me tell you what she said." Tei cleared her throat." 'I don't care if you dump her body in the Newark Bay just don't bring it here.' Then she hung up on me."

"Great. How about a husband?"

"Nope."

" Ex-husband?"

"Uh, no."

"Children?"

"Not a chance."

"Parents?"

"Died decades ago."

"I heard she had a nephew who was a lawyer. What about him?"

"Maybelle's Smithfield's son? Killed himself last year."

"Not a good thing. Anybody at all?"

"Well, she had a maiden Aunt Freda, whose like nine hundred years old." Tei stated looking over her notes.

"And?"

"She's half deaf. When she finally understood who I was, and what I was calling about, she yelled, 'A–a-ah!' Then hung up on me."

Baldwin frowned. "Figure out what to do with the body when the autopsy is complete. Find family somewhere, Wheeler. By the way, where are we with the Judge's autopsy report?"

"Dr. Clarefield said that he found something strange. He hasn't completed his final report. Said that he found something very curious."

"Curious does nothing for closing cases. Tell him to move his ass on that report. Close this case, Detective. Find the killer soon. This is a *Superior Court Judge* for God's Sake." With that last directive, he walked away.

Tei didn't appreciate his impatience. When she heard the authoritative iciness in his voice, it was a stone's throw away from a veiled threat.

Find the killer soon? She wondered what the hell that was supposed to mean. *What the hell does he think I'm doing? Sittin' here scratchin' my ass?* But there was a subtle message. Tei knew that if this case ever blew up, Captain Teflon would hang her. Before she could implode over the situation by dwelling on it, the phone rang jolting her back into reality.

"Homicide, Wheeler."

"Good morning, Detective Wheeler. I understand that no one has come to claim the body of Arabella Esel. Is that correct?"

"Who is this?" Tei was in no mood for a crackpot. She looked at the caller id and the name Brinkworth, S. appeared.

"My name is Mrs. Brinkworth. I'm a genealogist and friend of Detective Rodriguez of your office. Detective Rodriguez and I met at the McShand funeral. Is he in?"

"No he isn't. You know the deceased?"

"Which one? The dead lawyer or dead judge?"

"Well, I was thinking about the judge. Do you know the lawyer, too?"

Years of law enforcement experience told her that when the famous or the infamous were found dead, every lunatic element, from psychics to arm chair detectives, called with "information." Sometimes the information cracked cold cases. Other times, it was no more useful than a screen door on a submarine. She wondered what Mrs. Brinkworth had to offer.

"Well dear, I actually made the acquaintance of both. You see, by profession I've been a certified genealogist for years. I researched some Esel family history for a Claudette Johnstone, a thirty six year old niece of the Judge."

"Is she the daughter of Maybelle Esel Smithfield?"

"The Senator's wife? No, no. Claudette is the daughter of Elizabeta Esel Johnstone, the judge's other sister who died some years ago. The Esels were a small family. If you go to the Bergen County Surrogate's Office, you will find a will. Claudette is the only heir. Here's her telephone number."

Tei carefully wrote down the information. "Mrs. Brinkworth?"

"Do call me Sophiah, please."

"Sophiah, thank you for the info. This was incredibly helpful. Do you mind if I ask? Are you a friend of the Judge?"

"Oh, Good Heaven's no. I have no interest in Arabella Esel." The friendly voice become uncannily cold. "In fact, Arabella Esel couldn't be dead enough for me. But I am a Christian and she does deserve a proper burial. That's the only reason I called. To see that she gets a proper Christian burial."

"I see." Tei tried to keep her talking.

"That woman was so ill tempered, biased, and no more suited to be a member of the bench than I am qualified to be a concert pianist with my rheumatoid arthritis."

"Do you know anyone who would have wanted to kill her?"

"No, I don't. But let me say this. I'm glad I'm not the police officer on this one. I think you'll have so many suspects, you'll have trouble weeding them out. I must go, Detective. Some ladies are coming over for bridge. Can you have Detective Rodriguez call me?"

"Will do. What's your number?"

After jotting down the number quickly, Tei hung up the phone. The vitriol in the old woman's voice was evident, and she wondered if she'd just hung up the phone on the Judge's killer.

Back in the Prosecutor's Office, Peanut finished stuffing some of McShand's files into another box. "Done and done. Let's get out of here. You know, Mo, I half feel sorry for this guy. What a way to go! Is death the ultimate punishment?"

Great. I have to listen to a shithouse philosopher. Mo shrugged.

"Well, we all gotta go, right?"

"Yeah, but nobody deserves to die like this, right? Here he was a bigtime lawyer, and then he gets found spinnin' around in his car like an idiot."

"A poor man's punishment for his sins is that he spends the rest of his days dreaming about a life he can only view from a distance. My mother in Puerto Rico had a saying: '*La gente rica paga por sus pecados por su salud o sus ninos.*'"

"What's that mean in English?"

"Rich people pay for their sins through their health or their children. But at least, he doesn't have to worry about the rising costs of health insurance anymore."

"Now that's not fair. You know, I hear he gave a lot to local charities. I'm sure heaven has a little room for him somewhere."

"Or hell for that matter. We don't know about the man's misdeeds, do we?" he said pointing to the box of real estate files. "So what if he donated to charities? May be it's blood money given to ease his conscience."

"How about the judge?"

"What about her?"

"I mean she was a judge right? Died with dirt stuffed in her mouth. That's terrible."

"So what? You kiss ass, your lips get dirty. I'm sure that she ate in good restaurants and probably had a nice summer home somewhere. It cost her. She pissed somebody off enough to get dead ." Mo stopped in his tracks. "You know who I care about? The day old babies someone drops in a dumpster, and the teenage prostitute with the slit throat who was somebody's runaway daughter. Those are the people I care about. They deserve the dignity in death, they never got in life. And most times they don't even get it in death. Poor people deserve to have their killers brought to justice, just as much as the rich ones."

"But aren't the judge and the lawyer people, too?"

"Get off your soap box, Penatuccio and stop the mental masturbation."

"Okay, okay. Time for lunch, Mo?"

"Nah, not today. Some other time." Mo didn't want to eat lunch with him. He wasn't interested in listening to Peanut's liturgy on who deserves what justice. He left the office and walked into Cheffy's deli to grab a sandwich.

#

Before he could even open the wax paper around his pastrami on rye, Tei handed him a stack of messages.

"You're new girlfriend called."

Dropping everything on his desk, he ran his fingers through his hair and grinned. "Which one?" He wondered if it was the little nurse with the nice ass, or the demure blond X Ray tech he'd met at Clarefield's house last summer.

"The 82 year old one. I knew you liked older women, but what are you doing in your free time, Rodriguez? Hangin' out in nursing homes?" She handed him Sophiah Brinkworth's message.

Quickly Mo sat down, pounding numbers on the telephone. It rang once, twice, three times. He was just about to hang up until a sweet elderly voice picked up. "Hello?"

"Hi Sophiah, it's me, Mo Rodriguez. Like to see you sometime. That granddaughter of yours still like Spanish boys?"

Chapter 6

FOREST AVENUE
PARAMUS, NEW JERSEY
HOME OF THOMAS CLAREFIELD

"Thomas, you really must give sushi a chance. It's low in fat and high in fish oils. Very healthy for you. Let me change your mind," the woman cooed.

Clarefield lay on his back in his pajamas, highly entertained by the telephone conversation. "Raw squid is good bait for bluefish. And besides, I can show you a recent medical article explaining the various types of deadly microorganisms that can be transferred to humans by eating raw fish. I might change *your* mind, pretty lady."

"Listen, there's a wonderful place in Hackensack called Miyoshi. Let's have dinner there Saturday," she paused, "and dessert at my place."

"Are you the dessert? Can I bring the whipped cream?"

"Only if you're good," she giggled.

Evelyn Westlake was cute, and he enjoyed her enticements. This latest bit of fluff hung onto his every word. He liked women who did that. It was so nice to be admired. Good for a man's ego. He kept the coquettish picture she had given him in a faux art deco frame. When his next conquest came over for a visit, Tom simply switched photographs. So far this week, he preferred Evelyn. She was blond, beautiful, and twenty eight with a sexual appetite that clearly matched his own. The best part of Evelyn was that she was crazy about the 43-year old medical examiner. No man could have wanted more.

He continued listening to her chatter, until he looked at the upcoming date on the calendar. It was coming close to May 13th. Suddenly, the medical examiner lost focus on the conversation. He felt dizzy and sick.

"Evelyn, I have to go."

"Sure darling. Is anything wrong?"

"No, no. My beeper went off. Later." He hung up the phone.

Life for Thomas Clarefield was as complicated as he was. He was a big man, a unique combination of Scottish-Jewish descent. He knew how to play life at both ends of the ethnic spectrum being an active member of Duncan's Scottish Rite Masonry, and a member of the United Jewish Congress of New York. His Jewish grandfather, Edvard Klarrfeld, owned one of New York's premier foundries at the turn of the century. In order to travel in non-Jewish business circles, he changed the name to Clarefield.

Clarefield money was old money built on the work of immigrants. Young Thomas grew up with servants on a large Long Island estate. But unlike many in his class, he had the unique ability to understand common folk.

Between semesters in college and medical school, he lied to his parents about accepting research fellowships. Instead, Clarefield spent time sweating in the foundry with his father's men. He applied for the job as an iron worker under another name. Working under a cloak of social invisibility, he went by the name of Harry Smith, living anonymously as a member of the rank and file.

Clarefield Steel Inc. was so large, he could have died as Harry Smith, and no would have been the wiser. No one noticed the boss' son, because no one had ever met him. His father thought he'd hidden his privileged son far away from ordinary life.

Yet, every summer, young Thomas drank with the ironworkers, smoked cigars and fished with them in the Long Island Sound. It was a well kept secret for years. He enjoyed his "Harry" persona because secrecy and mystery intrigued him.

So did identifying an unknown dead body. Thomas got this strange intellectual high figuring out who the body belonged to, and why the person died. Having lived anonymously, he knew that there were many Harry Smiths in the world, unknown people with no connection to a past. How they lived, or why they died was pure speculation. The why and how questions fascinated him.

Sometimes the cause of death was so painfully obvious, such as the case of a young man who had thrown himself in front of a New Jersey Transit train. No mysterious cause of death there.

Then there was a hiker who came across some dried human bones in a field, wearing some disintegrated clothing. A black polyester fiber, traced back to a camera man's jacket at a popular New York radio station, ultimately identified both victim and killer.

An innocuous thread. An unknown face. Putting the pieces of the puzzle together, and finding an answer. This was the stuff Thomas Clarefield loved because death had become a strange mistress to him over the years.

He looked at the calendar again. May 13th. How could he forget? He felt ill just thinking about it. That was the day his wife and infant son died, the day Death met him head on.

Before becoming a medical examiner, Thomas Clarefield began his medical career as an obstetrician. Life was perfect for him back then. Rising into the ranks as a respected attending physician at a teaching hospital, he had a beautiful wife, a healthy one month old infant, and an expensive home in an upper class neighborhood. But more importantly, he loved bringing life into the world.

On May 13th, 1981, after a grueling five hour caesarian section, he had successfully delivered a healthy set of twins. When he had stepped out of the operating room, the police, and his Surgical Chief waited for him.

May 13th. How could he forget? A juvenile delinquent had set Clarefield's house on fire while he was at work, killing his wife and infant son.

He demanded to see the bodies in the morgue. The terrified young physician expected to see charred remains. Instead, their bodies were virtually unblemished, colored only by death's pale cast. Why did they look like that? It wasn't fair! His little family looked like they were asleep. It was all wrong! His wife should be waking up any moment to kiss him. The baby should be crying. It didn't make sense to him, since the police explained that the house literally crumbled around them.

A fatherly medical examiner explained how people die from smoke inhalation and heat rather than being burned to death by fire. He told him about the brave firefighter who went into the blaze, and searched for people knowing that anyone inside was probably already dead at that point.

With that, Clarefield broke down and cried. He had accepted that medicine was about life and death. He dissected cadavers, delivered an occasional stillborn, and watched people take their last breath in an emergency room. As a physician, he was *used* to death. But this was different. He never thought Mr. Death would pay him a personal visit.

The seventeen year old arsonist pled not guilty by reason of insanity. He hired an expensive team of psychiatrists to show that he was insane at the time he set fire to Clarefield's home. Indeed, if a jury found that he was legally insane at the time of the act, the young arsonist would spend the rest of his days in a forensic mental hospital instead of Rahway State Prison. Under that scenario, if he eventually proved that his mental disease was cured,

53

he'd return to society.

When Thomas Clarefield heard the arsonist's plea, the war began.

He reached out to the police and the prosecutor. He lectured freely at crime victim's groups, and hired private investigators to do background checks on the arsonist and his family. Thomas had a full court press with any newspaper that would listen, determined to let the world know that he wouldn't let this murderer hide behind some bullshit psychiatric defense. He called in favors from cadres of politicians, including senators and assemblymen. He wanted a death warrant, pure and simple, for the man who killed his family.

The juvenile's family had money, too, but that was no problem for Clarefield. He would simply outspend them. After two years of ceaseless criminal and civil litigation, he forced the juvenile's family to seek shelter of the bankruptcy court. And once "Mr. Green" failed to walk into the office, the expensive lawyers asked for adjournments and then vanished. The case went to the Public Defender's Office and the juvenile pled guilty to murder to avoid the death penalty.

Looking back, Clarefield would have preferred to have the kid executed on the street. It would have cost him significantly less in money and time. But unless he was able to pull the trigger, it wouldn't give Clarefield satisfaction, only a murder rap. In the long run, he had succeeded. At the end of the day, the juvenile arsonist would die in jail.

Revenge he had. Money he had. But Thomas Clarefield's cheerful days as an obstetrician were over. He lost his heart for it, and wasn't sure what to do with the rest of his medical career.

That was where Detective Mo Rodriguez came in. He had made the arrest of the arsonist, and over time the two men became close friends. Mo convinced him that he didn't have to deal with living patients anymore. Dead people need good doctors, too.

Such was the birth of Thomas Clarefield, pathologist. He made an eternal pact with the Grim Reaper. Where there was a homicide, he would find the killer.

Whenever he saw May 13th on a calendar it made his blood chill, his heart race, and brought tears to his eyes. So when May of each year came around, he'd distract himself by a vacation, making sure he was nowhere in New Jersey when that day came and went.

Thomas Clarefield really didn't want the wealthy twenty eight year old debutante. Instead, he wanted a place he could never go back to — the past. That's what made him a restless soul. He looked at the clock. Gaining control over his emotions, the doctor forced himself to pick up the telephone.

"Hello, Evelyn? I'm running right now, but listen. How about we try that sushi restaurant in two weeks? Sounds like a plan? Good Babe. Gotta run." After hanging up, he ripped down the wall calendar and called his travel agent. He booked a cruise to St. Maarten the week of May 13th.

#

Jack Halloran did an abysmal job of lifting the latent prints from McShand's office, but he did an excellent job of sanitizing McShand's files. He already knew whose fingers were behind those latent prints: the crazy self-proclaimed witch. Pulling off the road, he called his client from a pay phone.

"Hello, Mr. Cane?"

"Why, hello there, John. Did you find McShand's killer yet?"

"I'm very close to making an arrest, sir."

"How close?"

"Closer than you can possibly imagine, Mr. Cane."

"Glad to hear it. I've wired another ten thousand dollars into your account."

"Thank you, Mr. Cane. I'll be in touch shortly."

"I am sure you will. By the way, I've spoken with Mrs. McShand."

"She's on board with your plan?"

"Of course," Cane laughed. "Why wouldn't she? I own her. She said that she'd love to have sex with Rodgriguez."

Chapter 7

"Would you like a cup of tea, Detective?"

Before Mo answered, the cheerful old woman signaled a servant, who stopped folding linen napkins at the end of an exquisite old mahogany dining room table. She smiled politely at Mo, and proceeded to the kitchen. Sophiah Brinkworth's wealth was obvious.

"I like your style, Mrs. Brinkworth. You've got some great Victorian antiques."

"Oh Detective, don't be so impressed. I've had all this stuff in my family for years. I suppose some of its worth money. We used to call it junk, but now they call it vintage." She laughed.

"We should all be lucky enough to own junk like this, Mrs. Brinkworth."

"So tell me about yourself. And the judge, of course."

"Where do I begin? H-m-m-m. Let's see." The old woman's eyes looked to the ceiling. "We Brinkworths have been in Ridgewood since the town was founded back in the 1600s. Isaiah Brinckworth, that's Brinkworth with a "ck" and not just a "k," was an ancestor, a Protestant pastor on my father's side. My mother, Jane Mount, was from a prominent old family of doctors and educators, the Mounts of Brooklyn Heights. I taught in the Ridgewood school

56

system for almost forty years. Started back in 1959. Just about when you were born, I suspect."

"What did you teach?"

Mo watched the old woman become momentarily wistful. "First grade. It's such a wonderful age. The children, so innocent, so sweet. I really miss it. But part of the wisdom of getting old is admitting when you can't do something anymore. When I didn't see the sweetness in the children's faces and my patience was gone, I knew it was time to retire."

"So how does being a certified genealogist come into the picture, Mrs. Brinkworth?"

"So you know I'm board certified. Good, good. I like that. You do your homework."

"Didn't have to. Your business card advertises it."

Sophiah smiled as she brushed a wisp of soft white hair away from her face. "Genealogy has been my hobby since my retirement. And since I came from such an old family, well, it seemed like a natural vocation."

"Madame, are you ready for tea?"

"Ah, Celestine has returned." Sophiah gestured to the maid who stood in the doorway. "Cream and sugar, Detective? So, tell me about your family."

"Well, we came here from Puerto Rico in the 1950's. Typical story. We wanted a better life."

"Which immigrant doesn't?"

Mo drew himself up. "We're not immigrants, Mrs. Brinkworth. P.R. is a U.S. territory. Remember? I thought genealogists knew their history." Admonishing her lack of tact, he shook a finger in her direction.

"Touché, Detective. I meant no offense."

As Mo looked at Sophiah, he realized that she was truly mortified by her own comment, so he let her off the hook. "None taken. So satisfy me. Why were you at Terence McShand's funeral?"

Rheumatoid arthritis made her hands look like twisted vines. She could barely pour the tea. After her lips touched the rim of the porcelain tea cup, she set down it down on the table with trembling hands.

"Don't get old, Detective. That's the secret."

"And the alternative is?"

"What happened to that poor young man up there." She pointed to an ornate oval portrait with gold leaf frame. It was an oil painting of a young man, late teens with feathered, longish hair, and the same piercing blue eyes as Sophiah Brinkworth. He wore a light beige tuxedo with wide brocaded lapels. It was a dated-looking, high school graduation, or prom picture. Mo figured it had to be her son, but he played dumb.

"Who's he?"

"Who *was* he, Detective. That young man was my son, Martin Saunford.

57

He's dead. The painting was done back in 1977, Detective."

"I'm so sorry, Mrs. Brinkworth. No parent should ever bury a child."

"Drink your tea Detective, and I'll tell you a story. Go on."

Mo picked up his tea cup and looked at her with curious eyes. "I'm listening."

"Good." She watched him take a long sip of tea. "You're right. Children should never die before their parents. But things happen. I'm afraid." She sighed. "Martin had just graduated high school. I had his graduation picture copied into that oil painting. It was supposed to be a surprise for him. Never gave it to him, though. Don't know why. My son was remarkable young man, academically gifted. Had early acceptance to three Ivy League universities. He chose Rutgers because he wanted to stay in New Jersey. But somehow along the way, he got lost."

"Drugs?"

"Precisely. I finally realized he had a problem when I received a telephone call from a lovely Detective Bowers. She told me that she'd just picked my son up for driving while intoxicated. Back then, I had a lot of influence. The whole incident went unrecorded." Mo noticed that her face flushed beet red. "I'm truly embarassed by the whole thing."

"So what Mrs. Brinkworth? Kids lose control. Parents have to bail them out. Happens all the time. I wasn't a perfect teenager."

Her voice cracked. "But that doesn't *happen* in our family, Detective. It's different for us. We were pillars of the community. My mother was a member of the Daughters of the American Revolution. My father was on the board of the Metropolitan Museum of Art. But what do they say? 'Pride goeth before a fall.'"

Mo touched her hand. "This is your son we're talking about. Kids make mistakes."

"Martin's bad habits got worse. He began lying and stealing. Typical druggie behavior I'm told. He dropped out of college in his freshman year. Detective, my son should have been a doctor or a lawyer. But instead after years of drug use, he died naked, face down in an alley way." She paused. "Frozen to death."

The old woman kept an incredible sense of composure as she told the story. She exhibited some emotion, and her eyes filled up, but she was neither weepy nor histrionic. "I accepted long ago that Martin would only flit in and out of my life when he needed something. A whole year went by, and I didn't hear from him. As it turned out, he was living on the streets in California, pretending to be an artist. Asked me to send him money for art supplies, so he could hone his craft." She half laughed. "Imagine that. A starving painter living in Los Angeles. How unique."

"So what did you do?"

"Sent him fifty thousand dollars. Then I offered to put him into a private hospital in Beverly Hills. He wrote me a long, rambling letter thanking me profusely for the money, and the hospital offer, which he politely turned down. But that was my Martin. He would vanish and show up, vanish then show up. It was a pattern I'd grown accustomed to. So, when I didn't hear from him for several months, it was not unusual. Then one day something happened. This unkempt, dirty man appeared at my front door. I didn't recognize him right away. Then I knew, Detective, then I knew."

"Knew what?"

"That this episode would be his last jaunt on the street. Which is how I made the unfortunate acquaintance of one Terence McShand, Esquire." Suddenly, Sophiah Brinkworth's eyes were on fire.

"Did he have something to do with your son's death?"

"In a strange way, yes. You see, no one claimed Martin's body immediately. I didn't know he was dead, so the City of Hackensack buried him in a Potter's Field called Working Man's Circle Memorial Park."

"You mean the old Cemetery on Liberty Street?"

"It *was* an old cemetery. A developer, a scoundrel named John Wilkinson Cane, and his lawyer, Mr. McShand, converted the burial ground into million dollar condominiums. I sued the City, Cane, and his development company. I wanted to get my son's body back, so I could give him a proper Christian burial."

"Were you successful?"

"Yes and no, but mostly no. I delayed the construction of condominiums for seven months with a lot of litigation. Cost old Cane a lot of money, but Martin's body couldn't be located because the City of Hackensack either lost or destroyed the cemetery's burial records. The judge ordered Cane to relocate the bodies, but put no time limit on it, so he never did it. And this horrid woman judge yelled at me in open court. She said that I was a disgraceful mother to let my son die in the streets. If I didn't know his whereabouts when he was alive, why should I care about burying his body? All I can say is that my case was dismissed by a judge who sat like a handkerchief tucked in the breast pocket of the City's lawyers. And those beautiful luxury condominiums? They rest on top of fifty thousand dead bodies, one of which is my son, Martin."

"What judge handled your case?"

Sophiah gave Mo a mischievous grin, the same grin a child gives to a parent when his hand is caught in the cookie jar. "You know who, Detective. That's why you asked me the question."

"Arabella Esel," Mo whispered.

"Correct. So now you know why I hate Terence McShand and Judge Esel. Couldn't be dead enough for me. Murder victims? Fitting ends for both of them."

Mo reached out for her hand. "Sophiah, I know that you would never hurt anyone, but I have to ask you. Can you account for your whereabouts on—?"

"Of course, Detective, I understand. In the early morning of Mr. McShand's death, I had a hair appointment at Salon Chanteuse. On the morning that Judge Esel was killed, you and I were at the same place, McShand's funeral. Remember?" She winked at him.

"So you saw me?"

"Yes, you were with that attractive black woman. Detective Wheeler, isn't it?"

"Good surveillance, Sophiah."

No arthritis in the eyes, he thought. *I didn't think the old girl saw me.*

"I could never kill anyone personally, Detective. But getting back to the reason you came here today. I called a young lady related to the dead judge. She's ready and willing to take the corpse off your hands. If you don't mind, I'll take you to her house."

"What's your interest in the dead judge's relative?"

"We're both members of the New Jersey Historical Society."

#

Stuck in the death seat again, Mo was now a terrified passenger in Sophiah Brinkworth's late model Mercedes. From Ridgewood, they shot up Route 17, heading for Tuxedo, New York, to the home of Claudette Johnstone. Once again, he found himself stomping on the invisible brake on the passenger's side. He couldn't believe it. The old lady's driving made Tei's driving actually look good.

"Mrs. Brinkworth, can you slow it down, for Pete's Sake!" Mo watched the speedometer cresting eighty as the car wove in and out of traffic.

"Relax, Detective. You should be used to high speed chases." She smiled. "I may be a warbler on *terra firma,* but I move like greased lightning behind the wheel. The joints are creaky, but the eyes aren't."

"Mrs. Brinkworth, I'm begging you. Please! Slow down!"

"Imagine, a tough fella like you, turning chicken on me." At which point, Mo watched a green traffic light change to yellow. Instead of slowing down, the old woman floored the gas pedal, and blew through the light. Mo's jaw dropped.

"Look, once we hit the New York State border, I have no jurisdiction. If a New York State trooper pulls you off the road, I can't talk him out of a speeding ticket," he pleaded.

"That's okay, Detective. I expect no special favors. Besides we'll be at

Claudette's house in no time."

The unlikely pair crossed the New Jersey border into New York State. Passing everything from forested land to antique stores, Sophiah gave Mo a guided highway tour. She knew the area fairly well. But her memories were of farms and open land, not strip malls. She slowed down as they approached a strange looking restaurant that time eluded, the Red Apple Rest. Sophiah explained that it hadn't changed anything but its prices since 1949.

"You see that place we just passed? When I was young we used to call it The Apple. It was the place to go. They used to make the most delicious cherry vanilla ice cream. Fresh cherries as big as walnuts! Even Martin Saunford, Sr. said it was the best ice cream around. God rest his soul."

"Widowed?" Mo asked.

"Oh yes. Died of liver failure at forty eight."

"I'm sorry."

"I'm not. He was an abusive drunk. I blame him in large part for Martin Jr.'s death. He wasn't a loving man, Detective."

"Sorry, Mrs. Brinkworth."

"No worries. Ah, here's the road we need."

Sophiah cut a hard right turn off Route 17, and wheeled down an unpaved, unmarked road. For a mile, gravel underneath the Mercedes made loud crunching sounds. Sophiah drove around potholes the size of small wash tubs, as they went deeper and deeper into the woods.

"Where are we going?"

"Claudette's not far from here. Relax. This is a little piece of God's country, Detective. We only have another ten or twenty miles to go."

"Are you kidding, Mrs. Brinkworth?"

"Steady up, Detective. A little bit of old lady humor. We only have another quarter mile. Oh Mo, please call me Sophiah."

Finally, they reached their destination. A charming small Cape Cod style home appeared in the distance. Sophiah pulled up in front of the house, stopped the car, and shut off the engine.

"Should I lock the door?" Mo asked.

"You really are a city boy, aren't you? Not necessary up here. People still leave their doors open. Can you go around the other side and give me a hand, Mo?"

"You bet." Ever the gentleman, he went over to the driver's side and opened the door. With arthritic hands and a slightly hunched back, he saw that she probably weighed all of one hundred ten pounds soaking wet. She'd be a perfect crime victim, helpless looking, easily knocked down with one blow, or thrown across a room. Yet he sensed that there was this incredibly strong will trapped inside a tiny frail body. If Sophiah Brinkworth was spirited in her youth, nothing had changed, though age had taken its toll. After propping her up against the car, he reached inside and grabbed her cane.

"Hi Sophiah!" a cheerful voice called out.

"Good morning, Miss Claudette. And how are you today?"

"Lovely darling. And you?"

The sugary exchanges irked him, but over the years Mo realized that you get more flies with honey than you do with vinegar. He forced himself to be tolerant, and was pleasantly surprised when he saw the woman standing in the doorway.

For being a close relative of the dead judge who had looked one step away from a Holstein, Claudette Johnstone wasn't unattractive.

She was of average height, somewhat buxom, and not overweight. Mo noticed that she had kind eyes, and her voice was soft and gentle, almost melodic. She had naturally dark hair, quite the contrast from the dead judge's whose hair color resembled a Clairol lab experiment gone awry. But thankfully the pretty smile and warm dark eyes drew attention away from a smaller version of the hooked Esel nose. Mo enjoyed the look of her. However, this was not the time for him to think about romance.

"Sophiah, is this Detective Rodriguez?" she inquired.

"Yes, it is. And I think that he is very happy to see you. About your aunt, I mean."

Mo grabbed one arm and Claudette grabbed the other. They lifted the octogenarian up the small flight of stairs to the landing. In a nearby tree, a small baby owl swooped down and landed on a weak branch, causing it to bob up and down. Sophiah watched the wobbly limb, waiting for it to crack and send the hapless birdie crashing to the ground.

"Interesting. A baby barn owl. Wonder why he's out this time of day? For some Native Americans, Lakota I think, the owl is a messenger of death."

Mo smiled. "Not today, I hope."

Claudette gestured to Mo and Sophiah. "Please come in."

Mo contrasted the decorative tastes of the two women. Claudette's house was a tiny jewel box nestled among the trees in God's country, while Sophiah had a huge home in upper crust Ridgewood. Claudette painted her walls shades of muted pastels, warm mauves and pinks. Sophiah had expensive Victorian furnishings; Claudette preferred a mélange of vintage collectibles from various eras. Sophiah's home was sterile; Claudette's was simple and comforting.

"I guess you're wondering why I haven't come forward sooner. I apologize. I was hoping that my Aunt Maybelle would have claimed her sister's body. But I don't think that's going to happen."

"It's not." Mo cut right to the chase. "Can you tell me if there is anyone who'd want to see your aunt dead?"

Claudette blushed. "I'm afraid Detective Rodriguez, I don't know who *wouldn't* want her dead."

Suppressing a smile, he leaned forward. "Satisfy me. What was her problem with people?"

"Aunt Bella was the middle of three sisters. As a child, I think that things were awkward for her, she was the brunt of grammar school jokes. She was plump, not very pretty, but very smart. Her intelligence served her well later in life, I mean just look at her. She was a Superior Court judge, for God's sake. She had to be smart as well as politically savvy."

"Let me guess. She used her brains to get ahead, then spent the rest of her life paying back the grammar school bullies who teased her on the playground forty years ago."

"As much as I hate to admit it, that's probably true. Aunt Bella had a long memory. And she wasn't very stable, particularly if she went off her medication."

"What kind of medication did she take?"

"Stuff to control her anger. Prozac."

"Prozac? She was depressed?"

Sophia interjected. "You know what those TV therapist types say? 'Anger is depression turned outward.' "

"All I can say is that she was always acted a little mad at everyone," Mo stated matter-of-factly. "Was she involved romantically with anyone?"

"Well, she never married, and dated very infrequently. Recently she told me that she'd given up on men. One broken heart too many, I guess."

"I see." Mo smiled to himself as he thought, *like she'd have a heart to break. Made outta marble. Break that bitch's heart with a goddamn chisel.*

"Do you know of places she'd visit? People she associated with?"

"She was heavily involved in bar activities." She paused. "I meant the legal bar, not this kind of bar." Gesturing, she placed her thumb to her lips and shook it gently. "She was always invited to many affairs, but that seemed to decline after she left the criminal bench and went civil. She handled a lot of important cases."

"Important? How so? Every case is important if you're the litigant, isn't it?" Sophiah felt compelled to put in her two cents worth of opinion.

"I guess I used the wrong word." She glanced over to Mo who'd been writing away. "I meant to say high profile. The kind of cases that wind up making headlines. She handled the Dorothy Cane murder. Sophiah's lawsuit over her son's grave. Cases like that."

"Oh, that's right. I forgot about the Cane case."

Sophiah leaned in and raised an eyebrow as she looked back and forth between Claudette and Mo. "Personally, I think the bastard killed his wife. The government just couldn't convict the wily old fox."

"J.W. Cane," Mo smirked. "No matter where I go, I can't get away from him."

"Detective, is it true that whoever killed my aunt stuffed her mouth with dirt? That's what the newspaper said. Is it true?"

This was the part of the job that truly depressed him, telling the victim's family exactly how the victim had suffered. He knew the standard questions. "Did my child die quickly? The papers said he was tortured for eight hours. Is it true? Was she raped?"

He sighed. "Yes Claudette, it's true. I'm sorry."

A single tear rolled down her cheek. "Not your fault, I know. Just seems so cruel, so disgraceful. Was it the dirt that killed her?"

"I don't think so. As soon as the medical examiner finishes the autopsy, he's going to give me the final report next week. Then I think we'll know better how she died."

Claudette sniffled. "You know, no one really liked her. She once told me how her dry cleaner had deliberately ruined her suit, so she sued him. She couldn't keep a housekeeper, and all the law clerks she hired were the children of people who owed her favors. Most of them quit only after a few weeks. I don't think that she had any real friends. That's sad. She was tolerated by people because she was a judge, not because anyone really liked or cared about her."

"So what about you? Why are you willing to bury her?"

"Out of some peculiar sense of obligation, I guess. She wasn't nice to me, Detective. But she deserves a decent burial. It's the civilized thing to do." When Mo looked at her eyes, he felt sorry for her. This young woman was saddled with a chore he could never do. "When can I pick up the body?"

He was just about to respond when the little black beeper attached to his belt went off. "Excuse me, my office is calling. Can I use your phone Claudette?"

"Sure. In the kitchen."

Mo stepped out of the living room and into the kitchen. He rapidly dialed the telephone number of his office. Tei answered the phone.

"Homicide, Wheeler."

"What's up?"

"Mo, they caught a murder suspect on McShand."

"Who?"

"The witch guy."

"Now when the hell did *that* happen?"

"Jack Halloran. You better get back here."

64

His frustration echoed in the next room as he slammed the phone in its cradle. He knew something was wrong. He returned to the living room.

"Sophiah, we have to go."

"Anything wrong, Detective? I was just about to explain to Claudette how one goes about picking out the proper casket."

"Later, Sophiah," Mo snapped. "All hell's broken loose in my office." He reached for Sophiah's cane and helped her to her feet.

He turned to Claudette. It was probably not the right time, but he was somewhat attracted to the dead judge's niece. "Claudette, I have a few more questions for you but I can't stay right now. May I call you?"

"Yes, Detective, of course."

#

Minutes later, they were racing down Route 17 at breakneck speed in Sophiah's Mercedes. As a former teacher, Mo figured Sophiah was a patient observer of human behavior. He was preoccupied. She sensed it, but he wasn't in the mood to answer questions.

"You are awfully quiet, Mo. Anything wrong?"

"No, not really."

"You know, you are a handsome devil. If I had any notion that you preferred older women, I'd make a pass at you."

Mo's eyes widened. "What!"

"Just kidding. I was trying to take your mind off of whatever's bothering you."

"Oh, thanks."

She leaned over to him. "She's a cute little thing, that Claudette woman."

"She seems nice. Keep your eyes on the road, Sophiah."

"Ever married, Detective? I hope you don't think I'm prying."

"No, never went down that road. Almost did once, but being a cop isn't conducive to a stable marital life. Homicide ain't exactly a nine-to-five job. And the young lady I was engaged to couldn't have it any other way. I'm better off not married. I lived with a few women, though. I do alright."

"I imagine that you would. You seem like you really like women. Have a good relationship with your mother?"

"She lives in Aibonito in Puerto Rico, but yeah, we're close. We talk."

"I think you should ask Claudette out on a date."

"Stick to genealogy and driving the speed limit." He smiled.

"Touché again, Detective."

Mo ignored the comment. Too absorbed in his own thoughts, the detec-

65

tive watched dozens of trees move in and out of his sight on Route 17 as they crossed the border back into New Jersey. His mind raced along with Sophiah's car. The real murderer of Terence McShand was still out on the streets somewhere. They arrested the wrong guy.

Chapter 8

CRIMINAL PROCESSING UNIT
SHERIFF'S OFFICE
BERGEN COUNTY JAIL ANNEX

The Sheriff's department took his street clothes and replaced them with a bright orange jumpsuit with the letters "BCJ" emblazoned across his back. He steadied himself for the finger printing. Across the room, G.P. saw a small, metal table with ink pads and stacks and stacks of used identification cards. G.P. was horrified.

Being hauled away in front of his store patrons had no effect on him. Holding a criminal identification for a mug shot card didn't bother him either. But the thought of having the intake officer place every individual finger on a finger print pad touched by hundreds of dirty, lice infested felons made him weak.

The officer uncuffed G.P. while another officer stood back, observing the process. He brought G.P. over to the fingerprint pad set up on the stainless steel table. Without breaking stride, a muscular, well-built Sheriff's Officer squeezed ink from a fat tube, shaking it downward. With each squeeze, the ink tube made peculiar gaseous sounds which only increased G.P.'s queasiness. With each belch, G.P. felt a little worse. When the officer finally drained the tube of any ink, he ordered G.P. to give him his hand.

"Right hand."

"Okay. Here it is." Sweat poured off his hand.

"For Chrissake." The Sheriff's Officer handed him a paper towel. "Dry off your damn hand."

To his own amazement, G.P. saw the sweat dripping off his hand like running water. The only place where the droplets fell in greater quantity was around his hairline. When the Sheriff's Officer handed him a paper towel, he dried his hand, then wiped his forehead, too.

"Sorry, sir. Just a little nervous."

"Let's try this again." G.P. heard the annoyance in the officer's voice. The officer grabbed G.P.'s hand. Panic stricken, the terrified metaphysician flattened his hand like a starfish in the late stages of rigor mortis. He gritted his teeth as his breathing rapidly increased.

"Yes Sir-r-r."

"Knock it off, asshole! You can make this hard or easy. Your choice."

G.P. remembered the psychic protection meditation he'd taught his students in his Witchcraft 101 class. He meditated on the Gracious Goddess and built a pillar of white light around himself for protection against the demonic ink germs. He took a deep cleansing breath, as he envisioned a healing, protective white light wrapping around him like a ribbon tied around a birthday package. It worked. His mind felt strong, and he saw the white light ribbon, floating in mid air. The end of the ribbon had the face of a friendly, big eyed serpent, and it winked at him from the other side of the room. Drifting, the glowing airborne anaconda visible only to him, slithered over. When it finally reached G.P., the light snake wrapped around him, making him feel warm and cozy. The nasty voice of the intake officer grew farther and farther away. He saw the officer's lips move, his hands flail, but his voice kept fading, until it sounded like a seagulls squawking as they flew over a peaceful ocean. G.P. slipped away in a comfortable dream-like state. His mouth curled up into a silly smile, until he couldn't hear a thing anymore. All was silent and calm right before everything went black.

The guard reached for a wall telephone. "Get an ambulance in here! Inmate down!"

#

Mo raced into his squad room, bypassing everyone without his usual chatty conversation. He stood outside of Edgar Baldwin's office, only to see a full house: Ron Fulchess, Jack Halloran, Tei Wheeler and a young lawyer. Edgar saw Mo outside and waved him in. Overcome with that incredible sensation of get-out-the-Vaseline -I'm-about-to-be-screwed-again feeling, Mo opened the door.

"Mo, good to see you. Sit. We have good news. With the help of Ronnie Fulchess and Jack Halloran we picked up McShand's killer, G.P. Scalisi."

"The witch guy? So how did you make that brilliant determination? Through him?"

Mo pointed at Jack Halloran who sat poised like a cat across the room.

"Look, Ronnie and Jack were really helpful. Jack even found the murder weapon, and got a confession for us. This is what happens when law enforcement cooperates," Baldwin retorted.

"Really? What a neat little package. And where did you find the gun?" Mo's eyes were on fire as he spat the question to Jack.

"Same place you were looking, Mo. McShand's office."

"That's bullshit! I tore that office apart. There was no gun in that office. Unless, of course, you found it before I got there. I saw the fingerprint dust, Jack."

"Not possible good buddy. Ask the landlord. I met Mr. Desai *after* you came."

Baldwin picked up a brown manila envelope. "Sorry to burst your bubble, but here it is. Has Scalisi's prints all over it. You must have missed it."

Jack reached into his pocket and pulled out a crumpled soft pack of Camel cigarettes. "Look, I know this is a smoke free environment, but I feel like violating the law. The tension here is killing me. You guys don't mind, right?" Jack lit up before anyone responded.

"Take this." The quiet young man who had been observing the banter between the cops handed Jack an empty coffee cup to use as an ashtray. He looked at Mo. "Hi, I'm Harper Grey. I'm the new Assistant Prosecutor. I'll be handling the McShand murder prosecution."

"Mo Rodriguez." He eyed the thin young man, wondering where his loyalties lay.

"Detective, I understand you were the first on the scene. You dove on the car and rescued the corpse."

"Yeah, I did it. So, ah, Mr. Prosecutor, what's your take on all of this?"

"I don't know yet. I have to see the evidence. But it sounds like we have a pretty solid case against this Scalisi guy."

Edgar interjected. "You know, Mr. Grey here comes from the U.S. Attorney's Office. He's one of those big federal lawyers."

"How nice," replied Mo. He truly could have cared less. "So what's this about a confession?"

Ronnie Fulchess spoke up. "Well, you know I have a background in the occult. I spoke to him and he gave it up."

"Really Fulchess? So you spoke to him witch-to-witch? Is that it?"

"You know, I didn't like your attitude before and I like it even less now!" Standing up, Fulchess leaned in Mo's direction. "Let's face it. You couldn't close the case and I did. That's why you're all pissed off."

Mo lunged at Fulchess. Harper, half the size of both men, planted himself in between them. Edgar Baldwin grabbed Mo, while Jack held Fulchess back.

"Enough!" Tei yelled. "All you boys just sit your asses down for a minute." She turned to Fulchess. "Ronnie, Jack, could I talk to you guys in the interview room? I'm a little confused about some stuff. Could you help me out?"

"Now there's a wise woman," Fulchess glared at Mo. "Come on, Detective. I'll buy you and Jack a cup of coffee." Tei, Fulchess, and Halloran left.

Way to go, Tei. Mo wasn't stupid. Tei Wheeler knew him too well. Mo intended to grind Fulchess' face into Edgar's filing cabinet. By getting him out of the room, she quelled the flaring tempers.

Mo studied the young lawyer. "So, Mr. Prosecutor, what evidence do you have?"

The young man had dark hair, a well groomed beard, a dark suit and dark, introspective eyes. As far as Mo could tell, the eyes seemed sincere. "Apparently, from what Jack says G.P. Scalisi and Terence McShand knew each other well."

"How well?" asked Mo.

"A little too well," Edgar interjected. "Seems like our rich lawyer friend had two lives, one for public consumption and one private."

"How private?"

"That necklace around his neck? A little love token."

"From the witch?"

"Yeah. Scalisi admitted they were lovers."

"I can't believe this." Mo rubbed his head. "Something's wrong here."

Edgar's temper started to flare. "Mo, you are making me wonder if Fulchess isn't right. Professional jealousy. Let's look at the picture here. A confession, fingerprints, a murder weapon and a motive, a nice gay lover's quarrel." He looked at the young assistant prosecutor flanking him. "Sounds like a murder conviction to me. What do you say, Harper?"

"On its face, the case sounds solid, Edgar." Grey turned to the flustered Rodriguez. "Mo, can you call me so we can set up a meeting and discuss this case? I'd like you to walk me through the crime scene. Too new to the office for business cards yet, so I'll just use this note pad if no one minds." He tore off a piece of paper and scribbled. "Gotta run. I have suppression motions this afternoon, and I need to prep witnesses." After handing Mo a piece of paper he left, leaving Edgar and Mo to deal with each other.

"Look, I'm not attacking your abilities as a homicide detective. But it's rare when a killer just drops into your lap like this. I think that you should be grateful."

"And I think *you* oughta be looking at the facts a little closer. I met this man. Sure, maybe he's some metaphysical fruitcake, but I don't think he's a killer. And what's this with a confession? This crap comes out of the blue? I'm not buying it, Edgar. Something's wrong."

"I'm not here to argue with you. If you have some devastating piece of evidence that can prove otherwise, show it to me. But right now, we're moving on what we have. We don't need anymore. Oh yeah, don't go disturbing the crime scene."

"Thanks, Edgar."

Por nada, Mo thought as he left the office.

#

He ran back to his desk and frantically looked for Krishna Desai's telephone number on a card he'd stuffed in his wallet. When he found it, he punched in the number. A voice answered. It was Desai.

"Alloo?"

"Mr. Desai. It's me Detective Rodriguez."

"I spoke to my attorney today. He said that I am not to speak with you and only to talk to Detective Halloran."

"Mr. Desai, I just have a coupla questions. Please, I need your help."

"Do not call me anymore!" Desai hung up.

"Well, fuck you, too." He slammed the phone down and threw Desai's number into the garbage.

He glanced at the note Harper Grey handed him. Instead of a telephone number, Grey scrawled, "The Rusty Nail, tonight, 8:00."

"This just keeps getting better," he muttered.

Edgar poked his head out of the door as Mo walked down the hallway. "Either you or a social worker from the Victim Witness Unit meets with Inez McShand this afternoon. Tell her we found her husband's killer. I'll handle the other press matters."

"How about I just let her know we have a suspect?" Baldwin responded by slamming his office door.

Mo felt like the man in the circus who follows the elephant act. And he was already tired of shoveling other people's shit without a push broom.

71

Chapter 9

SKY'S END'S DRIVE
UPPER SADDLE RIVER
HOME OF INEZ MCSHAND

The young Guatemalan servant chatted with Mo, plainly overjoyed to speak to anyone in her native tongue. He asked to see Mrs. McShand.

"*La Senora esta dormiando,*" she informed him.

"Don't wake her up. I can come back."

Mo handed his card to the young woman. In return, she gave him a large gap-toothed smile. From the top of a long spiral staircase, Mo heard a familiar voice.

"*Eneida, quien es?*" the voice inquired.

"*Policia, Señora.*"

"*Digale esperar un minuto.*"

"*Por favor entrado.*" The young woman asked him to step inside, then took his coat. She directed him to a large addition attached to the main house. The room absolutely took his breath away.

It wasn't a dining room or family room, despite the large sectional sofas strategically placed throughout. It was some kind of lavish octagonal sitting room. The floors were imported Italian marble. The walls were painted a delicate eggshell. Rising from the room's center, was a large clear natural rock crystal waterfall, standing over six feet high. A clear steady stream of water flowed from an invisible source. The water's trail ended in a large beveled mirror pond. Above his head, was a sea blue sky with lovely, wispy clouds. Beautifully carved marble cherub heads mounted in each corner of the room looked down serenely. The window treatments were made from Victorian lace. Fresh American Beauty roses in large crystal vases were strategically placed and their fragrance, along with Pachobel's Canon in D, wafted through the room.

Mo could only give this room one description: opulence cubed.

"Incredible." Mo said out loud.

"I think so. I designed it. I call it my Summer Highland Falls' room after the Billy Joel song."

Inez McShand entered the room wearing a flowing white St. John terry cloth robe with gold brocade on the sleeves and collar. She wore stilettos with a bit of pink feathery fluff across the top, almost hiding her pedicured toes. Her hair was still sopping wet having just stepped out of a shower. She hastily combed it off her pretty face, and it fell into natural waves. Mo couldn't believe it. Old Widow McShand was a real piece of eye candy.

The stark white robe criss-crossed in front of her breasts loosely, teasing him with blushing decolletage. His larger head, the one containing gray matter attached to his shoulders, was there for one purpose. Mo needed to give information. That was it. He was the detective. She was the bereaved. Sex was not an option right now.

Aching testosterone aside, her demeanor troubled him. Inez was a far cry from the demure, overly polite woman he'd met at O'Brien's funeral home or in the morgue. Overt sexuality toward a complete stranger shouldn't be a character trait in the recently widowed. Mo figured she couldn't be that lonely yet. Maybe he was tired or paranoid, but the whole scene didn't work for him. He sighed with relief when Eneida intruded from an adjoining room.

"May I get you anything, *Señora*?"

Inez whipped her head around. "Nothing now, Eneida. You may go." Then she looked in Mo's direction and gave him a welcoming smile. "Perhaps we'll have coffee afterward."

"*Si, Senora*." Eneida curtsied and left.

"Are your girls here?" Mo asked.

"As a matter of fact they're not. And they're not coming home too soon either. I sent them off to my mother's house for the day once I knew you were coming to see me. They needed a break," she purred, "and so do I."

Mo plopped down on a beautiful tapestry covered settee near the waterfall on the other side of the room, far away from Mrs. McShand. "I have to be honest with you. This isn't a social call, Mrs. McShand."

She loosened her robe a little more. "Please. Call me Inez."

"I prefer to keep this professional. We found a suspect in your husband's murder. Name's Gino Patrick Scalisi. Anyone you know?"

"The gay witch?"

"You've heard about this guy?" He felt like someone had punched him in the stomach. "You never said anything to me about it."

She shook her head. "You know Detective, this is really old news to me. The witch wasn't his first lover. There were others. Many others."

"Really?" Mo salivated. It was the first time he had found a piece of information to latch onto. "Tell me more."

"Well, I do love all this." She opened her arms paying homage to her surroundings, pointing to the waterfall and skylight. "And I have two beautiful daughters to show for my marriage to Terry." She sighed and stretched back onto the couch. "How did I know that he secretly craved men? Those trips into New York for his monthly business meetings? What a bunch of lies! Ever hear of a bar called Tad's Leviathan Lounge?"

"No. And not a place I'd frequent, from the sounds of things either."

"I know you wouldn't." Mo watched as she leaned over, exposing more of her breasts to him. "You're a man who likes women. I knew that the first time I saw you. I bet you have sex with a lot of women, unlike my husband who stopped being intimate with me years ago."

Not information I need to know. Mo thought to himself. *She's outta control.*

"So are you telling me that your late husband cruised gay bars in his spare time?"

"Bars? Heavens no. Not just bars or clubs. Bookstores, shopping malls. He even had a tryst with my dog groomer. But look what happened. One day, he meets the man who killed him by going to some stupid witchcraft class. He wasn't interested in the occult. He was interested in that sniveling, queer little witch."

"And you know this how?"

"J.W. Cane contacted me. He said someone had anonymously contacted him. He showed up with Mr. Halloran and confirmed something that I'd suspected years ago. My husband had a secret life."

"So Mrs. McShand, how did you come to make Mr. Cane's acquaintance?"

"Well, Terry did a lot of work for John on his real estate deals. Now, *that* man is my kind of man, filthy rich. A total man. Did you know that any given day he's worth at least ninety million dollars?"

"I wouldn't have guessed."

"We socialized periodically, Terry, me, John and his flavor-of-the-month floozie, usually some self-proclaimed model or resting British actress. It was pleasant enough entertainment." Suddenly, her eyes went dark. "Then one day, John came to my house and told me that he had received an anonymous tip from a prominent member of the community."

"You mean someone outed your husband to Cane. Did he tell you who?"

"Never did. But John felt it was my right to know what my husband did on the side for kicks. I thanked him for telling me the truth."

"About him liking men?"

"Yes."

"I walked around for many years suspecting my husband was gay. John Cane offered me proof. You try staying married in name only. See how it makes you feel."

"That must have made you angry."

"Very."

"Why didn't you leave him?"

"The girls. I just couldn't do it to them. Children need a family, even a dysfunctional one like mine." She sighed. "You know, I know you don't like Mr. Cane, but—"

"How do you know *that*?"

"Because you think he killed his wife. He didn't. John's a good church going man, a philanthropist and very pro law enforcement. You have to get to know him. Oh, by the way, Investigator Halloran said so many nice things about you."

He only needed a split second for a decision. Either he would inform Inez McShand she was a naive screwball, or let the remark go. The grieving widow aroused his suspicions. Too much interplay between people who shouldn't be connected to each other.

"Yeah. Whatever."

"You know, Mo. I'd really like to get to know you better. Divorced?"

"Never married. Is that a crime?"

"No, but don't you get lonely?"

"I have a pretty active social life."

Suddenly the divorcee rose from the chair, and planted herself directly in front of him. As little droplets of water fell across her face, she opened the terry cloth robe slowly, allowing it to fall on the ground around her feet. The rock crystal waterfall poured in a steady stream directly behind her. Like Venus newly risen from sea foam, there stood the grief stricken Inez McShand, very naked, and in full view of a homicide detective, whose visit's sole purpose was to inform her that husband's killer was in police custody.

Mo gazed at her face, first. Then his eager eyes cruised the curves of her body, including her breasts, hips and finally a neatly trimmed pubic mound. He smiled. This situation was the stuff good porn flicks are made of. He saw the working title in his head: "Inside Inez" or "The Merry Widow of Bergen County." Mo was no saint. He stood up. The irresistible urge to jump on her came over him, particularly when she reached down and began teasing him by gently stroking herself.

But instead of giving in and taking the plunge, he quietly walked over to the coat closet where the maid hung his coat.

"I have to go Mrs. McShand. I came here to tell you that we found the guy we think killed your husband. I hope you and your family find some peace in that. Don't bother getting dressed. I'll just see myself out." Smiling and shaking his head, he walked out the front door, leaving Inez McShand standing nude in the middle of her Summer Highland Falls room.

"Come back here you bastard! Fuck!" she stomped on the floor in disgust. The sound of her heels on the marble, echoed throughout the room.

The phone rang. Nervously, Inez picked it up.

"Hello? No, he wasn't interested in sleeping with me, okay? How did you know he was here? Were you following me again? Of course, I tried to seduce him. What do you mean 'try' wasn't good enough? What the hell do you think I am anyway? Some whore?" She started sobbing into the phone. "Yes, I need a refill on the tranquilizers. No, I don't sound very tranquil now, do I?"

Her voice was shrill and hysterical. Inez McShand not only succeeded in humiliating herself in front of a total stranger, but she had managed to cry in front of J.W. Cane.

Cane despised weakness of any sort. Weak people were simply too easy to exploit, and Cane made a fool of her once again.

\#

As Mo drove away, he didn't know what to think. Liars, liars everywhere, not a one to arrest. The man jailed for McShand's homicide was probably innocent. Mo knew that the decedent's widow had no more interest in him than she did in a good game of Chinese checkers. The whole situation didn't pass his smell test. So when he arrived at his office, he was relieved to see Tei shuffling papers, cursing, and slamming down the telephone. A normal day on the job, is all that he wanted. Everything else was deranged.

He saw that Tei looked pissed off, probably after being on the phone for hours. Such was the life of a homicide detective. She looked up.

"So how did you make out? How did his widow take the news?"

Mo shrugged. "Took it pretty good."

"That always makes the delivery easier. That poor woman."

"Don't feel too sorry for her."

"Why?"

"Just don't." Mo glanced up at the clock. "Damn. The work day's nearly over."

"Me and the boys are having tacos tonight. Wanna come by for dinner?"

"Thanks anyway, Tei. But I'm meeting the new prosecutor for a drink tonight." Mo felt frustration making its way into his facial muscles. "And I feel a headache coming on. Damn."

"What the hell's eating you?"

"Too many dead people, Doll."

#

The Rusty Nail started out as an unobtrusive hole in the wall located on Essex Street in Hackensack. It had been there for decades. Once a haven for college students on the make in the early 1980s, the owners had redecorated the place in anticipation of upscaling the crowd. The plan failed miserably. Yuppies went elsewhere for their white wine spritzers. The regular drunks still missed the urinals, except they peed on the Laura Ashley wallpaper instead of latex paint. The Rusty Nail was a friendly enough place to do business, all kinds of business.

Mo arrived at 7:45. He nursed an ice cold mug of Stroh, and had just set his sights on a second frosty mug when Harper Grey strolled in.

"Hey, thanks for meeting me here. I don't have a lot of time, but I wanted to talk to you about the McShand murder."

"I'm all ears."

"Good." The young prosecutor smiled deviously. "You'll need them. I have something to show you."

Mo watched the young lawyer retrieve a manila envelope from his brief case. He quickly recognized the medical examiner's return address. "Bartender! Something cold for my friend here. So. What did Clarefield have to say about the prints found at the scene?"

The beer came over, and Harper took a long sip. "Take a look at the report."

Mo opened the envelope. The eyes of Harper Grey were all over him. "This came back from the State Police Crime lab. The prints aren't a match for Scalisi."

"That's right. But this report indicates that they are. This one is from Wellcan labs, a laboratory that does private contract work for the county. These prints match Scalisi's. What do you make of it?"

"One's wrong."

"Yes. I'm going to go to my supervisor and alert him of the discrepancy."

"A little more than a discrepancy, don't you think? They've imprisoned a man based on fingerprints whose results could have been dummied up."

Mo watched Harper with intense eyes. "Look Detective, I don't even know you. I'm putting myself out on a limb here okay? Don't get all hot and bothered yet."

"Sorry, but I got roasted over the coals in that office today."

"I know. I was there."

"And then I go to the home of the grieving widow, and she does a nice little flash dance for me in front of an indoor waterfall. Everyone's gone nuts."

Having vented his general disgust on the young prosecutor, Mo watched carefully to see his reaction. The young man looked thoughtful, not critical.

"Hey, I appreciate your problem. I think something strange is going on, but it's too soon to tell. You can't point fingers, too quickly. They want me to indict immediately, then have a press conference. I'm trying to stall, but everyone seems hot to push this case forward."

"Yeah, I know. What I don't understand is why they want you to take the word of this rent-a-lab over the good work of the State Police Crime lab. Makes no sense. What about this confession? Did this witch guy really give it up?"

Harper nodded. "Yes. Without getting a black eye or a busted rib by a cop. Like I said, everyone is pushing me to indict, then plead this guy out. If he won't plea, a committee is going to be formed to see if this should be a death penalty case."

"What do you want me to do?"

"Sit tight. I am going to talk to Scalisi's pool attorney. Find out what you can about Wellcan Labs. Maybe do some corporate searches. Also, I would advise you of something else."

"Yeah?"

"Stay away from Fulchess and Halloran."

Mo looked somewhat confused. "Fulchess, I have no problem avoiding, but Halloran was my partner for years. Up until today, I respected the guy."

"I know. But both guys are pushing this case. They must have their own agendas." He shook a finger at Mo. "And I don't want to have to prosecute you on an assault charge if you haul off and punch somebody. You're too hot tempered."

"I'm Puerto Rican, what can I tell you?"

"Just be careful. Gotta run. Here." Harper threw down a ten-dollar bill and left The Rusty Nail.

Mo looked at the wall clock. It was only 8:20. Too early to go home. There was plenty of valuable drinking time left.

#

Mo pulled into his driveway around 11:30, with a nice beer buzz. Salsa sat on the davenport with his nose and paws pressed against the window. Mo got out of the car and entered the house.

"Thanks for nothing, dog. You dirtied up my new window. What's the matter, boy? Rabbits bothering you again?"

The little terrier was a hunter of the extreme sort. If there were vermin around, he'd find them. Somewhere outdoors, a rabbit shook its little white bunny behind in the bushes, daring Salsa to the chase. Because it was too late to let Salsa out in the yard, and he didn't feel like hearing Salsa's barking all night, he carried the dog into his bedroom. He dumped him on his little bed of rags, next to the expensive, unused dog bed. Mo then ripped off his clothes and threw them in a hamper next to the bathroom. Giving his teeth a lick and a promise with his toothbrush, he laid across his bed when he was finished.

He could've had a sweet nocturnal fantasy about the good Widow McShand, but something about her repulsed him. The five beers he'd downed at The Rusty Nail finally had their desired effect. Sleep was just around the corner.

I gotta quit drinkin,' thought Mo. As he lay his head down on the pillow, he felt drowsy. A deep dreamless sleep was on its way, not plagued by his thoughts of the newly dead. It was the sleep of the righteous.

#

The next morning, Mo bounded in the squad room at nine. He looked eager. Today he was the Matador. He would not only kill the bull, but drag him across the ring by the *cojones.*

"*Buenos dias, Señorita Wheeler. Como estas?* I bring this to you." He handed her a cup of coffee in a brown paper bag. "Three sugars. Just the way you like it."

She tooked the coffee and sniffed. "Hm-m-m. What are you all happy about? Before I forget, Harper called. You have an appointment with the witch at eleven today."

Chapter 10

BERGEN COUNTY JAIL ANNEX
RIVER ROAD
HACKENSACK, NJ

No matter what time of the year it was, the jail always smelled of stale urine masked by various institutional deodorizers. When Mo walked in, G.P. Scalisi sat next to a Sheriff's officer, chattering away. Another officer stood nearby quietly watching.

Mo waved to the man in the doorway. A buzzer rang and Mo entered the building. "How's my boy doing, Officer?"

"Okay. He's actually pretty cooperative. But he never shuts up. Blah, blah, blah."

"Has he asked for anything? Anyone?"

The uninterested officer shook his head. "Nope. Didn't ask for anyone. Just asked for some hand sanitizer and cleaning fluids."

Mo made a face. "Cleaning fluids? For what? To commit suicide?"

"I wish. Nah. He's got this fear of germs thing going on. Has the cleanest cell in the place. Let me tell you. In this place, that is truly messed up."

Mo noticed that the guard turned away to see whose footsteps were coming down the hallway. Dressed in a business suit, the man walking his way offered his hand to Mo.

"Detective Rodriguez? I'm Bill Callis, a friend of Harper Grey. Normally,

I wouldn't permit you to interview my client, but Harper tells me that you think my guy's innocent."

"I wouldn't go that far yet."

"Well, if you don't believe that my guy didn't do it, why are we here?"

Mo cut him off. "Look, this is a search for the truth, right? We just don't know where it's going to take us. Isn't that what it's all about? Does your client still want to talk to the police? If not, let's end this here."

Callis nodded. "Trust me. He wants to talk." Both men entered the interview room, while a nervous Scalisi and his guard stood up. "Would you mind leaving?" Callis politely asked the Sheriff's officer. The guard nodded and left Scalisi alone with Callis and Rodriguez.

"Sit down. I'll grab this chair right here." Callis pulled a chair up next to his client. "You can begin Detective. If the topic goes anywhere objectionable, I will instruct my client not to answer."

"Fair enough." Mo leaned across the table. "G.P., you and I have seen each other before, right?"

G.P. crumpled a paper towel, wrapped it in another towel, and placed it carefully in a plastic sandwich bag. Like a robot, he stood up and threw the baggie in a nearby garbage can, and sat back down. "Yes."

"When we met, you denied knowing Terrence McShand, the victim, correct?"

"I never denied it, Detective. You just never asked me that question. Yes, I knew Terence McShand."

"Well, now I'm asking you. So tell me about it. Where did you meet?"

G.P. looked thoughtful. "He came into the Aura Quest. He was interested in learning witchcraft. He was my student for awhile."

"For how long?"

"About six months. Then things took an interesting turn. We expanded our student-teacher relationship." He leaned over to his lawyer. "Terry was such a good man."

"How so?"

"We became lovers."

Mo eyed the fragile looking man anxiously sitting before him. "So why did you kill him?"

"Ask my lawyer."

Bill Callis looked at his client. "G.P., you have to answer that question. Tell the detective what you know."

"He's dead. I killed him. That's all you need to know." G.P. replied quickly.

Mo looked at Callis. "Why did I come here and waste my time?"

"G.P., is there something you aren't telling us? I think there is," said Callis.

"Let me try something different here." Mo rubbed his forehead. "You were romantically involved with Terence McShand, correct?"

"Yes."

"Were you in love with him?"

"In a way."

"Did you ever give him any tokens of your affection?"

"I'd recently bought a gross of moon-lovers necklaces with a Goddess prayer written in Theban on the back. You know, the ones I mean. I gave you a bunch."

"What language is Theban?" Callis cut in.

"The Magician's alphabet. I was going to give it to Terry right before he died." G.P. sighed sadly. "The lover's necklace has two interlocking faces of the moon. Each lover keeps a half. I was going to give him half but I never did. We had a fight."

"What did you fight about?"

"He wouldn't leave his wife for me."

"So you never gave him the necklace?" Mo pretended to be only casually interested in his response.

"No. Then next thing I read was that he died."

Callis and Mo exchanged slight smiles. "Died? You mean after you killed him."

"Oh yes, yes, of course. That's right, after I killed him."

"Where's the necklace now?"

"Still gift wrapped back at the shop. I think I left it in my desk."

Mo looked at Scalisi's hands. They were red and blotchy. Blood droplets oozed out from the cracks in his skin along his knuckles. "Have you seen the nurse about that?"

"Yes, but she tells me that there is little I can do. I've washed my hands so much that I have disturbed the skin's natural environment." G.P. looked over at his lawyer. "Bill, did you bring triple antibiotic ointment?"

Callis opened his briefcase and handed him a white tube. Eagerly, G.P. rubbed the cream all over his hands, working it up and down each finger, cleaning them like a surgeon about to enter an operating room.

Mo placed his hands on the table. "Well, I've seen enough right now." He rose from the table and tapped on the glass window inside the visitor's room. The door buzzed and a guard came to take G.P. back to his cell. Mo started down the hallway.

"Have a good day, G.P., Mr. Callis."

G.P.'s lawyer trailed behind him for a few strides then jumped directly in front of him. "Aren't you going to say something?"

"Yep. Goodbye."

"You're kidding me, right? So this meeting was a monumental waste of time?"

"Sorry you thought so, Callis."

"That's it?"

"For now. All I have is a half of some wacky love necklace with no corroboration."

"What about the indictment? I hear they want to ask for the death penalty on this one if he doesn't plead."

"Yeah, that's the rumor."

"Goddammit, wait a minute." Callis was taller than Mo and got right up in his face.

"Detective, do you really think that man in there is capable of blowing another man's head off? Ask them to dismiss the indictment against my client."

"Isn't that the lawyer's job?" Mo shot back. He understood the thoughts running through Callis' head. Both men assumed that the other half of the necklace found on the dead lawyer's was lying around, gift-wrapped inside of the metaphysical store.

"I don't think you want to see an innocent man charged with a crime he didn't commit."

Mo went toe-to-toe with him. "If he's innocent, its your job to prove it, not mine. I'm just trying to get some facts here, *amigo*, so be a good man and get outta my face." He half felt like cold cocking him.

Callis backed down. "Just do the right thing."

"Yeah." Mo left the building, got into his car, and drove away. Callis went back to the interview room.

When Mo saw the nearest payphone, he pulled off the road and dialed his office. The phone rang ceaselessly until a frustrated Tei Wheeler finally answered.

"Homicide. Wheeler."

"Tei. It's me. Do me a favor. See if Scalisi has a mother or a father. I'm going to do some corporate name searches on the rent-a-lab."

"How did your meeting with the perp go?"

"Good, went real good. We make any progress on the dead judge?"

"What's this 'we' bullshit? No, I haven't found out who killed the judge. I thought this investigation is supposed to be a team effort going on here."

He glanced at his watch. Despite the fact the pay-phone had a perfectly clear connection, he didn't want to listen to her bitching. "Listen, Tei, I can hardly hear you. Bad connection."

"You're full of shit, Rodriguez! There ain't no bad connection—"

"Gotta fly. Oh, by the way, meet me at the Aura Quest in an hour."

"Why? What the hell am I going to do that for?"

"Can't hear you, babe. See you there."

Chapter 11

THE AURA QUEST

The only thing worse than conducting an investigation in the pouring rain is to conduct an investigation in pouring, freezing rain. With no umbrella or overhang to protect him, Mo leaned against the storefront window of the Aura Quest. Raindrops the size of almonds hit him on the face. He turned around and looked inside the store. Since the witch's arrest, the Aura Quest had been dark for weeks, and he couldn't see a thing.

Tei appeared moments later sporting a large golf umbrella. She was practically bone dry in spite of the downpour.

"You look like a Peeping Tom. Okay, wise guy. The landlord is visiting relatives in Seoul. Scalisi's behind bars, and we have no consent to search the defendant's place of business. Also, if I remember correctly, you were ordered to stay away from the crime scene. So don't we need a search warrant to be here?"

"I got the warrant in the car." He gave her a Cheshire Cat grin. "I'll go get it." He took her umbrella and left her standing in the downpour. Tei watched impatiently as he opened up the trunk of his car. He stuffed something under his coat.

"Aw, no you don't!" she yelled. "I know what you've got under that coat! Ain't no search warrant! You crazy!"

Mo ran back to her and handed her the umbrella. "Don't you like my search warrant?"

Since G.P.'s arrest, Mo couldn't access the store. Because of G.P.'s obsession with all things malevolent and microscopic, there was no way he'd consent to a strange, unclean person entering the place. Callis wouldn't let him in so this left Mo with one avenue of choice to gain access to the store. He proudly lifted up an industrial set of bolt cutters, then shoved them in his partner's face with the same enthusiasm a first grader has showing off a lost tooth. He guided Tei to the rear of the building, as he placed them under his coat.

"You're nothing but trouble with a badge. The devil with a Puerto Rican last name. If I get my ass handed to me on a sling because of this, you will pay Rodriguez, you will pay!"

"Keep walking and shut up." He handed her a pair of latex examining gloves.

"Damn you, Rodriguez," she muttered.

The pair walked around the back of the store and scaled a fence. Once in the yard, a double panel, rusty metal door connected the Aura Quest to the outside world. This is where he and Tei would go in. Mo remembered the last time he was there. Scalisi went somewhere down a flight of stairs which probably lead to a basement.

Cautiously, he looked around. Then he smiled at his partner. "Let's do it." From beneath his coat, he pulled out the bolt cutters and sliced through the metal padlock. When they opened the door, the two police detectives look downward. They were confronted with total and complete darkness. Tei turned to Mo.

"You first."

"Let me think about it."

"You brought the bolt cutters. How about a damn flashlight? You bring a damn flashlight?"

"Patience my pet, I'm on it." At which point Mo fumbled around, reached into his pocket and found a small penlight.

"A pen light! Rodriguez, is that the best you could do? I don't need an eye exam!"

"Watch this." When he turned the barrel of the penlight, the steps were visible. Switching their radios off, they went step-by-step down into the basement. When they reached the bottom, Tei felt something come from behind and lean on her shoulder.

"Mo, I feel something."

The pair whipped around, guns drawn. Mo shoved his gun and the penlight into a golden face wearing a black and white striped nemeth cloth. A replica of a huge Egyptian sarcophagus promptly fell open, revealing an empty funereal container where a mummy should have been.

"Jesus, Christ, what the hell is King Tut doing here? Find a damn light switch!" Tei screamed. Then with one push, she shoved the empty sarcophagus back into the corner.

Mo flipped a switch and lit the room. The sickening sweet aroma of incense and flowery perfumes permeated the walls, along with bleach and Lysol. Mo looked at the vinyl-lined shelves. Carefully labeled green and brown glass bottles stood in rows like little soldiers preparing for battle. Another wall held stacked boxes labeled 'candles,' 'gods and goddesses,' and 'jewelry.' Cans of Lysol were all over the place. It was the laboratory of a very well organized mad scientist.

Mo carefully lifted the glass stopper of one little bottle containing clear oil. He took a whiff.

"Hey, I think this is patchouli. I used to wear this stuff in high school."

Not quite recovered from her encounter with the plastic mummy case, Tei was unamused. "Yeah, I bet it went over real big with the ladies."

"Not as big as I would have liked." Out of the corner of his eye, he saw an exit. "Tei, look, more stairs. Let's go."

The detectives left the basement as the sky outside roared with thunder and lightning. Old wooden treads creaked with each step they took. When Mo reached the landing, he found himself in the center of the metaphysical store. He looked around.

"Hey, he replaced the glass from the last time we were here. Let's see if Witchypoo has an office around here somewhere."

Tei gestured. "There's a door."

Mo ran over and twisted the knob. "It's locked."

"I suppose you have another search warrant?"

"As a matter of fact, I do."

He reached into his pocket and pulled out a strange looking key. He stared at it for a moment. "This could probably open a vault in the Vatican."

"Just hope it opens the office so we can get our asses outta here."

Mo inserted and turned the key. The lock popped and the door opened to a makeshift office with a single bulb desk lamp, a metal table, and two small filing cabinets. As claustrophobic as the closet-come-office appeared, it was as psychotically clean as the rest of the Aura Quest. He reached into one of the metal filing cabinets and opened it. There was a checkbook, and the missing files from McShand's office, including an attorney's ledger. He took everything out of the filing cabinet and handed it to Tei.

"Hang onto this stuff." Mo noticed that as his partner looked at them, her eyes widened at the sight of the dead lawyer's checkbook.

"Mo, what the hell is this stuff doing here?"

"We'll find out soon enough."

Then he found what he came for. Beneath the piles of business records lay a small, carefully wrapped box in black tissue paper with little gold foil pentagram stickers scattered all over it. Attached was a heart shaped gift tag with handwriting. Mo read it aloud.

"To My Dear Terence, a man of infinite cleanliness, patience and talent. Love, G.P." He smirked. "Infinite cleanliness. Ain't love grand?" He jammed the jewelry box into the coat pocket of his recently cleaned overcoat. "Here. Grab the rest and let's get the hell out of here."

Tei's ears perked up. "I heard something."

"Probably just thun—"

Before he could complete the word, a shotgun blast blew out the new storefront window.

"Tei, get down!"

Glass shards flew in a thousand different directions. The detectives split up, each diving for cover behind anything they could find. Although Mo's heart raced, his head moved in slow motion. He heard heavy feet stepping over the debris in the store, and the sound of a gun being reloaded.

He turned a corner. A huge figure, dressed entirely in black with a ski mask, greeted him. Mo fired a shot and barely missed grazing the assassin's arm. Tei followed up. She dove behind some larger pieces of statuary. From the floor, she looked up and saw a large fishtail with an arm holding a huge bronze triton.

A statue of King Neptune? I'm an Aquarius. Maybe this is a good sign.

Before she could complete the thought, a gun blast severed the aquatic king's arm. The bronze triton flew off and impaled the floor, missing her head by inches, but pinning one of her braids to the floor.

As she lay on the ground, she tried to yank her braid loose. Seconds later, Tei found herself eyeball-to-eyeball with the man in black. She took aim and pulled the trigger, but nothing happened. When the clip jammed, the mask laughed.

"Oh shit!" Tei dropped the nine-millimeter glock and reached for a small revolver she kept in an ankle holster. Too late. Ski mask man reloaded faster and aimed at her head. Tei Wheeler saw the faces of her children pass in front of her from infancy to adolescence. Then came the sound of leaden thunder.

She closed her eyes wondering how the mortician would reconstruct her head after it was blown off. Piecing all those skull fragments would be a bitch. If he did a crappy job, she hoped that her mother would at least have the good sense to have a closed coffin wake.

Mo's bullet nailed the man in black, right in the chest. His shotgun blast missed his partner and hit the ceiling. Plaster flew in all directions. A water pipe broke just as the masked figure dropped to the floor.

Vest. That bastard's wearing a vest! Mo thought.

Police sirens screamed in the background, and the black figure managed to rise from a crumpled mass and stagger to his feet. Two other figures donned in black came out of nowhere. They grabbed the injured man and dragged him from the store. One of the figures grabbed the shotgun and pointed it back and forth between Tei and Mo.

Charging the trio would be either useless or deadly. They were completely outgunned. And strangely, the gunmen seemed more concerned about retrieving their ski-masked brother than killing anyone. The figures jumped in the back of a limousine and vanished. Mo ran over and grabbed his partner.

"Tei, you okay?"

"You and your shitty ideas," she said breathlessly. "Mo, we gotta get out of here."

"Yeah, I know, I know. I need those files." The files were scattered. He ran around picking them off the floor, including Terence McShand's ledger. By the time he came back, Tei was on her feet. The two bounded down the basement stairs and out through the supply room. They knocked over the mummy case as they bolted out the door. Seconds later, they were trapped in the backyard of the Aura Quest as the police sirens grew closer.

"Mo, we're finished if they find us here. What's the plan?"

"Follow me." Mo scaled a fence in back of the Aura Quest, and Tei followed him.

"You hungry?"

"You nuts?"

Mo smiled. "Italian food? Sounds like a great idea."

Right next to the Aura Quest was DeRicco's Trattoria. While the police entered through the front of Aura Quest, the pair strolled into the back entrance of DeRicco's. Mo and Tei stood paralyzed in the middle of a busy kitchen. Waiters and food trays flew in different directions. A man wearing a chef's hat looked curiously at the pair.

"Can I help you?"

Mo looked back at him sheepishly. "Table for two?"

Chapter 12

SURF AND SEA COUNTRY CLUB
DEAL, NEW JERSEY

Sitting in the power seat at the end of an elaborately carved chestnut conference table, he ordered his assistant to bring his latest round of prospectuses. Cane never asks. He demands.

Companies, individuals and limited partnerships sought him out for investment opportunities. FireCane, LLC, was one of New Jersey's most successful land development companies. And new investors were just dying to get in on the ground level with Cane's land development projects. After all, there's nothing like riding the coattails of a successful multi-millionaire builder.

Well, not all of J.W. Cane's projects had been successful. He did have one or two turkeys. The Glass Slipper Hotel and Casino was one of them. He chuckled to himself when he thought about them.

The "Cinderella Project," unlike the famous fairytale, had no happy ending for anyone but Cane. A lifelong friend of Cane had come up with the idea of building a huge 20-story hotel and casino on the Atlantic City boardwalk shaped like Cinderella's fabled glass slipper.

The "toe" of the slipper would contain a gambling casino, with everything from slots to Baccarat tables. The "sole" of the architectural shoe would pay homage to expensive boutiques like St. John, Fendi, and Chanel. Another area would contain expensive European health and beauty spas. Finally, the "heel" of the slipper would house luxury suites with rooftop dining, including a 5-star French restaurant. Patrons could dine under the moon and the stars, while eating pan seared fois gras with fresh mango chutney.

The project, constructed entirely in glass, required a flexible roof, which would open and close depending on the weather. Cane had announced that the Cinderella Project would aesthetically rival the works of I.M. Pei.

The Glass Slipper! How spectacular! How cutting edge!

How ridiculous! Cane thought to himself. Cane and his investors never got far in the development process. A builder dug a large hole in the beach next to the boardwalk with a backhoe. Cane sponsored an elaborate champagne reception for the ground breaking, then a month later another backhoe leased by the bankruptcy trustee came along to finish the job.

A federal court had ordered Cane to fill the hole up and repay investors through a Chapter 11 reorganization. Conveniently the corporation, Cinderella Enterprises, went bust and all the investors except Cane, lost their shirts. Contractors who bought supplies to build The Cinderella Project went belly up along with Cinderella Enterprises. Cane offered profuse apologies, but that was all he offered. Unabashedly, he continued to live a lavish lifestyle while in bankruptcy as he filtered Cinderella investment money into offshore accounts.

An occasional bankruptcy? Just the cost of doing business.

But then the luxury condominiums he built over Working Man's Circle Cemetery? Now *that* was a successful project. He remembered how that miserable old woman, Sophiah Brinkworth, had put the brakes on the works for over eight months. It really pissed him off. If her dirty vagrant son ended up in an anonymous grave, so what? Wasn't his fault. He named the luxury condos the "Working Man's Circle High Rise" after the old Potter's Field. What more did the old bitch want? Her son's memorial wasn't a tombstone. It was much grander. His body along with fifty thousand others, rested comfortably underneath the living quarters of the wealthy. Much better than a piece of granite with dates of birth and death scrawled on it.

With the help of his friend Bella Esel, Cane had the Working Man's Circle project built after only eight months of delay. He never removed the bodies. Cane figured the old lady would never survive the appellate process. And beside Judge Esel made him promise to dig up the bodies — eventually. The cemetery and the old lady were a nuisance that time would take care of without his intervention.

Then there were other parasites, like greedy McShand. How many times had he protected him from prominent people knowing about his aberrant lifestyle? Now Cane wasn't entirely homophobic, but had he known that his lawyer trolled Christopher Street in his spare time, he would have found a new one. Image was everything to Cane. He needed to maintain his own outward appearances.

But once McShand started moving and shaking things in county politics, Cane didn't have a choice. He had to protect his business interests. McShand would be an embarrassment to Cane if his dual lifestyle were to be found out.

Terence McShand was an excellent lawyer regardless of his sexual proclivities. He knew people in high and low places, and had mastered the art of offshore money management and the tax implications of foreign-asset transfers. McShand made millions, bounced them from one corporation to another, eventually dumping the mother load into an abyss of Caribbean banks. Cane appreciated the lawyer's talents in that regard.

Greedy, Greedy, Greedy. Kindness taken for weakness. Largess taken for granted. That was McShand's problem. Cane thought impatiently. *He had to go.*

McShand cost him a bloody fortune between commissions and legal fees. As if that weren't enough, the lawyer had the terribly bad taste to demand more cash. Not that McShand didn't have a right to it. Cane made him promises, then cut him out of a deal or two. Hey, the world is full of broken promises. He should've just gotten over it. After all, the Hackensack lawyer was nothing more than a small time defender of municipal parking tickets until Cane raised him up and made him a multi-millionaire. The developer never expected that McShand would try to extort him by threatening to go to the IRS.

Murder for hire is easy in New Jersey, depending on how you wanted the job done. Quick and dirty, a person of no social or political import could cost you about five grand. But if the person was *really* special and the homicide recipe required extra sauces and pickles, like torture and kidnapping, you were talking big money.

Cane decided not to kill McShand right away. Since he still had some use for McShand, he would fire a warning shot over the bow first.

On a busy Saturday morning, McShand found some raunchy pornography wedged between legal notices and supermarket circulars in the morning mail. Cane figured the little present would serve as an embarrassing reminder to McShand of his not-for-public-consumption life, which Cane would expose if McShand kept pushing him for more cash.

A few days later, McShand called Cane. He thanked him for the mailing, much to Cane's dismay. It really pissed Cane off that the lawyer perceived the mailing as nothing more than a sick joke.

Time to ratchet up the heat.

Next Cane sent someone on his payroll to give the lawyer a clearer message. On a balmy summer evening, Ronnie Fulchess paid a visit to McShand's house with several 8 x 10, black and white glossies of McShand and a young Latino escort walking arm and arm down Eighth Avenue. When McShand answered the door to his home and saw Fulchess armed with these photographs, Cane got the desired response. McShand went ballistic. Fulchess left the lawyer's home with a broken nose and a promise. McShand would kill him and Cane if he ever came near his family again.

That finished it. Unwittingly, that afternoon Terence McShand drew a line in the sand. A threat against *his* life? No way. Cane would kill him first. But it wouldn't be easy.

McShand was well-known, liked by many, and ubiquitous. The easiest point of execution would have been his home in Upper Saddle River, but his wife and children lived there. Too many witnesses. Better kill him elsewhere.

The assassin received specific instructions. Cane told him to tail McShand for a few days, figure out his schedule, and then kill him over the NJ border. Cane estimated that the job would cost him between fifty and a hundred thousand dollars, particularly if he wanted a little torture thrown in for good measure. His guesstimate was right on. To have Terence McShand strangled, shot, and a piece of his tongue chopped off cost him one hundred thousand plus expenses.

When the deed was done, an informant called Cane announcing the lawyer's untimely demise. The developer found it amusing that McShand was still mobile post-mortem.

He always did like that car, Cane thought quietly. *Such a nice clean kill.*

The phone rang and Cane picked it up.

"Cane here. I'm putting you on speaker phone."

"Is there anyone around Mr. Cane?"

"No my friend, I'm alone and the clubhouse is empty."

"Bad news."

"That's not what I want to hear. What's going on?"

"Mo Rodriguez and his partner paid a visit to Scalisi's shop."

"And?" Cane asked nastily.

"They took McShand's ledger and some of your real estate files."

"Imbeciles! I told you to clean up the place."

"We did. Guessed we missed a spot."

"Have him suspended or something."

"Don't worry, John. I'll take care of it."

"You better." He slammed the phone down. Mo Rodriguez, the bane of Cane's existence. The developer didn't think much of his investigative acumen. He thought his massive subpoenas were stupid, his interrogative techniques fruitless. But what really drove Cane to the brink of insanity was the cop's tenacity. Like a pit bull, once his jaws sunk into something, Mo's grip never let up.

When the 'not guilty' verdict came back in his wife's murder case, Rodriguez stormed out of the courtroom.

On the street photojournalists' cameras flashed. Cane posed for reporters flanked by his legal team. "The jury has spoken and justice has been served," he announced.

The newly acquitted Cane planned on heading off to Manhattan in his favorite private limousine, the Panther. The car had a hood ornament in the shape of a leaping panther, with eyes that lit up whenever the driver applied the brakes. Cane, the Panther and his latest girl were on their way to *Sign of the Dove* for a meal. After all, he was free both legally and spiritually. It was time to celebrate.

Unbeknownst to him, an unpleasant surprise awaited him. Someone sprayed painted "KILLER FREED" across the side of the black limousine. Cane recoiled. Horrified, but more importantly embarrassed, he hoped the newspaper folks were gone. His eyes scouted for the graffiti artist. Why would someone do this to an innocent man? Philanthropist, investor, family man— how could anyone do this to J.W. Cane? He looked up.

Across the street, stood Rodriguez in all his trench coated glory. He smiled and waved at the newly acquitted.

Cane took it in stride and smiled back. "You should have seen her body vibrate in the bath water like jello. It was magnificent, Detective."

"It's a shame you weren't in the tub with her, you murdering scum!" Mo yelled back.

"You're a sore loser, Rodriguez. A sore loser!"

Complacent with the verbal dig into the cop, Cane hailed a taxi. But he feared some day he would find the detective crawling up his ass all over again. Dead men tell no tales. Mo Rodriguez would have to join the ranks of his late wife and former lawyer. He would dearly pay for this kill, a hundred, no, two hundred thousand dollars.

Whatever it would cost him, it would be worth it to see Mo Rodriguez dead.

#

A lunch of freshly made gnocchi, half a carafe of Chianti and a large tiramisu sat in the bottom of Mo's stomach like a lead plate. It was a good thing he and Tei coated their stomachs with an expensive lunch, because their spirits sank as they walked into the office. Mo knew what was coming. He had scarcely taken off his coat before he was approached by one of his lieutenants.

"The Captain would like to see you in his office," he stated coldly. "Rodriguez, I like you, but what the hell are you doing?"

"What about me?" Tei asked.

"No. Just Rodriguez."

"Sure." Mo maintained his cool, but he knew whatever was about to happen wasn't good. Mo knocked on his door.

"Yeah, come in."

Mo sucked in a breath and entered. *Here it comes.* "What's up, Cap?"

"What's up?"

"Why don't you tell me?"

"Tell you what?" he asked innocently.

"Don't play games with me. Why the hell were you in Scalisi's store? The case is closed. We have the killer. End of story. What the hell were you trying to do? Disturb the crime scene enough to give the asshole defense attorney grounds for an appeal?" Baldwin's eyes were on fire.

"I don't think Scalisi did it."

"I don't give a rat's ass what you think. You have more nerve than brains. You nearly got a fellow officer killed, a mother with two kids, no less. If the defense gets wind of this, I have to explain why one of my detectives unlawfully entered the defendant's place of business. What the hell were you thinking, Rodriguez? Besides, I told you to stay away. You disobeyed a direct order."

"You want to know what I was thinking? I'm thinking like this stupid bastard rotting in the county jail is the wrong guy."

"Bullshit. He confessed. Prosecutor Grey's indicting tomorrow and he'll cop to a murder plea to avoid the death penalty. So I ask you *again* Detective. What were you doing in Scalisi's shop?"

"I was trying to find something."

"Find what?" screamed Edgar. "A way to exonerate a confessed killer? What the hell were you thinking?"

"Look, Captain, just hear me out. I found something in Scalisi's office. McShand's real estate transaction files and a ledger."

"So what does that have to do with anything? Do you have it with you?"

"Yeah."

"Good."

"Hand it over."

"I want to take a look at it first."

"Don't bother, Detective. There's no need to. You're not on this case anymore. Just give it to me. It's evidence."

Mo cracked a smile. "Let me change the subject for a minute. So. Do you have any idea who tried to shoot me and Wheeler? Somebody tried to blow our heads off, and forgive me for saying this, but you really don't seem too goddamn interested."

"I'm interested." Baldwin remained cool. "But I have a lot on my mind. What really concerns me is when a seasoned detective goes off half cocked, disturbs a crime scene, and builds a case for the defense. Let me have those files."

Mo threw them across the table and then stuck his face right in Baldwin's. "Let me make one thing clear, Captain, crystal clear. I'm on the side of what is right. Don't ever trash my integrity."

"I don't have to take this shit Mo, and I'm not going to." He crossed his arms. "As of now, you are on indefinite suspension, pending a full hearing and an internal affairs investigation. Out of the respect I used to have for you, it'll be with pay."

"What about the Esel investigation?"

"Once Wheeler gets her act together, she can handle it by herself. Hopefully, she's learned something out of this whole mess. Like when to stay uninvolved in a situation."

Mo flushed. The office was afraid of Wheeler. Mo knew Wheeler would hit the Department with a discrimination suit so fast their heads would spin. She was safe for now. But his own anger and frustration flowed through the veins in his neck. He looked at Edgar with pure venom.

"I have one more question. How did you know I was at the crime scene?"

"That matter is under investigation. I can't comment."

"That's the bullshit answer you give when you either don't know the answer, or you're hiding something. What kind of shell casings did you come across at the crime scene?"

"You're pushing it, my friend. Really, really, pushing it."

"You'll be surprised how far I'm going to push this thing." With that, he slammed the door and left. He was pissed for not copying McShand's ledger, except that he had something Baldwin didn't have. He patted his coat pocket, holding McShand's unopened moon necklace. Suspended with pay he was a free agent, and left to his own devices, Mo could find out who really killed the lawyer.

Chapter 13

ROUTE 17 NORTH
PARAMUS, NEW JERSEY

Tei Wheeler thought she must have killed a puppy in her last life. The Esel murder investigation was her divine punishment. Finding the killer of a victim nobody cares about truly sucks. And next to bubonic plague, Arabella Esel was as much beloved. Speeding up the highway, Wheeler had her work cut out for her. She was up to her ass in potential suspects.

"Back to the beginning," she muttered out loud. She'd canvass the area a second time. Perhaps with luck on her side, she'd discover a minute detail that might make a difference. And of course tonight, she'd attend the judge's wake.

Her beeper went off. She recognized the number and pulled into a gas station only to find a dirty, sticky pay phone. Tei called her partner.

"Rodriguez? Where the hell are you?"

"Home."

"It's the middle of the day. I think I know what the answer is but what's your lazy useless ass doing home?"

"Suspended girlfriend. Insubordination and conduct unbecoming." He laughed. "So do *you* think I'm insubordinate?"

"Always did. Now what am I gonna do? I'm stuck with this case all by myself."

"Nah. Not really. Let's just say I'm always with you in spirit."

"I feel for you, Mo. I got away with a scolding from Baldwin." Her voice sounded guilty. "Something funny is going on. Maybe *we* should've called Internal Affairs. You know they want me to testify against you."

"Figured that. I think this whole thing runs deep. Look, Tei, just worry about the dead judge. I have a hearing in four weeks where they'll decide whether or not to strip me of the badge." There was an uncomfortable silence at the end of the telephone.

"You know, Baldwin told me not to talk to you. In fact, he ordered me not to talk to you. He thinks you're a bad influence."

"What do *you* think?"

"Call me if there's anything I can do. Meanwhile, I'm going to interview Judge Esel's dry cleaner after I stop at her house and have a look around."

Chapter 14

QUEEN ELIZABETH CONDOMINIUMS
UPPER MOUNTAIN AVENUE
MONTCLAIR, NEW JERSEY
HOME OF VIRGINIA SCALISI

When the doorbell rang, Virginia Scalisi gently flattened any wrinkles on her dress. For sixty plus, she looked good. Her lipstick, a lovely mauve, matched her outfit. She'd just come from the beauty parlor and the graying hair around her temples was replaced by a newly dyed honey wheat color. After giving a quick glance to a mirror above a credenza, she rushed to the door and opened it, ready to rip out the heart of the man innocently ringing her doorbell. He never even had a chance to say 'hello.'

"What the hell are you going to do about my son, Hugo?" she cried. "This isn't fair. My son is no killer." With that, she broke down and sobbed. All that pent up confidence was spent in two sentences.

"Awfa Christsake, Ginny. Look, we don't know what he got himself involved in here. You know what I mean, Ginny."

"What? Because he doesn't like women?"

The big man nodded in response. "It's a problem in our business."

She waved her hands at him in disgust. "Your business. You're all hoodlums. All of you."

Ginny figured he'd tolerate her insults to a point. Once he saw the tears in her eyes, he'd realize she was only a mother fighting for her son's life. Her words had the opposite effect. Hugo's face grew red. It always did when he was about to blow up.

"You know, I like the way you matched that Persian carpet with that wallpaper you had brought over from Italy. Very nice, you got good taste Ginny. Always did. Always told my late brother, Santo, I always said, 'You know, Santo, your wife has good taste.'"

"So what's your point?"

"You wouldn't have this fancy-schmancy apartment, your goddamn Persian carpet, and yeah, and let's not forget your matching wall paper. You're sittin' your fat ass in a half-million dollar condo. Us hoodlums, my late brother being one of them, paid for all this shit. So can I come in, or are you going to let me stand in the hallway like a jerk off?"

Ginny calmed herself. "Come in already." She turned away and walked into the kitchen as her brother-in-law shut the door behind her. "My son is in jail, Hugo. He's facing a murder charge. But I'm telling you, he's no killer. What am I going to do?" She started sobbing, and Hugo grabbed her hand.

"Ginny, sit down. I would not have believed it myself. I agree. Gino Patrick isn't a killer, he's too soft that way. But I gotta tell you. I hear he confessed. The men I know don't confess to a crime unless they got something to confess to."

"He needs a good lawyer."

"He has the best pool attorney around. Billy Callis is a good friend of mine."

All Ginny could think of were the piles and piles and piles of documents on some overworked private lawyer's desk. If a lawyer's earning 400 dollars an hour on a private client, why should he pay attention to a file where the local bar association only pays him 35 dollars an hour? She was sure her son's case would receive no attention at all.

"How good of a friend?"

"Let's just say Billy Callis does the law gig for a hobby. He owns several businesses."

"Great. That's great. Another hoodlum."

"You know, I am trying to have patience with you, but I am sick of this hoodlum shit. So before you started to insult me, let me finish my goddamn sentence. Bill does the law thing for the sheer love of it. He doesn't need a pension or money. He will get the right treatment. I assure you."

"Gino Patrick isn't perfect."

"Far from it."

"But he's the only son I have."

"He's my only nephew, Ginny."

"So what's the talk around town?"

"Make me some black coffee."

"Okay." Retrieving a new espresso pot, Ginny walked over to the freezer and took out a container of imported espresso beans. "Keep talking while I do this."

"Well, what I hear from Billy is this. This dead lawyer was found driving his car around in circles. Seems like he got his head blown off and was strangulated."

"Strangled."

"Whatever. Anyway, they find this necklace around the dead lawyer's neck that's some kind of a witch thing, a charm or some bullshit like that. It gets traced back to the Aura Quest. Anyway, they start to question G.P., and he admits that he and McShand were cozy. Then he gives it up, confessing that he killed McShand. But I spoke to Billy Callis. He seems to think that the story is a fabrication."

"Which part?"

"Well, G.P. never gave the dead lawyer the necklace. But then G.P. back tracks and says, 'Oh yeah, I put the necklace on him after I killed him.'" He sniffed the air. "That coffee ready yet?"

"Give it a minute."

"Billy wants to try the case, but G.P. insists on pleading to avoid the death penalty."

"Hugo, if he spends the rest of his time behind bars, then he may as well be dead. Jails are dirty places. And you know how G.P. feels about dirt. What should I do?"

"Be a mother to him. Visit him. That's about all you can do. Let the lawyers do the rest."

"I have an idea, Hugo. Why don't you go see him?"

"I don't need to do that. As his Uncle, I'm overseeing his well being from afar. Besides, I got my own problems with the law right now. Gotta keep my own head above water, you know. First time I've been in town in months."

"I think it would make him feel better to know that his Uncle Hugo is thinking about him."

Hugo immediately looked at his watch. "Jesus, it's late. I have to stop at Foschini's. Lola wants me to pick up some bread for dinner."

"Send Lola my love. Wait, the coffee's almost ready. Let me pour you a cup."

"Nah, no time. Besides send Lola your own love. You don't come over and see us no more."

"Well, I've been pre-occupied. I'm working. I got a little job keeping the books for this printer in Montclair after Santo died. Pays nothing, but keeps me busy."

"Busy ain't a bad thing," Hugo stated thickly as he kissed his sister-in-law on the forehead. "Be strong for your son, Virginia. There's a rough time ahead." With that, Hugo walked out of his sister-in-law's house.

When she was sure that Hugo was gone, Virginia Scalisi ran to her bedroom. She moved an elaborately framed print of Thomas Gainsboro's "Blue Boy" and opened a wall safe. The widow pulled out a set of ledgers and bank books. Clutching them to her chest, she sighed with relief. The information contained in the books would keep Hugo honest in his treatment of G.P.

Her late husband had left her with copies of all his business interests— and Hugo's. He never told his brother about the copies, and Ginny never let on that she had them. If Hugo tried to screw G.P., the books would be a nice piece of evidence against him in a racketeering trial. It was the only insurance she had against her powerful brother-in-law.

"Hoodlums," she muttered. "Who the hell do they think they are?"

Chapter 15

CRIME SCENE INVESTIGATION
HOME OF THE LATE JUDGE ESEL
42 WALDWICK TURNPIKE
WALDWICK, NEW JERSEY

Screeching into the drive way, Tei slammed the transmission into park. She yanked the keys from the ignition and looked down. The tip of a tiny hand holding a torch poked out from under the car's floor mat.

"There you are," she giggled as she scooped up a tiny Statue of Liberty. "Get back up here, girlfriend." With a sweeping move, she jammed the little statue back in its plastic holder on the dashboard. When she finished, she loaded a clip in her automatic and secured her weapon in its holster. Digging around in her purse, Tei felt around for the keys to the Esel house. She'd taken from Mo's desk in the office.

As she stepped from the car, she admired the late judge's landscaping: a pampered green lawn with well placed trees and shrubs. Tei lit a Kool. When she had finished smoking about half the cigarette, she flicked the butt onto the macadam and walked up the steps to the front door of 42 Waldwick Turnpike.

She opened the huge oak door and entered a small vestibule attached to a hallway. A set of stairs led up to the second floor. At the hall's end, Tei saw a large Japanese vase. She walked over to the vase and turned it upside down looking for an artist's seal.

"Royal Satsuma. Yeah, right." She gently returned it to its place. "Hope you didn't pay a lot for this, Judgy Wudgy. Meadowlands Flea Market stuff."

She then proceeded to the living room. Like the late judge's hairstyle, it was immaculate and pristine. She took a small camera out of her handbag and snapped a few pictures. Then she stopped and stood back to take in a full view.

Everything looked like a dime store special. None of the furniture was extraordinary or well made. Tei couldn't help but notice the white bamboo end tables. She had bought the same pair of ugly things for $19.99 at Old Gilroy's House of Wholesale. Out of morbid curiosity, she picked up a large piece of what looked like a vintage Roseville floor-standing vase. The feel was right, the glaze and color was appropriate, but it was signed on the bottom "Made in Taiwan."

The dead judge's living room would have driven an interior decorator to suicide.

The walls didn't have enough coats of paint and the previous wall color came through. The faux maple coffee table was also courtesy of Old Gilroy's. The lacy curtains were Wal-Mart specials. Matching plastic, imitation wood sconces spray painted gold, were stuck on the wall. The Cappi di Monde lamps had the initials "A.E. 1980." Tei figured that old Arabella probably made them in an adult night school ceramics class. The final assaults to the eye were the white plastic logs in a faux fireplace and the white plastic marble-ized mantelpiece. Over the mantel, hung a red velveteen shadow box displaying a plastic, bejeweled statuette of a flute-playing pixie sitting crossed legged, very dated and very dusty.

"Can't believe this place," Tei stated, "land of cheap and home of the tasteless." She started to move toward the judge's study attached to the living room, until she heard a car door slam.

She opened her holster, stood by the door and waited. Out of the car stepped Claudette Johnstone. She exited and walked up the front steps. By the time she reached the landing, Tei opened the door. When they came face to face, the two women glared at each other.

"Who are you?" Claudette asked.

"Detective Wheeler, Homicide Unit. You must be the judge's niece. We may have spoken on the phone before." She extended her hand.

"Oh yes, of course. I thought Detective Rodriguez was on this case."

"Well, actually I'm helping him out on this one. He's tied up with another emergency."

"I see," Claudette replied suspiciously.

"You don't mind me looking around, do you?"

"Of course not. I'll just need the key when you leave."

Well, that's hot shit. These keys sat in Mo's desk for a week, but now because I have them, she wants then back.

"Not a problem. Would you mind answering a few questions?"

"Sure." Both women looked around the room at the same time. "You know, Detective Wheeler, I haven't been here in years. But I have to tell you. The place hasn't changed much. Still as tacky looking as ever."

Tei laughed. The comment broke the ice between them. "I guess that you're not a fan of your aunt's decorating either. So let me ask you. How well did you know your aunt?"

"What can I say? It's one of those things. I mean, she was family, would send gifts for birthdays and holidays. But she wasn't enjoyable to be around."

"How so?"

"Very bossy and opinionated. Easily offended and quick to offend. She didn't talk to my mother and father for years because at some family picnic, my father made fun of her teacup poodle. Asked her why she didn't get a real dog. Aunt Bella didn't speak to them for five years."

"Lordy, what happened to the dog?"

"Teacups can be nasty tempered. He bit her on the ankle, so she had him put down."

"Well, it's good to know she loved her pets as much as people." Tei rolled her eyes.

"I know what you mean." Claudette nodded.

"What about her fellow judges and lawyers?"

"Most paid homage to her in the courtroom but not out of it. You'll see tonight. I doubt if many people will show up."

"Funny. Think she would have made just one friend while she was a lawyer. Listen, can I take a look in the study for a minute? I saw some photos on the wall."

"Go right ahead."

Tei noticed that Claudette relaxed a little bit. She half felt sorry for her. After all, this chick just won the boobie prize of the year—a dead body no one wanted to bury. Tei entered the judge's study with Claudette trailing her.

It was a large room consumed by dark wormwood paneling. A standard issue government desk lamp and a small incandescent light fixture in the ceiling provided enough light for Tei to look at wall photos.

"Let's see. What have we here? Here's your aunt as a young woman. Wow, she looks different. Looks almost sweet."

"She was about twenty years old there. My father said that was the way she used to be—sweet. No one ever figured out when she went sour, if you know what I mean."

"Did she have any friends from college, law school, or anything like that?"

"No. I mean there was one woman, but she and Auntie Bella—"

"Let me guess. They had a fight and don't speak anymore."

"Correct. I think she got along slightly better with men than she did with women."

"Now this is interesting. Claudette, do you know who this is?"

It was a very large 8 x 10 glossy of the late judge with Terence McShand and another man. The smiling trio stood poised in front of a large water fountain at an expensive looking banquet hall.

"Yes. That's my aunt with Terry McShand and that developer, J.W. Cane."

"How friendly were they? I thought you said that your aunt didn't have any friends."

"Well, I think that they were strange bedfellows. I mean, she often said that she wouldn't be a judge if it weren't for Cane. She did a lot of land use stuff, and McShand appeared before her quite a bit. I think they may have socialized outside of the office, but I'm not sure. Like I said, Aunt Bella and I weren't close."

"Interesting. Two of J.W. Cane's acquaintances turn up as homicide victims. Now let me ask you. Why did you decide to step up to the plate?"

"And do what?"

"Bury your aunt? I mean, you just said you two weren't close."

Claudette's eyes filled up. "That's a hard question, Detective. You know, I was very interested in genealogy, so I joined a local chapter of the Garden State Genealogy Association. That's where I met Sophiah Brinkworth. Sophiah told me the story of her son, how he had died and how he's probably buried under some luxury high rise. I just didn't want that to happen to my aunt. Sophiah inspired me. I mean she's is a real lady, and believes that everyone, no matter how sad or bad, deserves a decent burial, even people like my aunt who she hated." Claudette wiped away a tear. "She kind of convinced me it was the spiritual thing to do."

"Did your aunt have a will?"

"Yes. She left everything to my mother and father. But since they're both dead, I inherit. Here's the name of the lawyer handling the estate if you want to speak to him. All her files are with him. I took them out of the house several days ago."

"Okay, thanks."

"Detective, I have to go back to the funeral home and finalize some things."

"How long are you waking her for?"

"Only tonight with burial for tomorrow. Will I see you later?"

"Yeah, I'll be there. But I promise to keep a low profile and stay out of the way."

"Will Detective Rodriguez be there?" Claudette looked hopeful.

Tei heard the teenage girl anticipation in her voice. Mo had this effect on women, whether it was intentional or unintentional. He was a charmer in looks and personality, but when it came to the ladies he had this commitment problem. He believed a man should have as many women as hairs on his head. Claudette happened to be a new strand.

"I think he's still tied up, but I don't know." Tei reached for the picture of Judge Esel, Cane and McShand. "Would you mind if I take this?"

"No, not at all."

"Oh by the way, here are your keys back." Tei handed her the house keys. "Thanks."

"It's okay Detective. Why don't you hang on to them? You may need to get back in here sometime."

Tei smiled. "Don't worry, they're safe with me."

"Detective? Find the person that killed my Aunt."

"Don't worry Claudette. I'm on your side. We'll get to the bottom of this."

#

A loud thunder storm raged outside, but nothing speaks volumes than an empty funeral parlor. When the doors opened at 7:00 p.m., the only people present were Tei and Claudette. Tei looked at the young woman sympathetically.

"You know, people are always late for these things."

"I don't think anyone's coming. Would you walk up with me to her coffin?"

"Sure."

Tei's motherly instinct took over. She grabbed Claudette's arm and together they walked up to the casket. Claudette looked at the body of her late aunt.

"They got her hair color right."

"Your aunt looks peaceful."

"I think this is the most peace she's ever had. She tormented a lot of people, but I think it was because she was so tormented." Claudette turned and looked at the empty funeral home behind her. "Nobody's coming Detective. Absolutely no one. This is so sad."

"There's a bad storm outside, honey. The roads are slick. Folks move slow in this kind of weather. I'm sure your family is coming."

"No. They called. No one from either side is coming."

"It's only 7:05. Give it time, honey."

Tei kept an eye on the wall clock. The hands moved rhythmically, 7:15, 7:20, 7:30, 7:45, 8:00. Claudette was right. No one was coming to Judge Esel's wake, absolutely no one. The upright heart shaped flower arrangement, and pink rose casket blanket were sent by Claudette. There were no mass cards, no other floral arrangements. If no one cared for the judge when she was alive, they cared even less now that she was dead. Anyone walking in the room would have thought it was a pauper's funeral, except the casket was nicer.

Finally, a door slammed, and feet stomped. It was the sound of someone wiping the mud off their shoes. Anxiously, the two mourners' heads turned.

This ought to be interesting, Tei thought quietly.

An elderly white haired gentleman with a cane walked into the room. He immediately went up to Claudette, after signing the guest book.

"Hello, dear. I'm Judge Walthers. Are you Arabella's daughter?"

"No Sir. I'm her niece."

"I see. I'm so sorry for your loss. This must be difficult for you."

"Thank you, Sir. Judge Walthers, have you met Detective Wheeler?"

"No, I haven't. So sorry, Detective. Where are my manners? Didn't mean to ignore you. Judge Anderson Walthers, retired, I'm happy to say."

Tei extended her hand. "An honor, Your Honor."

The old judge smiled. "Well, I just came to pay my respects to Bella. You know we used to eat lunch together, she and I. Nice lady. Dry sense of humor."

Claudette and Judge Walthers continued talking as the thunder clapped outside. Tei excused herself and went to the entrance of O'Brien's to see if anyone else came in from the storm.

In the vestibule, Mo removed his coat and started complaining to a funeral director. "What a crappy night out there. Whe-e-w!" He smiled at Tei. "Hello there, gorgeous. What's new? You look good in basic black."

"S-s-s-sh! You can get in a lot of trouble being here."

"Why, *Mami*? Just came to pay my respects to the old girl. Where is she?" He gave Tei a crooked smile. He turned to the funeral director standing aside and whispered loudly, "She's still laying down with her eyes closed, right?"

Tei slapped him in the arm.

"Ouch!"

"Don't be nasty. That poor girl inside feels bad enough. Don't make her feel worse."

"Hey, I'll cheer her up."

"I bet you will."

Mo entered the room and walked right up to Claudette. He watched as Judge Walthers looked up.

"Well, my dear. I don't want to monopolize your time. This young man is waiting for you. I'll just sit in the back of the room with Detective Wheeler." With that, the old gentleman stepped aside and headed toward the rear of the viewing room.

Mo looked at Claudette's large brown eyes. They were red and bloodshot from crying. Her hair was piled on her head, almost the way her late aunt used to wear it, except that Claudette was a distinctly younger, prettier version.

"Hello again, Claudette." He gently touched her arm. "How are you?"

A tear rolled down her cheek. "I guess I've had better days."

"I understand."

"Do you have any leads, Detective?"

"Call me Mo."

"Oh. Mo for Morris?

"No, no. Moraimo."

"That's an interesting name. An old family name?" She batted her eyes.

"Yes, there are several old Mos in the family." He chuckled. "Back in Puerto Rico."

Mo felt that Claudette was unabashedly flirting with him. He went with it. After all, it was fun, he was a man and she wasn't ugly like the old dead aunt.

"Really? I've never been to Puerto Rico. I hear it's a beautiful island." Claudette heard the door open again. She turned around to see who was coming. "Oh, Sophiah's here."

Sophiah entered, dressed in old fashioned funeral garb, a long floor length high neck black dress and several strands of jet beads. She was a walking anachronism, looking Victorian, but pleasant. She struggled with each step, yet she was a cheerful as ever.

"Damn rotten night for a wake. Plus, I had to drive the speed limit, that's why it took so long for me to get here. Oh, my arthritis kills me in this damp weather. Hello, Detective." She plopped down in a chair beside Claudette. "How are you, my dear?"

"Okay, I guess."

"Well look. It's a disgusting process, but it'll all be over by noon tomorrow. Once they plant her, you don't ever have to look back."

"Sophiah! Don't say that! This was her family." Mo looked strangely at the old lady.

"It's fine, Detective," said Claudette. "I understand what my aunt did to Sophiah. She has every right to have bad feelings."

"It's your call." Mo noticed Sophiah's attention was focused on the back of the room. She looked at Mo and winked.

"Claudette, isn't that Anderson Walthers?"

"Yes, it is. You know Judge Walthers?"

"Goodness, yes. Had a few of his children and grandchildren in my class. I think I'll hobble over and say 'hello.' He's a widower, you know. And at my age, you can't pass up an opportunity to chat with a fine gentleman." With that, she drew herself to her feet and walked over to Tei and the retired Judge.

Mo looked at Claudette. "I'm confused. That old lady insults your blood, and it doesn't bother you?"

"I understand her pain. My aunt humiliated her in open court and dismissed her case. Her son is gone. She's grieving."

"I just don't get it."

"Am I supposed to walk around hating her, Mo? That would make me no better than my aunt."

"I guess you're right. Probably not healthy either way." He looked at the wall clock. "Can't believe it's closing in on 8:35 already."

As Mo finished speaking, he heard men's voices in the vestibule. Just as the men turned the corner and entered the viewing room, a crack of thunder sounded like it split the roof in half.

"Well, I'll be damned, Claudette."

In walked J.W. Cane with two of his bodyguards. Mo watched as Cane ran straight to the casket and knelt before it. He closed his eyes and folded his hands in a pious state of prayer, while his two protectors stood guard. When he finished, Cane made the sign of the cross over himself, and rose from the funeral bier. He turned and walked over to Claudette. When he saw Mo Rodriguez seated next to her, he looked annoyed.

"You must be Miss Claudette. Arabella spoke so highly of you."

The woman was surprised. "Really? Thank you."

"Oh yes. I don't know if you know who I am."

"I do." Mo chirped.

Cane ignored the remark and kept talking. "I am John Cane, a developer. My attorneys appeared quite a bit in front of Judge Esel on land use issues. She was always fair and just."

"In other words, she gave you exactly what you wanted, right Cane?"

Cane looked over at his bodyguards. They looked back at him, waiting for his signal to attack. "As I was saying, she was always fair and just. I think that her untimely passing is a loss to the New Jersey bench and bar." Mo watched as Cane smiled at Claudette with the same fascination a snake has for a small mammal within its reach.

"Thank you for coming, Mr. Cane. I appreciate your condolences."

"Well, unfortunately I can't stay. But please if there is anything I can do..."

"She won't be calling you, Cane."

"Now Detective, I'm completely confused. You're not here in your official capacity are you?"

"None of your damn business."

"I see. Then there's not much left to say except for good night." He extended his hand to Claudette. "Here's my card. In spite of what Detective Rodriguez says, please call me anytime. Anything I can do for the niece of

Judge Esel would make me happy." Cane turned away. He nodded at the two men, then left the funeral parlor as quickly as he had entered.

Claudette turned to Mo, "I've never seen him before."

"I have. Miserable murdering bastard."

"What do you mean, Mo?"

"Some other time Claudette. Listen, it's almost closing time. I have to go." He leaned over and put his arm on her shoulder. "If Cane calls you, call me. Here's my office number and my home phone number. I have to go."

She looked at him shyly. "Do I have to only call you if Mr. Cane calls?"

"That's entirely up to you. Excuse me. I have to go."

Mo approached Tei who retreated to the back of the room patiently taking in the view. He saw that Tei was about to burst.

"See who sashayed in?"

"I know." She reached into an oversized pocketbook under her chair. "Gotcha a little something." Tei handed him a small brown paper bag. "Take a look at this when you have a minute."

The clock struck nine and after a short prayer, the funeral director announced that visiting hours were over. Out in the parking lot Mo opened the brown paper bag that his partner gave him. He looked at the picture of the dead judge and dead lawyer with their arms around J.W. Cane. For some reason, he wasn't shocked.

Chapter 16

BERGEN COUNTY MORGUE
HACKENSACK, NEW JERSEY
MAIN AUTOPSY ROOM

Seeing Cane the night before left Mo cold. By 9:00 a.m. the next day, he pushed his way into the morgue and pounded on the office door of Tom Clarefield. He wanted answers.

"Tommy, you in there? Open up, it's me. Mo."

"Over here." Mo's eyes followed the voice.

Hovering over a corpse, Clarefield shook his head with annoyance. "Mo, do you know why this old codger died?"

"No. And I don't particularly care right now either."

"Good. I'll tell you. Croaked at home, in his bedroom. Mr. Tyler's family found him, butt naked in bed, Playboy Magazine in one hand and a choke hold on Mr. Winky in the other. Too much excitement for a 99 year old. The old ticker just gave out. But I had to spend the morning gutting him like a bluefish, just so I could tell his family that Granpappy's heart gave out. The man *was* older than dirt. Ridiculous, I tell you. If he lived any longer, some- one was going to have to kill him with a stick." He picked up the Playboy and thumbed through the pages. "Ah, I remember this issue. Lots and lots of tits in this issue."

"Forget the tits for a minute. How did Esel die?"

Clarefield's eyes always danced, like a little kid plotting his next joke on the unsuspecting. But Mo noticed that when he asked about Judge Esel, the doctor's eyes darkened. His demeanor became somber. Something was wrong.

"Step into my office, Detective."

The two men entered Clarefield's cramped office. He shut his blinds and locked his front door.

"What are you doing that for?"

"Just being cautious. Wouldn't want the rats to see anything. Have you seen this?" The doctor handed him a memo written on the Prosecutor's stationary addressed to Mo by Captain Edgar Baldwin.

"I never received this."

"Funny, it was addressed to you and copied to everyone in the office. Look at the bottom. And by the way, you've been banned from the office. No one's even supposed to talk to you. You're a pariah."

He ripped up the piece of paper. "That sonavabitch, Baldwin. I can't believe this. Some weird shit is goin' down my friend. I think Cane is behind it. So. Are you going to kick me out?"

Clarefield smiled. "Yes. Immediately after I tell you about our dear Arabella here."

"Go."

"She died because she stopped breathing."

"What? A heart attack?"

"No. When I examined the body, I found some bruising about the base of the skull right around the cervical vertebrae three, four and five. But what wasn't obvious the first time I examined the body, were these two tiny breaks in the skin, pin holes, barely noticeable."

"Pin holes?"

"Yes. On the left and right. So I did a CAT scan of the area and *voila*." Clarefield threw some x-rays up on his flourescent box. "Take a look at her cervical vertebrae, right here."

"I'll be a horse's ass." Two slender straw-like objects on the X-Ray film were wedged on both sides of the cervical vertebrae.

"They were buried so deep, I almost didn't find them. Two hat pins with their heads broken off. A most macabre way to die. What the perp had to do was get behind the victim, and shove the pins in the vertebrae hitting the phrenic nerve on both sides."

"In English, please."

"Phrenic nerve fibers originate in the cervical spinal column and travel through the cervical plexus to the diaphragm, causing the diaphragm to contract. That's how you breathe. What happened to Arabella here, was that the pins jammed into the back of her neck severed the phrenic nerve connection. She suffocated."

"Is this a hard thing to do?"

"Hell, yeah. I mean the person is alive while you are doing this. Her neck had to have been hyper-extended, so someone held her head down. The bruising is consistent with that. So imagine what happened here. The person's struggling to breathe while the perp wiggles the pins around long enough in the back of both sides of the neck to cause her to stop breathing. By all means, not a pleasant way to go. But you know what? That isn't the real interesting part. That dirt stuffed into her mouth? High ammonia concentrate with human bone shards."

"Human bone shards?"

"Yep. That dirt didn't just come from anywhere. It had to have come from a burial pit or a tomb shaft where bodies were decomposing."

Mo looked away. "Graveyard dirt."

"Precisely. You know, Mo, the pin trick was used by Victorian mid wives to get rid of unwanted newborns. It was a common murder technique where a prim and proper lady may have cheated on her husband and then found herself knocked up with another man's baby. Mid wives would do the pin trick and then say that the baby died in childbirth. I can't believe anyone would use it on a 60-year old woman. You have any suspects in mind?"

"Yeah, but it doesn't make sense."

"The Brinkworth woman?"

"Yeah."

"That's what Tei thought, too."

"When did you talk to her?"

"She called me early this morning. Right now, she's at the funeral. The old lady is pretty frail, Doc."

"A frail person couldn't have pulled this stunt off. Our girlfriend wasn't exactly a midget. She was strong enough to fight back, but didn't have the opportunity. Look at this bruising about the back of the neck in this photograph. I'd hazard a guess and say somebody came up behind her." His coroner friend plopped down a color photograph clearly showing hand and finger marks around the back of the neck.

Mo studied the photo for a minute. "So she was held down by her hair and then jabbed with the pins by the other hand."

"I think so. But his old lady's *really* old right?"

"Ancient and arthritic. Under normal circumstances, I'd like her for this murder. Especially since she was involved in a cemetery case against a developer who buried over a graveyard containing her son's body. Judge Esel dismissed the case against the developer and humiliated her in open court. The old lady hates her. Oh, here's another lovely touch." He handed his coroner friend the photograph of J.W. Cane, the late Terence McShand and the late judge posing amicably for a camera.

113

"A judge's wake. Must have been packed with politicos," Clarefield said.

"Nope. Just another retired judge, the niece, and Sophiah Brinkworth. Then Cane shows up. But the Brinkworth-Johnstone connection is strange. She's very close to the dead judge's niece, who knows that she openly takes great pleasure in going to funerals of the people she hates. That's suspicious, and if it's not, it's just plain weird."

"My friend, there's no law against gloating over the demise of people you hate. I can attest to that." He pointed to a framed article of the arsonist's arrest. "I have regular fantasies of seeing that bastard laid out in a pine box. That kind of hate never really goes away, Mo. But I must say, this photo is truly interesting." Clarefield smiled. "What a lovely portrait! Two murder victims and a sleazy developer. Here you can have this back."

"I'm telling you, Tommy. Cane is involved in this somehow. He arranged to have these people offed. How do we tie this whole thing together? I'm running low on ideas. Oh, someone tried to kill me last week, just f.y.i."

"You're too much. Look Mo. You have to leave now. I can't be seen talking to you and I can't help you if people are watching me. By the way, how did you get in here?"

"I slipped in with the Joyous Workers."

"The mentally handicapped cleaning crew? You slipped in with a bunch of retarded people?"

"Yep."

"You're more pathetic than I thought."

Chapter 17

FUNERAL OF ARABELLA ESEL
HACKENSACK CITY CEMETERY
HACKENSACK, NEW JERSEY

There was no funeral mass at the local church for Judge Esel. Claudette decided it would be too depressing to have the St. Mary's Church pews filled with three mourners and elderly parishioners who attended funeral masses as a hobby. She, Sophiah, and Tei would go straight to Hackensack City Cemetery for burial and then to a repast.

Claudette looked up at the sky. It was a dull battleship grey. Early morning condensation caused an eerie smoke-like mist to move low across the ground. The scene haunted Claudette because the mist lingered at the bases of tombstones, resembling spirits who rose from the earth. She took comfort in the monotone voice of the priest calling upon God's blessing for the soul of her late aunt. It was good to know that God was around somewhere, especially in the land of the dead.

Leaning on her cane, Sophiah was very quiet and outwardly respectful. Between their genealogical club work together and her assistance with her aunt's funeral arrangements, Claudette appreciated the old lady's efforts and comfort during the funeral process. They should have been arch enemies, but they weren't.

"Is everything alright, Tei?" inquired Claudette. "You keep looking around."

"Oh, yeah. Just checking everything out. Part of the job." She stated quietly.

Just want to make sure no one tries to shoot me again. She thought to herself.

Claudette scheduled the repast at Solari's, a local restaurant. It was her aunt's favorite eatery, right near the courthouse and definitely haute cuisine. Tei hadn't intended to stay for the meal, but she did anyway. She hoped to gain insight into Sophiah's strange relationship with Claudette, somewhere between the veal saltimbocca and the tiramisu.

"So Sophiah, do you feel that you can get on with life? Now that the judge and lawyer have both passed?"

The matron bristled. "Detective Wheeler, I have always 'gotten on' with my life. Just because I found a certain enjoyment and finality in seeing Esel and McShand six feet under doesn't mean that I stopped having a full life. My son is dead and gone. Her burial doesn't bring him back. You have children, right? I hope you never know what it's like to lose a child. It's a fate worse than death. I should have been buried under that condominium complex, not my Martin."

"Did you kill Arabella Esel, Sophiah?"

Sophiah dropped her napkin. "Oh please. I wish I could tell you I did or that I paid some astronomical fee to have it done. I could never *personally* kill anyone, so the answer is no."

"Sorry, Sophiah, I'm a cop. I have to ask."

"Just doing your job, I understand." She popped open a locket on a large chain around her neck and glanced at a watch face. "Well, look at the time. Must be running along." Sophiah looked over at Claudette. Her withered hand reached for Claudette's arm. "My dear, can't say I'm sorry for your loss, because I'm not. But I am sorry for your pain because you are a nice young lady and fine genealogist. When someone dies, you never really get over it. Time merely places a greater distance between your immediate hurt and the loss. Be strong." She smiled at Tei. "Grief counselor told me that once. Seemed to make sense. Anyway, I'll see you at the club meeting next month. Detective, call me if you need anything." With that, Sophiah Brinkworth retrieved her coat from the hatcheck girl and left Solari's.

Tei looked at Claudette. "I think I insulted your friend."

Claudette pushed a lock of hair from her face. "You were doing your job. You have to ask the questions. Tell me. What did my aunt die from?"

The sadness in Claudette's eyes made the detective more uncomfortable than usual. "It was bizarre. Two hat pins were inserted in her neck, severing a nerve which caused her to suffocate."

"Good God."

"The coroner told me, what was even stranger was that the dirt packed in her mouth? Came from a graveyard."

"Who would do that?"

"Someone with a real axe to grind. Like your friend who just left."

"I don't believe it. Sophiah couldn't have done this. She couldn't."

"I agree. Too fragile. Could she have paid someone to do this?"

"No. She's also pretty religious, and keeps her conscience close by. Even though she hated my aunt, I don't think that she could actually kill anyone."

"Well, the medical examiner said you would need a lot of physical strength to do this. Sophiah probably would not have been physically capable of committing the act. Were there any other lawsuits besides Sophiah's over the cemetery's conversion?"

"I don't know." Claudette sighed. "Here I saved these for you." She pulled out a series of articles from The Bergen Daily and other regional newspapers from her purse. "These are what the newspapers have said about my aunt's death."

Tei read the headlines. " 'Judge on Cemetery Case found Dead-Possible Foul Play Involved;' 'What Her Peers Really Thought-The Dark Side of Judge E.' "

"As you probably noticed, more people wanted my aunt dead than alive."

"I know. But there's a stone cold difference between someone wishing that someone would drop dead, then actually killing the person. Let's go over your aunt's schedule again."

Over dessert, Tei took copious notes about the judge's routine as best Claudette remembered it. Tei would do a second canvass of the courthouse personnel working that day. She felt that a break in the investigation was coming soon.

Tei was sure of it.

Chapter 18

BERGEN COUNTY JAIL ANNEX
VISITOR'S ROOM

As he entered the visitor's block, G.P. Scalisi watched his mother's foot tapping away. Patience? Virginia Scalisi had none. He tried to hide his bandaged hands. It was too late. She saw them and rushed over to pick up the telephone on the other side of the bullet-proof glass.

"Gino Patrick, what have you done to yourself? Your hands, my God."

The guard gestured the orange jumpsuit to stand up. G.P. picked up the phone on the glass wall between them.

"Sorry Mother. It wasn't intentional you know. This place is filled with germs and I'm trying to protect myself from the microbial world. Guess I got carried away."

"Aw, Gino Patrick, it kills me to see you like this." A tear rolled down her cheek "Just look at you. Orange was never your color."

"Not going to a charity ball, Mother."

"Where's your lawyer?"

"Bill Callis is supposed to be coming here this morning."

"Is he treating you right? Your Uncle Hugo says he's a good man."

"Well, Mother look behind you. Ask him yourself."

The ever dapper Bill Callis stood behind Virginia. "I am a good man, Mrs. Scalisi. I don't care what that old bastard Hugo says about me." He put his arm on her shoulder. "How you doing, Virginia? Can the three of us talk?"

She nodded. The guards escorted Bill Callis, G.P., and his worried mother off to a small room, leaving a prison guard outside the door.

Callis slammed his briefcase down. "Let's get to the point. G.P., why the hell do you want to plead guilty to a crime you didn't commit?" Virginia Scalisi nodded in agreement. But before he could answer the question, the guard stationed outside the door knocked and entered.

"You have another visitor."

"I thought we were only allowed two people at a time." Callis asked.

"I'm makin' an exception for this one," the uniform replied smugly. With that, Mo Rodriguez walked in behind the guard.

"Look. Unless you're here to tell me that you've convinced the prosecutor to withdraw all charges against my client, I think that you should get the hell outta here."

Mo turned to Mrs. Scalisi. "Detective Mo Rodriguez, Ma'am." He extended his hand to G.P.'s mother. "Bill, save your line of shit for jury summation. I have something in my pocket you may want to see."

"Let's have it, Rodriguez."

Mo looked over at G.P. "You never gave your little love token to McShand did you?"

"I don't know what you mean, Detective."

"I think you do." He pulled out the little gift-wrapped box with the affectionate note written to the late lawyer. "Here. You never gave McShand the other half of the necklace." Mo noticed that Callis was about to jump out of his shoes, he was so excited. G.P.'s face went white.

"Where did you get that?"

"From your oogie-boogie witchcraft shop. I also snagged a ledger. The ledger your boyfriend gave you for safe keeping. So, you want to tell me about it?"

Callis jumped all over him. "He isn't saying a thing until you give him immunity."

"Okay. I don't believe he killed Terence McShand. But the whole problem I have Counselor, is that he said he did. What's up with that?"

G.P. took a breath. "I killed him. Why won't anyone accept that? So just let me plea on Monday, and I can die of streptococcus or whatever viral thing lives in the New Jersey prison system. It's better that way—for everyone."

Mo knew G. P. was lying. "Did someone threaten you G.P.? Is that why you are willing to cop a plea?"

"Look, I killed the guy. It was a lover's spat that got outta control. You're my lawyer right? Tell him to stop badgering me."

"Give him a chance, G.P. He's trying to save your life, dammit!" Callis threw his hands up in disgust.

"Why? What kind of life do I have, Bill? Selling oils and incense to people who want love or money? I'm just a mountebank, the village quack. I don't have a life. If it all ends tomorrow, so what? At least I'll be germ free. Who's gonna care?"

"I care Gino Patrick. I'm your mother. Or did you suddenly forget that?" Virginia Scalisi wiped her eyes. "Listen, if my brother-in-law threatened you, I have stuff on him. And you can bet on that one, Mr. Callis."

Mo watched Billy Callis give her a sarcastic half grin. "What kind of stuff?"

"Before Santo died, he told me that he'd found another set of books in his warehouse on West Street. There were records on a whole bunch of businesses, he didn't know nothing about. He was going to ask Hugo why he was screwin' around and dealin' outside of the family behind his back. But then my sweet Santo had a heart attack. Oh G-a-a-a-wwd!" G.P.'s mother let out a plaintive wail so loud, that the prison guard stationed outside rushed in.

"What the hell's goin' on in here?"

Mo took charge. "Nothing officer. The prisoner's mother is just a little upset. We're fine."

"You sure, Detective?"

"Yeah. We're cool." The guard nodded and left.

Mo took in the whole scene. Lovely, absolutely lovely. A desperate mother who thinks her son is getting railroaded, a defense attorney in cahoots with a mob chieftain, and a gay witch about to plea to a murder he didn't commit.

Oh how, he wished he were back in the burglary unit!

"Mrs. Scalisi, I'm sorry about your husband, Santo, but did you know what was in those books?" He eyed Billy C. to see his reaction.

"I looked through them once. Lots of canceled checks, copies of corporate registrations, bookkeeping crap. Had that dead lawyer's name all over them."

Mo tried to maintain an outward calm. He was about to burst. No, he was about to explode all over the little room. "What dead lawyer?"

"You know, Terence McSheehan or something. The guy that was shot? The one all over the newspapers?"

It was beautiful. Now he was finally making headway into McShand's murder case. The fog started to lift around him, and the anxiety in Billy Callis' face was obvious.

"Virginia, do you have a copy of all the stuff with you today?"

"Yes."

"Can I have it?"

"Only if you think it will help exonerate my son."

G.P.'s face blanched white. "Look, we've been over this. I killed a man. I did the crime, I want to do the time. Keep my mother out of this." He turned

120

to his lawyer. "Billy C., if you don't arrange for me to plea out to murder, I'll fire you and represent myself. Then I'll do whatever I want!" G.P. pounded his bandaged hands on the plexiglass window in the interview room. "Guard! Guard!"

The prison guard stepped inside the room. G.P. shoved his hands forward preparing to be cuffed. The guard looked at Mo for approval.

Mo nodded. "Do it." The guard cuffed the little man in the orange jumpsuit and led him away. Mo looked over at Mrs. Scalisi. "Ma'am would you mind leaving me and Mr. Callis alone for a minute?"

"I'll wait outside." She got up and left.

Poised, Mo was ready for battle. "So, Billy C. can we both agree he's protecting somebody?"

"Yes, I'd say that's a fair appraisal."

"Now for the sixty four thousand dollar question. Who?"

"Listen, are we on the same side here for once? I mean, do you really think that skinny mental case with the bandaged hands is capable of strangling somebody, and blowing half their head off?"

"Roger that. I never thought he did it. Oh, and by the way, I nearly got my ass blown into the next century. I went into Scalisi's shop to have a look around with my partner."

"Find anything?"

"Yeah, I did. That ledger his mama was talking about. Except I don't have it anymore."

"Yeah. I know. Edgar Baldwin took everything. He told me how you entered the shop illegally and asked me if I wanted to press charges against you. How's the internal affairs investigation going? You're not even supposed to be here right now."

"You can shove Edgar and Internal Affairs up your ass—sideways. That's not why I'm here Callis."

"Look, I think my guy is being framed, and so are you. That's why we're even having this discussion."

"You going to press charges against me?"

"Hell no, and I'll deny this statement if asked publicly. Your boss wanted me to file charges against you so bad, I could taste it. I thought cops stick together. He called my office and ratted you out about the break in. I'd watch your back if I were you."

"Great. All I want to do is find a killer. I don't have any other agenda. So let's look at what we have. I have this and this." Mo laid the glossy photograph of Judge Esel, McShand and Cane down next to the unopened necklace that never made its way to the dead guy. "So where we taking all this?"

The lawyer looked thoughtfully at the picture. "Esel gave McShand a lot of deference. Sometimes it was because he was right, sometimes because she felt like it. Most times it was because McShand was hooked into J.W. Cane. He's the man that pushed her nomination through the Senate hearings so she could become a judge." He sighed. "The necklace was probably planted on McShand's body. Your thoughts?"

"Along the same lines as yours."

"Forensics?"

"He was strangled with a garotte then shot in the head as an after thought. We found a few fibers which we're still trying to match up in our lab. But the most damning results implicating Scalisi came from the state rent-a-lab. I want to know why that happened."

"This whole thing stinks."

"Yep. It sure does, but sheer smell doesn't make a man plead guilty when reasonable doubt looms in the background." Mo eyed the lawyer with prurient fascination. "Since you and I are tryin' to get a love fest goin' on here, tell me something. What's your relationship with Hugo Scalisi?"

"How is that relevant to anything?" Callis asked defensively.

"Let's just say I'm thinkin' like our little witch buddy is afraid that someone is going to kill his useless ass, or kill someone he cares about. Let's just say I'm thinkin' like his mobster Uncle threatened him. Maybe someone else. Maybe someone like you, Callis. Maybe G.P. stumbled upon something and your livelihood's hangin' on a shoestring. That's why G.P. kept McShand's bookkeeping. Someone has something on somebody here." He flashed his bright I-gotcha-by-the-short-hairs smile.

Callis picked up his brief case. "Go to hell. I'm done here."

"Chickenshit."

The big man slammed his briefcase back on the table inches away from Mo's face. "I'm no coward Detective. But let's see who's the real chickenshit here."

"I'm all ears, Billy."

"Since you're *so* sure that I have all these mob connections, let me take a look at Ginny's Scalisi's copy of her dead husband's records. I'll get Hugo on the phone."

"Bullshit. How do I know you aren't going to take them and burn them to protect your gumba, old man Scalisi?"

"Ginny won't give you the records if I tell her not to. And old Hugo will tell you to piss up a rope if you can even find him. I promise you that."

"If I hit her with a subpoena, she'll give me her underwear. And the old man? He can sit and rot in jail under a material witness warrant. Oh, and I'll find the old man. Count on it."

"Not if I press charges against you for obstruction of justice and any other goddamn charge I can think of. You're on a suspension right now, correct?"

Mo was in the County Jail where he was tight with all the guards and administrators. Callis was a bigger man, but he could have caught him off-guard, and thrown one good sucker punch to that tanned chiseled face. Watching the blood splatter from his nose onto his monogrammed shirt may have been fun, but this was not the time. Callis had him boxed in a corner. After all, he *was* suspended.

"So what do I get if I let you take the records from Mrs. S.?"

"You have my word that I'll look at them and turn them over to you immediately once I've reviewed them."

"Your word? That's it?"

"Yes."

"So I'm supposed to take the word of a mob lawyer?"

"I don't see where you have a lot of choices right now, Detective."

Mo rose out of his chair slowly. Callis had him. "Okay, maybe you're right. But now I'm going to promise *you* something. If I don't have Virginia Scalisi's files hand delivered to me or my partner in twenty four hours, you'll find me with a search warrant for your office, Counselor. Work fast."

Billy Callis nodded. "I will." He turned to leave. "The plea agreement is ready. But I can stall Harper for a few more days."

"What about your boy in there?"

"What about him?"

"He's about to turn into Clarence Darrow. How you gonna stall him?"

"Don't worry about it. Listen. About delivering those files to your office. I can't deliver them to you directly. Do you have someone you can trust? I don't want the originals to wind up in the hands of Edgar Baldwin."

Mo shook his head in disgust. "Baldwin already has the originals. The ones I nearly got killed for. Give the files to Detective Tei Wheeler when you're done."

Callis suppressed his testosterone for a minute before bolting out the door. "Look. I really believe we're on the same side here."

"We'll see."

As the two men engaged in idle talk about the New Jersey Devils' latest triumph, Mo wondered, really wondered, what part Billy Callis and Hugo Scalisi played in these murders. He knew Callis was right: the man sitting in the jail cell with the bandaged hands was not McShand's killer.

Callis had forgotten about the unopened necklace. Mo stuffed it back in his pocket when the lawyer wasn't looking.

He had no intention of giving it to him.

Chapter 19

The Joyous Workers' building was an old bank which had been carefully converted into a sheltered workshop for the mentally handicapped. Cigarette butts littered a poorly manicured lawn. The landscaper, a big man with a rake, stood near the building's entrance. As Tei walked up the steps, she noticed another man peripatetically moving around the building. He puffed on a cigarette, barely inhaling, and leaving a large cloud of smoke behind him.

"Hello there, Sir." Tei chirped. "I'm looking for Ina Sierra. Is she around?"

Without breaking stride he put the cigarette out under his feet. "You wanna see Miss Ina? Miss Ina's inside running our work group theory meeting. Do you know what work group theory is? No? Well, I'll tell you. It's like this. Before we can go out and work, we talk about it, you know, what it means, showing up on time, knowing how to push a broom the right way, knowing how to be nice to people. You still wanna see Miss Ina?"

"Sure."

"Follow me." Tei was amazed by the man. He was well over six feet, but had the childlike innocence of a ten-year old. The big fellow moved around the room of the sheltered workshop program clumsily, bumping occasionally into a chair or desk. Tei watched his head turn around periodically to make sure she was still following him.

"You still there, Miss?"

"I'm right behind you."

"Let me show you a few things on the way to Miss Ina's office." He pointed to a group of people bagging little plastic parts. "These guys here are doin' piece work. They put pieces in the bag and then get paid for them."

"I see."

"They do really well. They make almost five dollars an hour. Mr. Sylvano here is the supervisor. Hi, Mr. Sylvano!" A gentleman looked up and smiled at Tei.

From his size, he was clearly able to carry the day if the sheltered workshop people got out of control. A bald man with a large physique leaned over one of the sheltered workshop members, helping him count pieces. Light skinned, he could have been black or Hispanic, Tei couldn't tell, but she was interested.

For some strange reason, when she looked at him she had a "moment," that sensual fraction of a nanosecond where the eyes of two people attracted to each other lock into a romantic gaze. An odd feeling, the swell of emotion for this complete stranger overwhelmed her. The last time she felt something this schoolgirlish was a long time ago. She blushed.

He walked across the room. "Can I help you?"

"Yes. I'm Detective Wheeler and I'm looking for Ina Sierra, one of your caseworkers."

"Oh yes, of course. I knew you were coming. Ina took the day off but she told me to expect you. My name is Sylvano Lake. I'm the program coordinator here." His eyes were light, honey colored, and penetrating. "Let's step into my office."

The pair walked into an office and Sylvano closed the door. "We have a fragile client population. It upsets them when they hear about things like death, particularly homicide. Their lives are hard enough."

"Mr. Lake, what kind of patients come here?"

He smiled at Tei. "Detective, we call them clients. They need social services and we provide them. 'Patient' infers sickness. But clients are people in need of a service. That's the philosophy of the Joyous Workers, positive not negative. We tend to screen people in. Most of the population comes from the state institutions like Greystone Park. Our job is to help them adjust to the outside world. My staff monitors their medication and supervises a housing program. We bought some apartments down the road. Our clients live there at night and come to work here during the day."

"You mean those apartments on North Street?"

"Yeah. What's the matter Detective? You're looking at me like I have a third eye."

Tei wondered how to put it delicately. She and Rodriguez pulled the bodies of a two heroin dealers out of a house on North Street a few months back. "Well, you know it's not the best area. And these people, like you said, are kinda fragile. North Street's tough down by the railroad tracks. I know. I grew up there."

"Then you and I have a lot in common. So did I."

"Really?"

"But getting back to the clients, we have a security shuttle bring them from the program to the apartments. Once people are in for the night, they're not permitted to leave. If a client has a problem during the night, we have an emergency alert system with Hackensack Hospital's Six St. John Wing."

"Oh sure. I know that ward. The flight deck."

He rolled his eyes. "Detective."

"Sorry."

He smiled. "It's okay. I love these people, but it does get crazy around here sometimes. Real crazy."

"Like crazy enough for someone to kill a judge?"

Sylvano Lake looked truly shocked. He really believed in his clients. Tei found it both touching and naive.

"Detective, the people in this program have severe mental handicaps. They aren't the violent, predatory types. I'm not giving you their medical records. And you can't just come in here and invade their privacy. There are laws against that. Get a court order."

Tei stepped out of the momentary sex dream fantasy she was having with Sylvano Lake and became a homicide detective again. "Here's a subpoena. I've already cleared it with your facility's corporate counsel, so you have to honor it, or at least part of what's requested in it. And if I do need people's medical records, I will get a court order. Look, I'm not interested in people's case histories. You have sign-in books when your clients are on the job. All I want to do is look at some program work records, maybe talk to a few clients who were in the building that morning. Someone may have seen something the morning Judge Esel was killed. Your crew was in the building at the time of her death, Mr. Lake. "

He relented. "Come with me." Their eyes locked again, but this time the message was not romantic. "I'm just concerned about the agency's exposure, if some how we're found liable for the judge's death. This program doesn't get a lot of money to begin with. If we get hit with a lawsuit, we're done."

"Don't worry. You get county money to run this place right?"

"Yeah."

"Your agency has the same immunity arguments as the police do if sued civilly. Let's move on."

He led her through the sheltered workshop. Each section was busier than the one before it. Several large shrink wrap machines sealed small tool packages. Sylvano stopped and turned to Tei. "These folks have made it through the work adjustment piece of their program just fine. Soon, they'll be able to return to the work force and leave the Joyous Workers behind. It's great to see people move on."

"But what happens if..."

"They decompensate? Stop taking their meds? Crack up? They come back. They're always welcome here. We have an open door policy once you're a program member." He softened a bit when he talked about his clients, but Tei recognized he was really pissed off about having to show her anything at all. When they reached his office, he pulled out a black and white marble composition book. "What day did she die?"

"April 10th."

He opened the book. "Here's the list of the clients who were cleaning in the courthouse that morning."

"Who's Al?"

"Alfred Wicks. Aw, c'mon. You don't think Alfred killed a judge? He's harmless, I mean, look. He has the I.Q. of an eight year old. You know Al?"

"Al tried to get in to change the judge's garbage the morning we found the judge's body. He left before I could interview him."

"Detective, you're not going to inquire as to his family or disability, are you?"

"No, Mr. Lake. All I want to hear is what he has to say about the morning we ran into him in Judge Esel's chambers."

"Alright then." He opened the door to his office and called down to his staff in one of the workshops. "Gloria, send Al up here for a minute. A police officer wants to talk to him"

Several minutes later Al came trundling up the stairs and into Sylvano's office. With each step, he took large deliberate bites of his lunch, a ham sandwich with lettuce, tomato and mayonnaise. Tei knew exactly what he was eating because most of the meal hung out of the side of his mouth. He promptly wiped his face with his coat sleeve and shoved the dangling sandwich shreds back into his mouth with gusto. He licked a dollop of mayonnaise off his hand.

Out of the corner of her eye, she saw Sylvano Lake watching her every move. She would have to question carefully.

"Hey Al, remember me?"

"Yeah. You're the lady police officer. Where's your boyfriend?"

"The other police officer, Detective Rodriguez? He isn't here today. Listen Al, do you remember the morning we first met?"

"Uh-huh. That was the morning I couldn't change the judge's garbage.

You wouldn't let me in."

"Right. Are you always the person who changes the judge's garbage?"

"Uh-huh. Everyday, I did it. Except the morning when the judge got sick. Then I didn't do it."

"You didn't?"

"Nope."

"Why?"

"The other guy told me not to."

"What other guy?"

"Well, I saw this new guy. But he was assigned to clean the second floor."

"New guy?"

"Yeah, Marty."

Sylvano interjected and turned to Tei. "I know every single one of the clients here. We don't have a Marty. And our program is topped out. We haven't had a new admission to the Joyous Workers Program since end of January."

Tei and Sylvano were on the same page. "Al, tell me and Mr. Lake more about Marty."

"He's my new friend. And do you know what? He drives. How about that? He don't have to take the Joyous Workers' transportation bus. He can come and go the way he wants."

"Do you hear from Marty, anymore?"

"No. I only really seen him the one day. The day the judge got sick."

"Do you remember anything about the car he drove that day?"

"It was white."

"How about the type of car? Buick? Pontiac?"

"It was big."

"Was it an old car? New car?"

"It was big and white."

"White like snow?"

"Yeah, dirty snow. Like Marty's hair and moustache."

Tei looked at Sylvano. "He means grey, Detective."

"So Al, Marty has grey hair and a moustache and a grey car."

"Uh-huh."

"Now, is he tall like you?"

"Uh-huh. But he didn't have this." Al pointed to his protuberant gut. "He had a muscle belly. And he was a good cleaner too. He helped me do my usual rooms."

"Did you and Marty clean Judge Esel's room?"

"Well, I usually do hers first. 'Cause you know why? 'Cause she says that if I don't do hers first, she'll complain to Mr. Lake and make him fire me and get real help. Yup, that's what she told me."

Tei tried not to lose patience. To get from point to point, Al made her work for it. Questioning Al was like interrogating the world's largest seven-year old.

"Al, listen to me for a minute. Did you clean Judge Esel's office the morning she got sick?"

"No, my friend Marty wanted to do it. He sent me outside to go get some coffee for me and a pack of cigarettes for him and he said I didn't have to pay for the coffee." He gave Tei a barbarous smile displaying jagged yellow teeth. "Wasn't that nice of him?"

"Oh yeah, real nice. Do you remember what time Marty went in to clean the judge's office?"

"It was the usual time."

"What time was that?

"When our bus gets in."

Sylvano cut in. "That's usually about 7:30 or so."

Tei continued. "Okay. So Marty went in all by himself and cleaned the judge's office."

"Yup. Can I sit down?"

"Sure, Al. What happened after that?"

"Well, Marty and I cleaned a few of my offices and then he just left."

"Do you know where he went? Did he say where he was going?"

"No."

"Did anyone else see Marty besides you?"

"No, because they were already in the building along with Miss Ina, the work crew supervisor. And Marty said that he would only talk to me because I was special. I cleaned for a judge."

"That's why you were special?"

"Because I clean the judge's office." Al's face twitched slightly at the mouth. "Can I go now, Mr. Lake? My stomach hurts and I don't want to talk anymore."

Sylvano cued Tei. "Detective, I think Al needs a break. There are some other things that I can show you."

She took the hint. "Thank you Al. You were very helpful. I'm going to give you my card. If you think of anything, any little thing at all, call me. I hope you will contact me through Mr. Lake. Promise?"

Stumbling to his feet, Al rose. "Okay." He looked at the card and began spelling. "D-e-t-e-c-t-i-v-e W-h-e-e-l-e-r. Okay, I can remember that: W-h-e-e-eler. Mr. Lake, can I take a coffee break early?"

"Sure Al."

Tei watched him leave the room. "I bet he loves his coffee, God bless him."

"God bless them all, Detective." He opened a book. "I think you should see this. It seems like an extra worker signed in on the date that Judge Esel was killed."

Tei looked down at the last name on the long list. "Worker Number 25. Martin Saunford. Incredible."

"You know this man, Detective?"

"Yeah. I do. But there's a slight problem, Mr. Lake. He's been dead since 1977."

Chapter 20

HOME OF HUGO SCALISI
GLEN RIDGE, NEW JERSEY

He settled down at his desk with a small, half-filled snifter of Opal Nera. Gently his fingers played with a large envelope from Mount Sinai Hospital Center. He wondered if he had the guts to see his fate type-written in black ink.

His personal physician informed him by phone that the results of his last CAT-scan weren't good. The cancer would have been extremely treatable if caught in its early stages. Not good news for a man like Hugo Scalisi. He didn't care. Cancer is cancer. He ripped open the envelope and read the medicalese: "...a massive calcified lesion at the inferior half of L5-S1 with an obvious abnormality." In short, Hugo Scalisi had a bone tumor on his spine.

How could cancer catch a man like him? Cancer victims were skinny with no appetites, night sweats and weight loss. He ate like a horse, weighed more than he should, and slept like an infant. The only reason he even signed up for the damn CAT-scan was because he had a nagging low back pain that kept him up most nights.

Hell, that's the last time I go for a check-up, he thought to himself.

"Ah well, whatcha gonna do?" he griped. Hugo threw his hands up in the air fatalistically, then drank the entire glass of black Sambuca in one gulp. He closed the envelope and stuffed it in the back of his drawer, where he knew his wife wouldn't see it.

If Lola saw the report, he was finished. That was the last thing he needed. First, would come the tears and gnashing of teeth. Then, she wouldn't let him out of her sight. Next, she'd start lining up the novenas and call his children. Within a short amount of time, his whole family would converge upon his house and start the death watch. No more Soppressatta, fresh mozzarella, or prosciutto. They'd force him to drink broth. All his good Cuban cigars? Right into the garbage. In short order, they'd have him buried and entombed before he even croaked. He wouldn't be able to do business, because he wouldn't be left alone long enough to even make a single phone call. No booze, no broads, no good food. What the hell kind of life is that? A life that would colossally suck the big one. The best thing to do was hide the radiology report. He'd worry about treatment later.

A ringing phone roused him from his daydream-nightmare. Hugo expected a call from a local union boss to discuss circumventing some state regulations. He was somewhat surprised to hear his accountant, Joseph Monaco, at the end of the line.

"Joey, what's up my friend? You took a look at the books I brought you from Ginny? Excellent. Any good reading?" He grabbed a pen and paper. "Really? Give me the names of all the companies and who the checks are made out to. Deliver it to my house tomorrow. And thank you my friend. Have a good night." He slammed the portable phone down then picked it up again. He called Billy Callis at home.

Callis picked it up on the first ring. "Go."

"Billy boy. I just got off the phone with our accountant. Seems like we got a little problem with our books."

"Problem? What problem?"

"Yeah. Seems like we got a rat inside our organization."

#

As much as Mo hated to admit it, he somewhat enjoyed the suspension. He managed to eek out a few extra hours sleep, and conduct inquiries without reporting to anyone. It was nice of old Baldwin to suspend him with pay! But knowing his supervisor as well as he did, any extended professional courtesies weren't going to last much longer. Edgar wanted his head as a trophy. It would guarantee his position as Chief of Detectives. Time was short.

By now, Mo figured that there was some kind of connection between McShand, Esel, and J.W. Cane. The two victims weren't randomly killed. Hell no. They were executed because they had damaging information about something or someone. Maybe one of them had pictures of Cane, naked with little boys.

The doorbell rang. Mo put down his beer. Still a little paranoid from the shoot out at the Aura Quest, as he passed a small desk, he reached in and grabbed a revolver. Baldwin made him turn in his badge and gun, but no one said he couldn't have a little home security.

B-a-a-a-r-r-r-i-ng! Mo hated that sound. It was a doorbell even an Avon lady would hate, if Avon ladies even made house calls anymore. The noise woke Salsa from his nap and he trotted over to the door to greet the stranger.

"Who is it?" Mo asked pleasantly with the revolver cocked behind his back.

"Mo? It's me. Claudette."

"Just a minute." He dumped the gun back in the drawer of the desk. He ran upstairs to his bedroom. Quickly, he sniffed his arm pits to make sure he didn't offend. Then he grabbed a black T-shirt and pulled it over his head. He opened the door.

Dressed in a red cropped jacket and a long black thigh slit skirt, Mo thought how lovely she looked. Sexy business chic worked for her.

"Not that I mind that you're here, but how did you find me?"

"Well, I went down to police headquarters."

"You make the place sound like Gotham City from Batman or something. So what happened at police headquarters?"

"I was looking for you and your boss, Captain Baldwin? He-"

"Let's get something straight. He's not *my* boss."

"I'm sorry. I just have some issues with Edgar right now."

"He asked me a lot of questions. He wanted to know if there was anything he could do, why did I need to speak to you, stuff like that. It made me kind of nervous. Luckily, I ran into Tei and she told me where you lived. I wanted to get away from Captain Baldwin. He gave me the creeps."

"He is a creep."

"I hope I haven't imposed on you by coming here."

"Nah. An imposition is when my relatives from Puerto Rico are supposed to stay for a week and they move in for three months. C'mon in."

"Captain Baldwin also told me that you were being investigated internally?"

Mo laughed. "What? My kidneys aren't working or something?" He always got a charge out of civilians trying to use police lingo. "If you're asking me whether I'm the subject of an internal affairs investigation, yeah, that's right. I'd like to know about it myself. And I'm doing a little of my own investigating." Suddenly, his rickety old couch looked very inviting. "Would you like to sit down?"

In the soft living room light, he realized that she was actually prettier than he remembered. Her hair was jet black, her eyes were an endless, deep brown. Mo slipped his hand into hers and gently led her over to the other side of the room. She came willingly at first, but then paused right in front of the bay window.

"I love the view. I bet you can almost see lights from New York in the distance."

Mo shrugged. "It's an okay view. I just put the window in about a month ago. On a clear day you can —"

Before he could even finish the sentence, Claudette warmly wrapped her lips around his and melted into his arms. Mo felt his temperature — and another part of him — rising to the occasion of a passionate lingual kiss. Pleased with the situation, Mo's hands immediately found her breasts, and he began to gently massage them under her blouse. She purred responsively and reached down, gently stroking the growing prominence between his legs. Mo salivated. The sexual tension between them was incredible. He felt a rush. He really wanted her.

Ah, so much for a shy genealogist. He always knew how wild those librarian types can get. Salsa who'd been trotting around went to the window and started barking.

He interrupted his kiss. "Salsa, shut up."

He placed his lips over hers again. Wrapped in a tight embrace, the two clung to each other. Mo found himself whirled around in front of the window with Claudette. For a split second in time, he felt outside of himself in an utter euphoric state. He sensed the potential for some really hot sex. Her jacket and blouse fell to the floor, and the two moved around in rhythmic circles, like a pair of courting birds. Her eyes were closed, and she inhaled deeply. Salsa continued barking.

"Salsa, shut the hell up!" Mo yelled. The dog's incessant yelping forced him out of his dream state. His eyes opened. A red laser beam appeared on Claudette's back. He pushed her to the ground and covered her body with his.

B-A-A-A-M! A car screeched off. Mo heard police sirens in the distance. A single shot penetrated the bay window leaving a round center hole and a huge spider's web of glass in his new window. The projectile was imbedded into his living-room wall.

"Stay down until I tell you to get up!" Mo slithered over to his desk on his belly and retrieved his revolver. Unbeknownst to him, little Salsa slithered right behind him then went under the sofa for cover.

Mo ran outside, ready to turn the neighborhood into a shooting gallery. Too late. The gunman and his car were gone. A police cruiser slammed into park. Out came a uniform who pointed a gun at Mo.

"You drop the gun!"

"Aw shit! Wait a minute! I'm a cop!"

"Drop the gun now!"

He raised his hands in the air and let the gun's barrel face downward. For a half second, he thought the night should've been better. Only minutes ago, his arms were around a pretty woman. What the hell happened? Now he was cold, shirtless, left with his fly unzipped and the fond memory of an erection. *Boy, does my life suck!* He thought disgustingly.

A second cruiser pulled up. Another uniform came out with his gun drawn. Right behind him was Edgar Baldwin. Mo glared at him.

"So Captain, what brings you here? Looking out for my well being again?"

Baldwin turned to the uniforms. "It's okay. He's one of us."

"You know, Captain. I'm a little fucking sick of people trying to kill me. I never saw this kind of action when I was a beat cop."

Baldwin looked in the direction of the shattered bay window. "Are you alone tonight?"

"As a matter of fact, I am," he said, zipping up his pants. "I was just about to take serious advantage of myself when some asshole shot out my front window."

Peanut the criminalist pulled up behind everyone else. As he exited the car, Baldwin directed him into Mo's house.

"Mind if we look around?"

Mo hoped that Claudette had the sense to hide somewhere or ditch out the back door. His instincts told him that Baldwin was looking for something or someone. Probably her.

"Come on in. Hey Peanut, you can begin by taking the bullet out of the wall in my living room."

The criminalist nodded. "I'm on it."

The sirens and cops brought out the whole neighborhood. Faces looked out of windows. Moments ago, street lights were the only illumination on the small Hackensack street. Now every single house on the block was lit up. The unexpected gunshot had made him the center of attention.

As he walked into the house, he let the door slam in Baldwin's face. He heard Baldwin mutter something like "dickhead" under his breath, but at the moment he had other worries. He sighed with relief when he looked at the floor. Claudette's jacket and blouse were gone. So was she. The woman was conspicuously absent.

"Tell me what happened, Mo."

"I walked past the window to get to my kitchen. Next thing I know: K-a-b-o-o-m! And my brand new window gets destroyed." He pointed to the gunshot hole and glassy spider web that was once the window. "I grabbed my gun and went outside."

"Looking for?" Baldwin asked.

"Looking for my mother's ass! Who do you think I was looking for? The bastards who tried to kill me! Again!"

"We'll get to the bottom of this."

"That's so damn reassuring. My partner and I nearly got nailed last week. How did you help me then? You suspended me. Now someone tries to cap me again. Do me a favor. Don't help me anymore. I'm liable to wind up dead."

"Got it!" the criminalist announced. With a pair of tongs, he gently removed a bullet from the wall. "Hmm, looks it came from a Remington 700. Have to see if there are any shell casings outside."

Baldwin continued the interrogation, taking notes. "Did you hear or see anything?"

"I thought I heard a car take off from in front of the house. Don't ask me if I got any license plates. I was too busy dodging bullets. Any luck on finding the shooters from the witch's shop?"

"We got some stuff, but it's inconclusive."

"What a surprise." Mo sneered. "So, how is it that you showed up at my house so fast?"

If the question flustered Baldwin, he didn't show it. "I was in the area and heard the call come in. That simple."

"How convenient. You don't live in my neighborhood."

"Screw you."

"I think you already have, Captain. So if you don't mind, I'm going to go in my basement to find some plywood so I can close up my damn busted window."

"Did Claudette Esel come to your house this evening?"

"Who?" Mo replied coyly.

"You know who I'm talking about. The judge's niece. She came looking for you at the office."

"Oh. You mean the one I used to work at before you had me suspended."

"The attitude's not going to help with your internal affairs hearing next week. And if you've been having relations with a relative of a homicide victim..."

"Let Peanut finish up his work. Then you can get the fuck out of my house."

Baldwin shook his head. "You have no idea who you're playing with."

"Neither do you. So get out while you're still in one piece."

With that Baldwin turned toward the door. "Larry Miller is outside. He'll take the rest of the investigative information."

"Whatever."

After Baldwin left, Lieutenant Larry Miller came in. Mo gave him what little information he actually had, leaving out the fact that Claudette Esel had paid him a visit earlier. When all was said and done, he stared at the shattered window in front of him. He hoped he still had some plywood in the basement from the last home repair project.

He opened the basement door. Salsa who had been all but invisible for the past hour or so, stood behind him barking. "So dog, looks like you're gonna use me for cover, eh?" The dog whimpered and crouched down low behind his feet, then ran back under the couch.

The darkness made him uncomfortable. Maybe the attempt on his life wasn't a one person job. Maybe somebody was left behind in the basement to finish him off.

He remembered a 2 x 4 he kept at the top of the stairs from some left over carpentry work. Instinctively, he grabbed it. Salsa started to follow him, then turned tail and ran back into the living room.

He flipped the light switch. Step by step, he went down the basement, half wondering if he'd be shot at again. When he reached the bottom step, he heard a noise and turned around.

Whimpering, Claudette came out from under the stair case.

"Mo, I'm frightened."

He sighed with relief. "Oh, darlin'. Don't worry."

Sometimes women need answers, sometimes they need quiet listening, and sometimes they need hugs. He dropped the wooden plank, and wrapped his arms around her drawing her into a tight embrace.

"C'mon. Let me take you upstairs. You're safe now."

She turned and stumbled, nearly falling on the first tread. Without hesitation, he scooped her up in his arms. Passing through his living room on the way to his bedroom with Claudette in his arms, he winked at Salsa who peeked out from under his couch.

#

When he opened his eyes, Mo lay on his back naked. Claudette's head rested across his chest breathing gently. He leaned over and kissed her forehead as he glanced over at the digital clock on his bureau. Two-thirty in the morning. Damn. He couldn't believe it. He and Claudette had been making wild hot monkey love for over four hours. Marathon sex. Nothing wrong with that. He closed his eyes. Then he remembered.

"Oh shit. The window."

Jumping up, he threw on a pair of gym shorts and ran downstairs. Salsa had made himself at home on the couch. Mo had this issue about animals on furniture, but Salsa snored so peacefully that he didn't have the heart to wake him up. And quite frankly, the dog saved his life. A little bit of couch time was a small reward.

Thirsty from his romp in the hay, he discovered a half can of beer on the kitchen counter. Could he justify drinking this early in the morning? Yes.

Fair game for food. Must be five o'clock in the evening somewhere around the world. Cornflakes in a can. He downed it in one huge gulp.

The phone rang. Mo picked it up.

"Yeah?"

"Detective Rodriguez?" a raspy voice inquired.

"Who the hell is this?"

"No need to get your balls in an uproar. I'm calling because of a common interest and a mutual friend."

"Tell me who you are first."

"Not important. I understand that you were nearly shot this evening. That's terrible."

It was either the shooter calling, or some other God-forsaken psycho who wanted him dead.

"I wasn't too pleased about it myself. So why are you calling me?"

"Justice. For you and me."

"You have my interest."

"Seems like there's a lot of dead people floating around and nobody's got answers. You interested in finding out who really killed that stupid fucking lawyer, right?"

"Yeah."

"Well, I'd like to invite you to a party tomorrow night. At a mansion in Deal."

"Why should I do this?"

"I already answered that Detective. Justice. You want it as much as I do. You'll get your justice your way. I'll get mine."

"Is that so?"

"Yeah. Oh, by the way, this ain't a "come-as-you-are" kinda thing. You'll be recognized by certain people. So I got a little disguise for you. A friend will leave the stuff near a dumpster outside of the Prosecutor's Office cafeteria. You put on the disguise, someone picks you up. You work the party."

"Work the party? As what? A circus clown?"

The voice laughed before it coughed. "You'll see."

"Who's the somebody who's going to give me this disguise?"

"I'm a friend of the gentleman who took McShand's books."

"I know who you are!"

The voice laughed. "See you at the big blow out on Friday, maybe." The voice hung up.

He stared at the telephone's receiver. Mo could hardly believe that he'd spoken with Hugo Scalisi. No one in law enforcement could ever get close to the old man. The Feds had been trying to nail him for years, but when the trail heated up, Scalisi and wife took up residence on Jesse's Secret, a yacht moored in a bay off the isle of Nevis. Only the seagulls could reach him there. Scalisi wasn't stupid. Nevis, unlike Switzerland and the Cayman Islands, had no cooperation agreement with the United States concerning money laundering. Dirty money still had a home on the tiny isle of Nevis.

Word out on the streets was that old Hugo came back in town for medical reasons. That really didn't matter. Mobsters don't make telephone calls to cops unless they're pissed off and it's an issue they can't handle within the "family." Obviously, something in Terence McShand's books crossed into Scalisi's turf and he wasn't happy about it.

"Mo?" Claudette stood in the kitchen doorway as she buttoned the top of her blouse. "Listen, I have to go."

He walked over and embraced her. "Why? I wanted to make you breakfast."

"Well, it's already after three, and I have to open the library tomorrow."

He laughed. "So you're a librarian and a genealogist?"

"Yes."

"That's great."

"Well, I like it. It's a new children's library in Hackensack. The funding came from that man ..."

"Yeah. I know who the money came from. Cane, the man at your aunt's wake."

"I never met him before that night."

"I know. Nice guy, right? He just donates the money he steals from other people to worthy causes anonymously, the scumbag." He sighed. "But I guess if it funds a library for underprivileged children, at least some good came out of that shitbag."

"That's all you can hope for sometimes. Listen, I never told you the reason why I came here. When the estate lawyer went through my aunt's papers, he found a bank account with twenty million dollars in it."

"Holy shit. That's a lot of coinage. You're a wealthy woman."

"That's what's weird, Mo. Aunt Bella wasn't worth a lot of money. I have the bank book with me. Let me show it to you." She left the room, came back with her purse, and pulled out a blue bank book.

"See? There are four, five million dollar deposits every year, for four years. My aunt never had that kind of money."

"May be returns from investments?"

"Aunt Bella didn't believe in the stock market. And these weren't dividend checks, either. They were wire transfers."

"From who?"

"Don't know yet. But when I do, I'll let you know."

"Cool."

Mo escorted his newly found love interest to her car. He was pleased to see that the neighborhood was quiet again.

"I have to go, Mo." Claudette outlined his mouth with her fingertips. He grabbed her hand and gently kissed it, one finger at a time. As he did, he felt a sudden rise in his groin.

"Look, I'm not very good at boyfriend thing," he confessed.

"Neither am I."

"Will I see you soon?"

"Count on it."

Minutes later, Claudette drove away. He looked across the street to his house. While he stood in the street, freezing his ass off wearing only gym shorts and sneakers, Salsa yelped at the broken window.

"Yeah, dog, hang in there. I'm coming."

Chapter 21

"So Doctor, the dead do come back to life." Tei complained. "And they come back as retarded maintenance men who kill people."

Clarefield was completely undisturbed by her declaration. "Well, look. Here's what I think happened. Your killer was familiar with the dead judge's schedule, which means he either worked there or knew someone who did. Must have figured out the retarded maintenance crew was an easy in. But there's some tie to the old gal and the cemetery. Whoever committed the murder used the name of Sophiah Brinkworth's deceased son. The killer was trying to either hide his identity or send some kind of a perverse message. Did she have any other children?"

"She never spoke of having any, only the vagrant son."

"Are you sure Martin was her only kid?"

"I don't know. But it would have to be. Look, Sophiah was born in 1912. Martin Saunford was only 29 when he died in 1987. That means he was born in '58, so Sophiah Brinkworth was 47 years old when she gave birth to him."

"Whew! That's a change-of-life baby if I ever heard of one."

"More like a change-of-life-make-you-want-to-jump-off-a-cliff baby. Damn! Pee, poop, diapers and puke at forty seven. Not in my life."

"Don't have any sloppy sex, and you'll have nothing to worry about."

"Honey child," she purred as she gave him butterfly kisses, "right now, I'd be up for any sex sloppy or otherwise. Don't you have any nice doctor friends for me?"

The cheeky medical examiner looked at the ceiling. "Black or white?"

"Preferably black, but I'm open-minded." They both burst out laughing.

"You slay me, sweetie. Now, let's get back to your old lady for a minute. What if Martin Saunford were a second son and not an only child?"

"I never asked her if she had other children."

Clarefield looked thoughtful for a minute. "Let's run the name Saunford nationally and see if anything turns up on NCIC."

"Good idea. I once caught a rap sheet on a guy from 1934."

Clarefield started typing into the computer's criminal data bank.

"What did the poor bastard do?"

"Curbside cruising and annoying girls."

"What's wrong with that?"

"Shut up and keep typing." Tei ordered.

Clarefield kept pounding away at the keyboard. "Dammit, it's not taking my password. You try it."

Tei switched places in front of the tired 386 computer. She kept typing until she heard a blip, a boop, and saw a map of the United States.

"Okay. I'm in. Now, let's see. I'm just going to type in the word 'Saunford' and see what comes up."

The screen was small, but fourteen Saunfords popped up. "Okay. We can rule out these ten Saunfords right off the top."

"Why?"

"They're black. This lady doesn't strike me as the type to be messin' with black men. Now we got Patrick Jay Saunford, deceased, so he's out. Willie Saunford, incarcerated since 1987 and he's still in so he's out. Michael Saunford, doing life for a homicide without parole, so he's no good. Wait, look at this last one. Andrew B. Saunford. Born 1939. Did time for armed robbery, drug possession, a bunch of burglaries. But look at this. Convicted of homicide in 1962."

"That made him about 23 years old at the time of the murder."

"Yeah. He was paroled in 1988. He did 26 years for murder."

Tei sat back in her chair and looked thoughtful. "So if this is her son, that means he must be about fifty one years old. I have another idea. MARS."

The Municipal Arrest Record System would let them know if Andrew had been behaving himself. She quickly typed in her password. A bright green State of New Jersey logo popped up. She typed in the name 'Andrew B. Saunford.' "Here he is. An arrest warrant for unpaid parking tickets. Looks like he paid up everything and the arrest warrant was withdrawn. But he's still VOP. Here's the name of his parole officer."

Minutes later, Tei was on the phone with Andrew B. Saunford's parole officer. During their brief conversation, Tei wrote furiously on the back of an envelope. When the conversation was over, she gave her medical examiner friend a complacent smile. "Andrew Brinkworth Saunford. Paroled in 1988 to the custody of his mother, Mrs. Sophiah Brinkworth in Ridgewood. He was coming in twice a week for drug monitoring and stopped suddenly, about April 9th. Since he violated his parole, there's an outstanding warrant."

"Last address?"

"His mama's house in Ridgewood."

"Question. Do you think he killed the judge because Mrs. Brinkworth told him to do it?"

"Don't know. But I still think the old gal's in on the whole thing." She got up from the chair and checked her holster. "It's time to go see Mama and her oldest boy."

Clarefield always admired Tei's spunk. "Go for it," he said as he smiled. "Just be careful."

"I intend to. But I have to make a pit stop at the public library first tonight. Then I'll catch old Mrs. B. in the morning."

#

The main branch of Hackensack Public Library on Main Street closes at 9 pm. Tei pulled up at 8:00 on the nose, which meant she had one hour to learn everything she could about a 28-year old homicide. She could start something tonight, but unless she had an extraordinary amount of luck, looking through old newspapers would be a two or three day job.

When she went into periodicals room, a skinny little woman behind the desk logging in the micro-fiche was less than happy to see her.

"Can I help you?"

"Yes." Tei pulled out her tin. "I'd like to see *The Bergen Evening News* from 1962. I'm investigating a homicide."

Tei studied the woman's face. One word fit her: desiccated. She may have only been thirtyish, but she wore pumpkin colored, polyester pants and candy striped blouse that bore a faint resemblance to an old barber shop pole. Her frowsy blond perm made her head looked like a greasy chrysanthemum, and the lack of facial make-up dumped another fifteen years onto her face. Plus, she had an attitude sharper than the six upright Dixon pencils neatly arranged in a holder on her desk.

"Am I supposed to be impressed by that badge?"

Tei figured she had to be patient with this woman. But she couldn't believe that this bitch was both nasty *and* ugly. God could leave you with one bad trait, but why punish you with two?

"Can I see the newspaper from 1962? And spare me the attitude."

She skittled away like an unhappy cockroach. Moments later, she came back with twelve reels of microfiche.

"Since you obviously don't know what date you're looking for, I brought you all twelve months. Sign the films out here."

Tei nodded a half-hearted thanks. She grabbed the first reel dated October 8 through 15 1962, and threaded it through the micro-fiche machine.

The headlines splattered across *The Bergen Evening News* announced the Yankees won the World Series in an amazing game. An avid baseball fan, Tei couldn't resist reading the article. She remembered her father telling her about that win. It was phenomenal. Had the web of Bobby Richardson's glove not snagged Willie McCovey's ball in the bottom of the ninth inning, the San Francisco Giants would have won the 1962 World Series.

Damn, she thought. *I gotta stop reading this stuff. I'll never find that homicide.*

Her eyes glanced down the rest of the page. In a tiny corner, underneath the long World Series story, was a byline. "Saunford Boy Found Guilty by Jury-Mother Collapses in Court After Verdict Rendered. Page 10." She turned to the article. After speed reading it, she made a copy and ran to the nearest pay phone. Frantically, she punched in Mo's telephone number. He answered.

"Yeah?"

"Are you always so damn cheerful?"

"Well, nobody's tried to shoot me tonight so I guess that's a good thing. What's up?"

"I think I know who killed Judge Esel."

"On a personal note, I don't really care. But then, I do have a morbid intellectual curiosity, like I always wondered where poop goes after you flush the toilet, and the sound of one hand clapping, that kind of stuff."

"Would you please be serious for one minute? Sophiah Brinkworth had another son. One died a vagrant, another was convicted of homicide in 1962. Listen. I found this newspaper article. Here's what it says: 'Sophiah Brinkworth Saunford, Bergen County society matron, collapsed in court today when the jury found her son, twenty three year old Andrew B. Saunford, guilty of murder. Last year, Saunford took a shotgun to his father, Martin Saunford, Sr., in the living room of their Ridgewood home, while his mother watched. Saunford pled self defense claiming that he tried to prevent his father from beating his mother while in a drunken rage. Prosecutor Robert Acquavino, convinced the jury that the killing was an intentional premeditated act over a change in his father's will excluding him from the Saunford millions. Saunford will be sentenced next month.' Mo, can you believe this stuff?"

"*Mentirosa*! And to think old Sophiah told me that her old man drank himself to death."

"Drank himself to death? With a twelve gauge shot gun? Andrew Saunford probably sprayed his father's brains all over the living room wall. What's a *mentirosa*?"

"A liar, it means liar."

Tei jumped when she felt a tap to her shoulder. The charming librarian stood behind her.

"Excuse me, the library will be closing in ten minutes. I assume by the mess you have left on the table, you're done with your so-called investigation?"

"Mo, hold the line for a minute." Tei covered the receiver with her hand and turned to face the sarcastic periodicals guardian.

"Yes, ma'am, I am through, and you can have the micro-fiche back. Then you can put your bony ass on a broomstick and fly home."

"How dare you!" The librarian turned and stormed away.

Tei couldn't resist one final tweak at book hoarding harpy as she stomped off. "By the way, this month's Cosmopolitan Magazine has some great make over tips. Do us all a favor. Read it!"

"Do you always pick on harmless librarians?" Mo snickered into the phone.

"I can't stand her. The bitch was rude from the get-go. And ugly."

"Now, now Tei, just because you're a big gorgeous woman, ain't no need to pick on the less fortunate. Get back to Brinkworth."

"I checked with parole. Saunford did 26 years in and got released March 31st to Sophiah Brinkworth's custody. Started skipping parole the day before Esel died."

"Is he VOP?"

"Yup. But I bet his Mama knows where he's hiding."

"What's the plan?"

"Gonna pay little unexpected visit to Mama Brinkworth. Listen, how you doing, Mo? I'm worried about you. The office is talking."

"Talk is cheap."

"Heard that somebody tried to shoot you again, and Edgar says you kicked him out of the house before he could complete the investigation."

"True, true, all true. Only thing is, I shoulda kicked Baldwin out sooner."

"He also says that you've been messing around with Esel's niece. Says he's going to hang you at the Internal Affairs hearing next week. You're in deep shit."

"True."

"Which part?"

"Never mind."

"Mo, I think you're being set up, and you're falling for every goddam trap Baldwin's put out for you."

"Don't worry about me. I'm okay. But don't go trying to take down Andrew Saunford all by yourself. He's a killer. Wait for me. Promise?"

Tei smiled sweetly at the other end of the telephone. "Oh sure. I promise."

Chapter 22

The thought that Johnny Cane would be over in a few minutes jolted her out of her depression. With Marilyn and Irene out of the house for the rest of the evening, Inez McShand was ready to do business.

The anti-depressants did what they were supposed to do, keep her functioning day-to-day. She knew that she wasn't the best mother, or the worst. Inez often complained to other people that she wished she'd never had children. Of course, she also wished she never married her bi-sexual husband. But how did she know her handsome consort turned into a raging queen when the sun went down?

Living in the worst of both worlds, she was a 39 year old mother and widow. All she had left was a pile of broken dreams, lots of money, and the emotional crumbs of attention that a sociopathic developer threw at her when it suited him. Her usefulness to Cane was over when she failed to seduce the homicide detective assigned to her husband's case. If Rodriguez slept with her, she would have reported a rape. But she underestimated the cop's ability to resist temptation. Or may be she just gave up too quickly.

Inez wasn't quite ready to give up on Cane just yet. He owed her. In exchange for money and some more prescription tranquilizers, she gave him her husband's whereabouts the night he died.

The big fundraiser for the Ocean Hill Preservation Society was Friday. In the not too distant past, Inez was Cane's steady escort for evenings like this. Since Terry's death, Cane became colder, more distant. Inez heard that he had another new, younger, plaything by his side. Other than visiting her for an occasional romp in the hay, Cane had cast her aside. She was disposable.

But she was dysfunctional, not stupid.

One day, in the throes of a major depression, she had this epiphany. She had been used. When she confronted Cane, he laughed at her. Now when he came over today to pick up his clothes, she would have the last laugh. Her silence would cost him dearly.

The doorbell rang. The maid wasn't there. Perfect. The door bell rang again. She pinched her cheeks to give them color and mentally prepared her opening line to Cane.

"You really don't think you can get rid of me that easily," or "Surely, you don't think you can hide from me," she would say dryly. Maybe she would just say, "You owe me you sonavabitch!" and punctuate the statement with a hard slap to the side of his face.

The doorbell rang once more. When Inez looked through the glass, she saw a figure. It wasn't Cane, but Inez recognized him. It was his driver, the other person in Cane's seedy little world who kept secrets for him.

In their friendlier moments, Cane demanded they have sex in the back of his limousine, under the persistent watchful eyes of Cane's chauffeur. The driver always leered in the rear view mirror, watching their every gyration. It didn't bother her because she was usually pretty spaced out between the booze and the drugs. So as usual, here was the voyeurist driver, ready to pick her up and take her to Cane's waiting pants. The horny old bastard probably wanted to bang her in the nearest no-tell motel, if he didn't plan on getting some ass during the limo ride.

Inez opened the door halfway. No time to scream for help. There was a muffled noise and Inez McShand crumpled backward, dead, with a single bullet hole right between her eyes.

Chapter 23

BERGEN COUNTY JAIL ANNEX
HACKENSACK, NEW JERSEY

G.P. finished making his bed and the bed of his bunk mate, Lorenzo McKrane. Lorenzo was six foot four, and weighed in at about 260 pounds with limbs like tree trunks. He'd just finished a mandatory seven year stip of a ten year sentence for aggravated assault, armed robbery and drug dealing. He would cut your heart out as soon as look at you. Just G.P.'s rotten luck. Bad enough his cell mate was a violent maniac, but far worse was that he was a slob who spat on the floor when he felt like it.

McKrane had moved for a sentence reconsideration after seven years of good behavior, playing the model prisoner. If G.P. pled guilty, he'd avoid the death penalty. McKrane might be moving on, but G.P. was going nowhere fast, so to occupy his time, he catered to his cell mate's every demand.

McKrane watched with amusement as G.P., his personal slave, tidied up their cell.

"Hey Witch, last time you made my bed, the damn sheet came off. Make sure the edges are tucked in."

"You got it, Mr. McKrane."

"You got one of them win-me-at-court spell kits? I don't really believe in that mojo bullshit, but why take my chances?"

"Right here, Mr.McKrane." G.P. handed him a small draw string bag.

"What the fuck is that smell?"

"Planetary oils and herbs"

"Planet what? Forget that shit." He threw the bag back at G.P. "You got a cigarette?"

"Right here, Mr. McKrane." He handed him a half pack of Marlboro's.

"Witch, I didn't know you smoked."

"I don't. I bargained the cigarettes for some hand Sanitizer. Besides, smoking disgusts me. Do you know what they do to tobacco plants? First, the seedling tobacco plants are coated with pesticides. Then they're harvested through hundreds of dirty hands. I even read once that migrant farm workers use human feces to—"

"Shut the hell up!" McKrane flung the cigarettes back at him. "You one sick-ass motherfucka. Why you got that germ thing goin' on?"

"I think it started when I was very young. I was never much for making mud pies or anything like that. The thought of worms and insects living in filth just made me nauseous. I much preferred to learn how to bake cookies. You know, Mr. McKrane one time —"

The inmate slapped his hand across his forehead.

"Oh man, I hope they convert my sentence. I can't stand listening to this shit anymore. I couldn't have me a regular con. No, instead I get me a sorry ass motherfucka who think he Mr. Clean." McKrane rolled on his back and looked at the ceiling. "What are you goin' to say you guilty of, tomorrow?"

"Murder."

"What? *You* kill somebody?"

"No, not just anybody. A lawyer."

"Why? You lawyer lose your case on you?" McKrane inquired curiously.

"No. It's more complicated than that."

"I gotta tell you. You don't look like you could kill nobody. I mean, just look at your sorry ass. You about 90 pounds soakin' wet. Plus you got that germ thing goin' on. Man, I've seen killers in my day, but like my Latino brothers would say, you don' look like you got the *cojones* for that sorta shit."

"Well, that's what I'm pleading tomorrow. Murder. Believe it." G.P. wanted to change the subject. He would do what he had to do and that was that. When a correctional officer appeared, he stopped straightening up the cell.

"Yes, Officer Burns?"

"Scalisi, you got visitors."

G.P. looked surprised. "But Visiting Day isn't until tomorrow."

The guard was uninterested. "It's your lawyer and some other people."

"What other people? " G.P. asked.

"How the hell should I know? I ain't your social director." He opened the cell. "Stick out your wrists." G.P. stuck out his wrists and then yanked them back. The action pissed off the prison guard.

"Excuse me Officer Burns, but before you put the cuffs on me did you..."

The guard cut him off. "Yeah, yeah, I wiped the cuffs off with alcohol. Now give me your wrists before I lose my patience and spit shine the damn cuffs."

McKrane nearly fell off his bunk laughing at the guard's remark. "Mr. Clean done strike again!"

G.P. smiled nervously as he walked in handcuffs down the hall to the Visitor Reception Area.

#

When he entered the room, his Uncle Hugo sat directly in front of him. Dressed to absolute perfection, he gave his nephew an unusually warm welcome.

"G.P. Nice to see you nephew! Sit down son, *Che fa?*"

"I'm okay Uncle Hugo. What brings you here?"

"Not just me. I'm here with some friends. Look behind you." G.P. turned around to see prosecutor Harper Grey, his defense attorney Billy Callis, and three other men in the cookie cutter dark suits. He looked at the agents.

"Those suits government issued or do you all shop in the same place?"

His Uncle Hugo took a deep breath. "Let me introduce you. You know Billy Callis, of course, and Mr. Grey from the Prosecutor's Office. The gentleman to your right is Mr. Albert Smith. He's a lawyer from the U.S. Attorney's Office. The man next to him is Agent Reilly from the IRS and this is Agent O'Hara from a government agency that's my personal favorite, the F.B.I. The F.B.I.," he sighed. "I know them well. They've been chasing me for years, and ah, Agent O'Hara here, even has a particular love for me."

G.P. watched the tall blond agent give his uncle a hostile glare. "Don't get cocky. Just consider yourself fortunate this go-around, Scalisi."

"Fortune favors the bulls, Agent O'Hara. Now Gino Patrick, I bet you are wondering why I am sitting in this room with all these lovely members of law enforcement who, under regular circumstances, would normally be my arch enemies."

"It did cross my mind, Uncle Hugo. You've been running from the Feds for years."

"But these circumstances ain't regular. I'm here to tell you that you don't have to plead guilty to a crime that you didn't commit."

Despite the fact he felt like a cornered rat, G.P. pulled himself together and summoned his courage. "I killed that goddam lawyer. We had a lover's quarrel, I got jealous and I did him. End of story." G.P. got up and tossed a chair across the room. His uncle just smiled.

"Nice display of bravado. Now sit your ass down, Gino Patrick. You didn't kill that man." Hugo looked at Harper Grey. "Explain it to him Mr. Prosecutor."

"G.P., some books and records were turned over to us by your attorney, Mr. Callis that gave us positive proof that Terence McShand was killed by someone else."

"Who?"

"Not at liberty to say right now, Gino. I'm sorry."

"Now what Mr. Grey didn't tell you here, is that Bill Callis turned over some records that your mother had. And Mr. Grey and Mr. Smith, because they are businessmen like me, were smart enough to give me complete immunity from any of my past problems like money laundering, racketeering, tax evasion, homicide..."

"Homicide was never on the table Scalisi, you know that."

The old mobster laughed. "Oh yeah, yeah. I forgot. But I was supposed to provide them with something. What do you call it Mr. Grey? Collaboration?"

"Corroboration. G.P., your uncle will corroborate the stuff in Terence McShand's ledger so that it connects the right people with Terence McShand's murder. In the near future Mr. Smith and I will be talking to you again. We have some questions for you, but for now you'll be released."

"You mean you're going to let me go?"

"Yes. You didn't kill Terence McShand and we know that. You were trying to protect someone, weren't you?"

G.P. put his chin to his chest, and looked down. "Yes. I was."

Hugo looked at the other men in the room. "Gentlemen, would you wait outside for one minute. I know you bastards are going to listen anyway from outside the damn door, but just make believe you're gonna try to give us some privacy."

"Two minutes, Scalisi." barked Agent O'Hara. The lawyers and the federal agents exited the room leaving G.P. and his Uncle alone. At least visually.

"Gino Patrick, I may have misjudged your character. You were trying to protect your mother despite all your nuttiness. My brother, Santo, would have respected that. Therefore, so do I."

"Are you apologizing to me?"

"No!" The old man yelled back. "You're still a friggin' nut job who could fuck up a one car funeral! But for once, you demonstrated a little heart. You tried to be a stand up guy and be strong for your mother." Biting his tongue, he looked at the wall. "We can talk about this at my house during the holidays."

"I can come over?"

He sighed. "I don't know why I'm offering this, but yes, G.P., you are welcome at my house again."

G.P. reached over and hugged his uncle. "Thanks Uncle Hugo."

"Yeah, yeah. Now get off me."

Outside, O'Hara and Reilly listened to the conversation of uncle and nephew. Agent O'Hara couldn't resist commenting about the warm family reunion. "So Reilly, how long do you think it'll be before the old man has the crazy nephew fencing stolen goods for him?"

"After he gets released?"

"Yeah."

"I give it a week."

"What about Rodriguez? What'll we do with him?"

"I'll take care of it tonight."

"He's pretty tough."

"We'll see. Hell, yeah we'll see."

Chapter 24

BERGEN COUNTY COURT HOUSE
HACKENSACK, NEW JERSEY

Sitting at home waiting for the day to end, drove him crazy. He wanted to do what he does best, work the streets. But when the face on the kitchen clock said 5:30, it was time to move. He had a party to attend.

For a split second, he thought that may be Tei was right. May be one of Baldwin's buddies made that phone call to him to lure him out. This whole meeting thing was set up. If someone planned to ambush him, he wasn't going down without a fight. Mo was sick of being shot at, sick of verbal threats, and damn sick of dead bodies. It was his turn to get a gun and take care of business.

The police property unit located in the basement of the county court house had a weapons storage section, consisting of guns and ammo confiscated from the street. It was a little-known secret to the outside world and it was loaded with assault rifles, shot guns, pistols, kevlar vests, and ammo, but Mo needed a code to get in. His suspension made him *persona non grata*. Prosecutor's Office policy mandated that the entrance code change whenever an investigator is on a suspension. Thank God for Tei! She gave him the new code.

Friday nights of a court house paycheck week were a wash. At 4:30 p.m., a person could lose their life if they got underfoot during the mass exodus of court house employees. By 5:30 p.m., the stampede was long gone. That's when he would make his move.

When he reached the court house, he parked his car and went down to the basement. Mo knew the near-retirement Sheriff's officer guarding the treasure trove of weapons. The old man usually made Mo sign in, but he could've left the building with a surface-to-air missile launcher and this codger wouldn't have noticed. He punched in the code, 3593, into the upright metal buttons. The door buzzed and he walked in. Much to his dismay, the Sheriff's officer wasn't the tired old man he'd hoped for. A new young new recruit sat in his place.

Shit, this is exactly what I don't need right now, an eager beaver, Mo thought.

"Can I help you?" the officer asked.

"Yeah, I'm on the job tonight. Big sting operation. Have to sign out some heavy artillery."

"What section are you in, Officer?"

"Narcotics."

"Name?"

"Wheeler."

"First and last name."

"What?"

"Your name?"

"And you are?" Mo leaned forward and read his name plate. "Officer Anders. David Anders."

"Your first and last name, please."

"Oh sure." He thought quickly. "Detective Tycovich Wheeler. People just call me Ty. Like to keep it simple. No one ever pronounces Tycovich right anyway." Mo knew that when the real Tei Wheeler found out about this, he would be the newest soprano in the Viennese Boys Choir, after she castrated him.

"Let me check the list." The young officer looked in his computer and couldn't come up with a Tycovich Wheeler. "Can't find your name. I got a Lindell Teishia Wheeler, but she's a detective in homicide. Can I see your badge please?"

"Sure." Mo fumbled for his badge in his jacket. "Damn. Can you believe this? I left my tin out in the car. Let me just sign out some stuff, and I'll get right back to you." He started walking in the direction of his locker.

"No Detective!" He yelled. "Since I don't know you and you forgot your I.D., I'm calling central dispatch to verify your identity." He picked up the telephone.

Mo started walking back. "Okay. I'm wrong. Here's my tin. Look right here." Innocently, the young officer looked in Mo's direction. Mo reached into his coat jacket and came back with a fist. He slammed it into the side of the man's head, knocking him off his chair. He picked Officer Anders up from the floor, finished him with a head butt, leaving the young sentinel unconscious. Then Mo propped him up in the chair, and grabbed a newspaper out of the garbage. Opening it up, he steadied the pages between the unconscious officer's fingers, covering his face. If anyone walked in, all they would see is a man behind a newspaper.

"Sorry Pal." He ran for his locker and ripped it open. Mo donned a Kevlar vest over his street clothes, consisting of black pants, a black pull over and a ski cap. He pulled out a long, black, beat up leather coat from his locker which he'd altered to suit his street needs. The designer features included a holster for carrying a sawed-off shotgun, and several pistols inside the coat's lining. The sawed of shotgun wasn't exactly legal, but tonight he wouldn't stand on legal formalities. He shoved a small revolver in an ankle holster, and lined his coat with extra clips for his nine-millimeter Glock. He heard a low moan coming from the desk where Officer Anders sat, so he looked for the nearest Exit sign. Pushing the door open, he set off an alarm, and ran like a bastard.

Ready for a street war, he ran out of the building and looked for the infamous court house cafeteria dumpster. His heart sank when he turned the corner.

He found the dumpster—with over forty heavy-duty garbage bags stocked piled all around it. Where the hell was he going to find a disguise in this mess? He kicked a trash bag. It broke open and the contents spilled all over the ground. A rat picking through the refuse in the broken bag ran across his feet.

"This blows!" he yelled out loud.

Behind him Mo heard the sound of tires on gravel. A dark blue panel van slowly crept down the alley toward him. Mo looked at the brick walls around him. The outside door to the kitchen was locked, and unless he was Spiderman, the windows were way out of reach. Trapped. He did the only thing that made any sense to him. He quietly reached for one of the weapons inside his coat as his heart pounded.

The window of the panel van rolled down. A head with long blonde hair and a beard wearing a Miller Lite baseball cap called him.

"Rodriguez, look behind the dumpster."

"Do I know you?"

"You will in about ten minutes."

Without taking his eyes off the man behind the wheel, Mo moved around the dumpster. Sure enough, behind the garbage, he found a brown paper bag. He opened it quickly and saw some coveralls, hair dye, and a few other things.

"C'mon Rodriguez. We don't have time. Get in."

Maybe this was his execution. He held a concealed hand gun and walked around the back of the van, half waiting for a bunch of skells to exit with guns blazing. When he reached the passenger's side of the van, Mo opened the door and pointed his gun at the head of the driver.

"Who-oa! It's cool. Look I'm on the job. F.B.I."

"Where's your badge?"

"Okay, okay. Look I'm going to reach in my pocket. Everything's cool. Don't shoot. My name is Special Agent David O'Hara."

Mo watched the agent carefully retrieve his identification. Mo took it into his hands without taking his eyes off the driver. Once Mo saw the i.d. was legit, he dropped his gun.

"Rodriguez, get in. We don't have much time."

"Alright." Both men looked around when they heard sirens in the background.

"Move it! We got to get our asses outta here. Those sirens are for me."

"What the hell did you do?"

Mo jumped in. "Never mind. Shut up and drive us outta here! NOW!"

O'Hara threw the van in reverse and peeled out of the alleyway at 50 miles-per-hour. Tires screeched, and the van headed down River Road to Route 80 East toward New Jersey Turnpike South.

#

Mo wanted explanations and he wanted them now.

"So why are the Feds involved?"

"Long story. We've been investigating corruption in your office for a couple of years now."

"Names."

"Edgar Baldwin, your ex-partner, Jack Halloran and a few others. We hadn't had a break in the case until McShand got offed."

"Who called me the other day? Hugo Scalisi?"

"Yeah. If you can believe this, Scalisi's cooperating with us. Listen, I hate to be a pain in the ass, but you gotta put that getup on. You can't be recognized at this party. Your life depends on it. So does mine. Start with the hair dye."

"Great." Mo reached into the bag. He found a comb and a tube of men's hair dye called "Runaway Red, No. 7." He squeezed the tube and a sticky, orange gel came out. He rubbed it through his hair and eye brows. Immediately, Mo's sandy blond hair color mutated into an ugly reddish orange. A scraggly beard rested in the bottom of the bag along with thick horn rimmed

157

glasses and a New York Mets baseball cap. He looked at O'Hara. "You've got to be kidding me. I'm a Yankee fan."

"No, I'm not kidding you. You think I've ever had this much hair in my life?" O'Hara exclaimed pointing to his faux rock star, Louis the XIV mane. "And I don't drink beer I drink Scotch. There's latex cement in the bag for the beard. You're not entering a beauty contest. Oh, and you have another present at the bottom of the bag."

He looked down and saw McShand's ledger. Callis remained true to his word and returned the file to him.

When he finished primping, he pulled down the passenger's side visor and got a gander of himself. His hair was a bright orange. He wore a glued-on beard, thick glasses, and the baseball cap. Then he stepped into the back of the panel van and put on a set of heavy brown Car Hart coveralls with a Regal Valet patch over the left breast pocket. Within minutes, Mo transformed from an ominous study in black to what could only be described as a nearsighted leprechaun who happened to be a Mets fan.

"Why was someone trying to kill me?"

"You stumbled onto something that implicated a lot of people. McShand kept the books for John W. Cane, who had a couple of Bergen County's finest on his payroll including the late Judge Esel. Apparently, McShand wanted a little more of this." O'Hara rubbed his thumb and index finger together. "McShand confronted Cane and tried to extort him. But the plan backfired. Cane had him killed, then tried to pin the murder on the gay witch guy who was McShand's lover at one point."

"Do you know who strangled McShand?"

"Not quite sure yet. We think it's someone at this party tonight. But who-ever killed McShand also tried to kill you. We matched bullets from the witch shop to your house. But here's where the crossover gets a little strange. Be-sides local law enforcement, Cane had some of Hugo Scalisi's people on his payroll."

"Why is that so unusual? He's a developer. Scalisi controls the unions. A match made in heaven."

O'Hara smiled. "More like match made in hell. Scalisi didn't know about it. These were pay offs he didn't approve."

"Holy shit. Now that *is* strange."

"Old Hugo didn't know about it until you and his personal lawyer stumbled upon that second set of McShand's books."

"The ones that came from the Aura Quest."

"Yep."

"Edgar's on Cane's payroll. Sonavabitch, why didn't I see it?"

"That's why your boss was trying to bury you. And that's why you are here tonight."

"What's the deal?"

"Ever park cars?"

"Yeah, as a college student at the Saddle Brook Marriott years ago."

"Good. That's what you'll be doing tonight for a while. Then we're going in for Cane, your boss, your ex-partner, and a few others involved in Cane's scam corporations, including Wellcan labs where they've been doctoring evidence."

"Jesus, this is unbelievable. You said others. What others?"

O'Hara looked pensive. "This is the dangerous part. Word has it that Scalisi wants to exact his own revenge tonight. He's pissed off."

"So will he be there?"

"Nah. He screws with us he blows his immunity deal. But that's not to say he wouldn't send someone else in to do his dirty work."

"What's the connection between Judge Esel and Cane?"

"She took about twenty million bucks in pay offs. But Cane didn't kill her. He needed her for all his shady land deals. Someone else did. Any ideas in your camp?" Mo wondered if he should mention that his partner was actually onto something. But he also knew how greedy some Feds could be when it came to taking credit for other cop's collars. If Tei was closing in on something, why shouldn't she get the glory?

"Nah. Fresh out of ideas. So besides parking cars, what's the game plan?"

"This place is crawling with civilians. We have to nab Cane and his cohorts without turning this charity ball into a shooting gallery. Most of the guests we know, but not all of them. Scalisi's people might be mixed in."

"So arrest them too. Who cares? You know O'Hara, it woulda been nice to have known about this little investigation. I've spent the last couple of months dodging bullets."

"I'm sorry Mo. Harper Grey knew, but we couldn't tell you."

"*Muchas gracias por nada.*" Mo looked out of the window. "Just in case you don't know what that means, many thanks for nothing."

O'Hara looked back somewhat embarrassed. "Sorry about that."

"Yeah me, too."

Chapter 25

As Mo and O'Hara drove through Asbury Park, an abandoned shell of a development project greeted them. The two continued on Ocean Avenue. Soon they would be in Deal, a private community exclusive to those who had money, lots and lots of money. O'Hara gave Mo a run down of The Tides, the mansion hosting tonight's *soiree*.

"Cane bought this place in the early eighties when it was just a big, broken down shack."

"I've been through Deal before. I dated a girl who lived in one of those broken down mansions."

"What happened?"

"She was kinda of a snob and I was too poor for her blood. I think she thought that she was doing her social conscience a favor by dating a poor Puerto Rican boy from Hackensack."

O'Hara laughed. "Yeah, I dated one of those kinda broads once. Don't feel bad. Rich girls don't like poor Irish guys from Kearney either. Let me finish telling you about The Tides."

"Go."

"Some rich guy built it the 1930's for a Hollywood movie actress, but she never lived long enough to see it. It's an art deco palace. After she died, the former owner just sealed the place up and abandoned it. Fell into a complete state of disrepair until —"

"Let me guess. J.W. Cane came along."

"Yup. Bought it for a song and refurbished it with all period pieces. Tonight most of the action will be in the Main Ballroom on the first floor. There's a study in the back of The Tides. That's where we think Cane's meeting Edgar Baldwin, Jack Halloran and a few others. Our surveillance shows Cane uses that room to conduct business. Our goal is to arrest Baldwin, Fulchess, Halloran and Cane, and try to get out quietly."

"You really think we'll get out quietly when we start cuffing people?"

"Hell no, but we gotta try." O'Hara glanced at a road sign. "Okay, we're out of Allenhurst. We'll be at the Tides in five minutes."

The two pulled up in front of open wrought iron gates. A burly attendant with a glowing nightstick stopped the van.

"You two can't be guests. What's your business here?"

"Regal Valet sent us for the night."

"Yeah, okay. Park this piece of shit on the back street where no one can see it. Then stand in front of the mansion. Wait until the cars and limos pull up. Help the ladies out, then park the car around back."

"Gotcha," said O'Hara eagerly.

"By the way, you get paid at the *end*, when the night's over. I've had too many of you bastards get paid and skip out before the night's done. Am I clear?"

"Yessir."

Mo and O'Hara parked their van on a small street far away from The Tides. Walking quickly, the two made their way to the front of the mansion.

For a minute, they forgot that they were there to apprehend organized crime suspects. An architectural paradise, The Tides could have been a stately Rhode Island mansion were it not located on the Jersey Shore. Row upon row of manicured shrubbery lined the extensive frontage of The Tides. Two gargantuan marble columns and a large marble staircase ascended to beveled glass doors, where a butler stood guard. The back of the mansion opened to the beach and the ocean roared in the background.

Servants stationed throughout the mansion accommodated the evening's guests. O'Hara and Mo watched a steady, simple traffic pattern. Cars and limousines pulled up in the horseshoe shaped driveway directly in front of the mansion. Black tuxedos and their escorts exited their vehicles and entered the stately home.

As the two men stood in front of The Tides, a long haired valet smiled with relief. "Dudes! Thank God you're here. Need a smoke break. Name's Mirage. Yell, if you need something, man."

"We're large and in charge, Mr. Mirage." chirped O'Hara. "What kinda name is that?"

"It's like, the name of my new band. I play bass. You should check us out at D.J.'s. in Belmar someday. Later." He walked away.

Mo rolled his eyes. " 'Mr. Mirage.' You're lame. What a line of horseshit."

"Roll with it brother, just roll with it."

After Mirage left for his break, the two fake valets replaced him. A brand new Mercedes sedan pulled up. Four women between the ages of one and two hundred tried to get out of their cars. Mo reached in and helped the elderly driver to her feet, while O'Hara assisted the other three passengers.

"Thanks, dearie. Just remember. Don't get old no matter what they say," rasped the driver. "Be a sweetie and grab my cane."

Mo reached in. He snatched an ornate parrot head walking stick and handed it to the old matron. Once the four ladies were out of the car, they linked arms. Step at a time, they slowly made their way into The Tides, tittering all the way into the building.

Mo looked at O'Hara. "It's gonna be a long night. I'll take the car around back."

When Mo returned moments later, a Cadillac pulled in. It was a late model El Dorado triple black, with cherry red pin striping. Mo recognized the car. He turned to O'Hara.

"Looks like some of our skells have arrived. You take this one. I can't get too close even with this leprechaun beard.

Jack Halloran, Edgar Baldwin and Ronnie Fulchess exited the car. His ex-partner, Jack, flung the keys at O'Hara who missed catching them in mid-air. They promptly fell on the ground. Jack didn't bother picking them up for the attendant. Instead, he yelled over to him.

"Make sure my car has no scratches on it or else it's coming out of your paycheck." O'Hara glared at him until he heard the sound of whirling blades. As he looked up into the starless sky, he tapped Mo on the shoulder.

"Rodriguez, I almost forgot. There's a heliport behind the mansion. Another escape route."

"Yeah. Cane probably needs it for quick getaways." As he looked at the El Dorado, an idea popped into Mo's head. A smile burst across his face. "Let me park this one for you."

"You sure?"

"Yeah. They're far enough away." The detective with the faux red beard and hair hopped in the new Cadillac. He promptly cleared any phlegm from his throat and spat on the passenger's side floor mat. Then he revved the car's engine, slammed the transmission into drive, and stomped on the gas pedal, leaving long skid marks on the pristine white asphalt driveway. A small crowd of people standing nearby gasped. The El Dorado's passengers turned around, mortified by the speeding valet who vanished into the night. The valet manager ran over.

"Hey! What the hell does your friend think he's doing?"

"Don't mind him," O'Hara grinned. "He's just a little enthusiastic. He loves those big ol' Cadoos."

"When he comes back, tell that asshole to slow it down or else he is fired."

"Will do." The annoyed manager stormed away as O'Hara snickered.

Seconds later, Mo came back. While O'Hara parked another luxury car, a stretch limo pulled up just as Mirage returned from his cigarette break. Mo recognized the limousine's distinctive hood ornament, a leaping panther. His nemesis had arrived.

Exit businessman Cane wearing an expensive tuxedo with a white fringed opera scarf, a dated Michael Douglas look. After giving a glance around to see if he was noticed by onlookers or local press people, Cane extended his hand to help an elegant woman step from the car. Mo held the door quietly as he watched Cane's escort rise to her feet. The pair walked hand in hand, cooing like lovesick teenagers. Without taking their eyes off each other, the couple made their way up the marble stairs. At the top of the stairs, they paused. The woman waited while Cane returned to the idling limousine.

Mo felt ice chips flowing through his veins. "Claudette," he mumbled. "I can't believe it. It's her."

"You know her?" inquired O'Hara.

"Just a little bit. That's Arabella Esel's niece. She just inherited twenty million from her late aunt." He sighed. "Unreal."

Cane returned outside and approached him. Mo hoped he wouldn't be recognized.

"My chauffeur will be joining us inside. Would you mind taking the limousine around the back?"

"Not a problem."

"Thanks, my good man." Cane promptly handed Mo a ten dollar bill. He opened the door. The chauffeur pushed him out of the way and ran to catch up with Cane. Mo remained unreactive. He had to stay cool. He put aside the fact the woman he'd slept with a few nights ago was now probably sleeping with someone who wanted him dead. Without thinking twice, Mo ripped up the ten dollar bill and threw it to the ground.

#

Outside the wrought iron gates of The Tides, Hugo Scalisi, his driver, Carmine Cusi, and his associate, Gaetano Giacomo waited impatiently.

"Boss," asked Gaetano, "you sure you're alright with this?"

"We got a coupla of our own on the inside, right?" Hugo asked casually.

"Yeah, more than a couple. Some are in the kitchen, but most are circulating as waiters. I made arrangements for you to go in through the kitchen. We pull around back. Carmine here makes like you and him are working in the kitchen, and then you're in. You do what you have to do and get out. Fast."

"Excellent, excellent Gaetano. Good job. You will be rewarded in due time."

Gaetano paused before reaching into his coat pocket. "Mr. Scalisi, why don't you let Carmine and me handle this? We done this stuff before."

Scalisi waved a hand at him. "What? And let you have all the fun? No sir. This was a personal attack on my family by this traitor jerk off. I'm handling this myself." He smiled at his henchman. "It ain't like I've never done this before. Besides you forget something. I'm dying anyway. So if someone shoots me or I get caught? So what? Be like Jack Ruby killing Oswald. What loss? I'm a dead man anyway. You got what I need, Gaetano?"

"Yes Mr. Scalisi." He gave him a handgun with a silencer attached. "Good luck, Mr. S."

"Thanks." Scalisi drew a long breath. "Now Carmine, get me into that mansion."

#

The speeches began about nine. According to the program O'Hara picked up, the mutual admiration speeches would last until ten, before cocktails and dancing. All the guests were assembled in the main ballroom listening to presentations. At the first opportunity, the two law enforcement agents dumped their parking attendant outfits. Breathless and pumped, it was show time.

O'Hara held a small walkie-talkie. He looked at Mo. "Okay. Everything is in place. Here's the plan. We're lucky. Our bad boys decided to ditch the party speeches. Word is they're boozing it up in the back drawing room like they usually do. Our agents are circulating and we have a SWAT team on stand by."

"Cane is mine, O'Hara. You owe me that much."

He nodded. "Done Rodriguez, done."

"Aren't you supposed to deputize me? I'm not a Fed. Remember?"

"You were a street cop in Newark, right?"

"Five years." Mo ripped off his elfin beard.

"Consider yourself deputized. Let's go!"

O'Hara and Rodriguez walked briskly to the front door of The Tides. A tuxedoed butler halted them at the door.

"Your invitation?"

Mo answered. "Get the hell outta my way." He flashed his tin and walked past the butler with O'Hara right behind him.

No time to spare, gotta move, Mo thought.

It seemed like it took them forever to reach the drawing room. As they stood outside the door, they heard men's laughter.

"Sounds like a party, O'Hara."

"According to the floor plan, the room has one exit. And we're blocking it."

Suddenly, the laughter stopped abruptly. Mo whispered. "They shut up."

"Shit. They know we're here." The F.B.I. agent looked at the closed door. "On my count, one, two, three ..."

With guns drawn, they kicked open the door. Cane, Fulchess, Baldwin and Halloran stood in a half-circle unmoved.

"Federal Agents!"

Leisurely, Cane put his hand in his pockets. "I can't believe I'm seeing this. F.B.I.? Really, I didn't think the Feds were that desperate for recruits. Rodriguez, don't you ever call it a day?"

"Not until you're in an orange jumpsuit Cane!"

Jack Halloran interjected. "You know, I tried to protect you Mo. But you couldn't leave well enough alone." He reached in his breast pocket. "I didn't want things to be this way."

A single gunshot struck O'Hara from the back. He dropped to the floor moaning. Without hesitation, Mo turned and fired behind him. His bullet caught the shooter, Cane's chauffeur.

"Fuck! I'm hit!" the man grabbed his shoulder and stumbled out of the room. Ronnie Fulchess jumped in front of Cane and became his human shield. Baldwin, completely bug eyed, froze in his tracks.

Jack Halloran and his ex-partner gave each other steely eyed stares. Halloran made the first move. "Sorry, buddy. I tried to warn you to stay out of this. But this is how it has to be." He pointed a revolver at him.

Mo fired first. Now two lawmen lay on the floor. Blood flowed. Agent O'Hara moaned in pain. Jack Halloran took a bullet through his heart. His blood pumped out on the plush carpeting underneath him. Within minutes, Mo's ex-partner was stone cold dead. The night wasn't going as well as Cane expected. Suddenly, the millionaire saw an opportunity. He rushed to a floor length glass window and flung a chair through it. He jumped out the window landing on the lawn a few feet below. Fulchess followed him. Both men ran into the darkness as the ocean roared in the distance.

The only ones left in the room were Mo and Baldwin. By now, the guests heard the gunshots. Pandemonium started when a man dressed in a bloody chauffeur's uniform stumbled into the main ballroom. Women screamed. Party goers fled out the front door of The Tides, frantically looking for their cars. The gala was officially over.

Mo looked at Edgar. "Looks like all your friends abandoned you, Edgar, Now it's just you and me." He threw down the gun. "Come here, you little prick!"

Baldwin put on his false bravado. "Face it! Your career's over Rodriguez! Pulling a gun on a Superior. Interfering in a federal investigation. I'm going to put you so deep in the system you'll never see the light of day!"

"I don't think so. Especially since you're the subject of this damn investigation!" He pounced on Baldwin, grabbing him by the throat. Baldwin made all kinds of gagging noises. Mo relented momentarily, long enough to let him catch his breath before he started punching him in the head.

"How does it feel, Edgar?" Mo tightened his grip around his neck. "How does it feel to be the prey for a change?" Mo's choke hold made Baldwin's face look like a honeydew melon about to burst.

"Don't move! Federal Agent!" The agent saw O'Hara laying in a pool of his own blood, his body shivering, his skin sweaty and white. He yelled into a walkie talkie. "Agent down! I need paramedics in here!"

Baldwin found his voice. "Help me. P-p-please! Agent, this man tried to k-k-kill me. I'm Captain C-c-Baldwin from Bergen County. Tr-r-rying to apprehend this sus-s-s-spect." Weakly, he pointed to Mo.

"You! Get off him!" ordered the F.B.I agent. "Stand up!"

"Shit. Look, I'm a cop." Suddenly Mo was overcome with this nightmare that Baldwin had successfully framed him — again.

"I know." The agent tossed him a pair of handcuffs. "Cuff him Detective, don't kill him."

Mo gave Edgar an evil grin. "My pleasure." He knelt down. As he rolled Baldwin on his stomach to cuff him, he body slammed Baldwin into the floor one more time for good measure. He turned to the agent holding O'Hara.

"Listen. Cane is on the run. I gotta fly."

"I got O'Hara. Go."

Mo lept through the window and bolted into the night.

#

The bleeding chauffeur stumbled into the kitchen. He grabbed a towel and tried to apply pressure to his shoulder. He'd killed many people in his day, but he simply couldn't believe someone actually shot *him* for a change. It wasn't fair. He closed his eyes, trying to ignore the burning pain in his shoulder until he heard a familiar voice.

"I treated you like my family. And this is how you repay me, you lousy bastard." An older man dressed in black and white checkered cook's pants and a white shirt stood behind him.

"Mr. Scalisi, what are you doing here?"

"I'm here to kill you, then piss on your corpse when I'm done." Old Hugo loaded a clip into his gun. "You cheated me by cookin' the books after my brother died. Then you killed that lawyer and tried to pin it on my nephew, makin' him confess to a crime he didn't commit. Hell of a way to do it, Lino. By threatening to kill a man's mother." He pointed the gun at Lino De Simone's chest. "And if that weren't enough you went to work for that scumbag developer, Cane."

Lino panted. "Maybe if you weren't such a cheapskate, old man." He pulled a gun out of his jacket and shot Hugo. As the old man dropped, he managed to get off one shot that struck De Simone in the groin.

"A-r-rh!" He screamed in pain. De Simone grabbed his crotch, his hands red and sticky from his own blood. He was so busy trying to determine what remained of his manhood, he failed to see two other chefs, Gaetano and Carmine, enter the kitchen.

"Holy shit, Boss! Carmine! Where the hell's our people? Get the Boss outta here. I'll finish this."

Carmine carried the bleeding old man out of the kitchen, leaving Gaetano to finish off the job Hugo Scalisi started.

DeSimone didn't even think to reach for his gun. He rocked back and forth holding his crotch and pleading. "No, please, Gaetano. We go back, remember? Cane will cut you in if you get me to a hospital."

Gaetano smiled. Then he dumped his entire clip into De Simone's body, leaving him dead on the kitchen floor. He stood over the bullet riddled corpse, relishing the moment until he heard voices. Gaetano started to exit the kitchen, but found time to run back and spit on De Simone's corpse.

"That's for Hugo." Gaetano vanished right before a SWAT team stormed the kitchen.

#

From a distance, there was so much commotion at The Tides that Mirage figured no one would notice if he helped himself to a few personal belongings of the guests. He heard a lot of noise, but hey, not to worry. Some major league partying was going on. He snagged the keys of a Beemer, a Porsche Carrera, and a stretch limo. Armed with a only flashlight and his trusty screwdriver, tooling around an alarm system was his specialty. He had just one more duty to perform before he started stealing.

"Time for that smoke break." Mirage lit up a joint and inhaled deeply. Great head rush. He smoked half, and decided to save the rest for his next break. Now in a nice weed induced haze, he'd feel less guilty about ripping off the rich.

The Porsche would be the first hit. Since he had keys, Mirage didn't need to disarm the alarm system. Sliding the seat back, he checked out the stereo.

"Damn, too recessed." he muttered. "Can't yank it out." Frustrated, he slammed his fist on top of the dashboard. The glove box opened and out fell out a gold Rolex wristwatch, and a pair of Ray Bans.

"There is a God." He pocketed the watch and put the Ray Bans on top of his head. The Beemer was next. He exited the Porsche whistling a Grateful Dead tune. He walked by the limo. From the underside of the car, Mirage saw a dark stream of reddish liquid dripping on the asphalt from beneath the limo.

"Yowee, massive transmission fluid leak man." Mirage knelt down and looked under the car to check it out. Some of the fluid got on his hands. "Wow, this's some sticky shit." He got down on the ground all the way, to see where the leak came from. It was dripping from trunk. Mirage looked at the limo keys. To open or not the trunk. "I think I'm gonna regret this, man." Carefully, he inserted the keys and popped the lid.

The top portion of a petite woman's body stuck half out of a garbage bag. Her eyes were frozen open, with a bullet hole dead center in her forehead. The body was carefully molded to fit around the limo's spare tire well. Mirage swallowed. The rocket scientist now knew it wasn't trans fluid on his hands. It was some dead lady's blood. He leaned over the corpse. Where did all the blood come from? After all, it was only one bullet to the forehead. Nobody could bleed that much, right?

He prodded down the top of the garbage bag with the screwdriver. The next sight pulled him out of his buzz and slammed him back down to earth.

The woman was disemboweled. Her guts were splayed around the inside of the garbage bag. Blood was everywhere. It was much more than poor Mirage could handle. He puked on the ground then ran from the site without any idea where he was going.

#

The heliport at the Tides was set close to the beach. Fulchess and Cane had to cut through a large garden before they reached the heliport. Fulchess, ever the loyal dog, followed at Cane's heels. He'd given up his soul and everything, absolutely everything, in exchange for wealth and power from Cane. The developer promised him millions for his cooperation in burying the McShand murder. Fulchess agreed to lie, obstruct and kill if necessary.

Moving quickly, suddenly Cane stopped short.

"You alright. Mr. Cane?"

"Be better in a minute," he said breathlessly. He reached into his pocket for a nitro pill. "Just a few chest pains, happens once in awhile."

"You havin' a heart attack Mr. Cane?"

"No you idiot!" he barked. "I'm just out of breath, that's all." Cane heard the whirl of the helicopter propellers in the background. "Good. We're close."

"Where's your girl, Mr. Cane?"

"She's already in the helicopter."

"Great Mr. Cane. Don't worry, Sir. We'll get there. What's the plan?"

"We'll 'copter over to a private airport in Pennsylvania. Then on a plane to the Isle of Margarita off the coast of Venezuela."

"Great plan, Mr. Cane."

Cane was highly amused by the way Fulchess salivated and hung onto every word he said. Though he enjoyed leading Fulchess around by the nose, it also repulsed him because the man was a mental weakling. No matter, though. Cane would keep him close by until Fulchess outlived his usefulness like so many others before him.

Finally, the heliport was in sight. Fulchess and Cane stood along the outer perimeter of the pad. The area was well lit. Cane saw Claudette waving to him from inside the helicopter. Propellers whirled. A man directing the ground activity ran over to Cane.

"Good evening, Jensen!" Cane yelled above the noise.

"Good evening! Mr. Cane, there's only room for one other person."

Without hesitation, Cane turned to Fulchess. "Ron, I'm so sorry about this." He pulled out a pistol and shot Ronald Fulchess dead, then turned to Jensen. "Get me out of here!"

Manipulating people and situations were so predictable Cane found it all rather boring. Cane's business motto, "always expect the unexpected" was something he often said but never truly believed in. Nothing was ever truly unexpected.

Except for Mo Rodriguez. He was highly unpredictable and that always pissed Cane off.

"Don't move!" Mo yelled with a raised pistol. "I'll kill you, you bastard!"

"I can't believe this! Rodriguez, you're like old chewing gum on a shoe! You just won't get out from under!"

Adrenalin heightened, Mo's attention caught the ground crewman. Jensen drew a weapon from inside his breast pocket. Mo fired and dropped him. Claudette screamed and pounded the glass from inside the helicopter.

"You're under arrest!"

"Not on your life!" Cane started to draw his pistol again. Instead of firing at the cop, he fell to the ground clutching his chest. The gun landed on the pavement. Mo ran over and grabbed the weapon. Cane was pale, barely breathing, but still alive.

"You ain't lookin' so good ol' boy." Now brandishing two guns he ran in the direction of the helicopter. He ducked under the helicopter's propellers, stood outside the cockpit and pointed his guns at the pilot.

"Shut this thing down or I'll blow your head off!" Mo yelled.

"Don't shoot! Okay!" The pilot killed the engine. As whirling propellers slowed to a complete stop, an anonymous pilot and Claudette Johnstone stepped out of the helicopter to the waiting arms of law enforcement agents.

Mo looked sadly at Claudette. For a moment, she seemed almost embarrassed. He wanted to hold her until he remembered, she tried to get him killed. He had to let her go, but not without saying something first. As an F.B.I. agent cuffed her, he stood in front of her.

"So what was the plan, honey? Waltz me in front of the window so your boyfriend Cane had a better line of sight?"

Tears streamed down her face. "It wasn't like that. I swear."

"Yeah, right."

"Mo," she whispered quietly. "My back had the laser on it. I would've taken the bullet not you."

In his heart, he thought that maybe she did care. He shook his head.

"Detective, did you want to talk to this suspect?" the agent asked politely.

"Nah. Get her out of my sight." Mo forced the words. For a split second in time, his heart actually ached. He turned away. Too painful to deal with.

From out of the melee, Mo saw Assistant Prosecutor Harper Grey coming toward him.

"Am I suppose to be happy to see you?"

"Probably not. We have a lot of dead bodies here, Detective. There'll be a lot of paper work to fill out. You know, you'll have to turn in your weapon and get a loaner."

"I don't need a fucking lawyer to tell me what police procedure is."

"Can you give me a quick run down on the body count?"

"Halloran drew on me. I shot him. Cane's driver shot O'Hara. I shot the driver. He took off bleeding. Cane kicked out a window with that guy there." He pointed to the late Ronnie Fulchess. "Me and Edgar Baldwin were left alone in the back drawing room. Him I would like to have shot, but I didn't."

"Ah yes, Edgar, who's now very contrite and singing like a canary."

"That prick? He's probably singin' about what everybody else did not his own bad acts."

"What about Lino De Simone?"

"Who's that?"

"Cane's driver."

"Like I said, I shot some guy in the shoulder. When last I saw the scumbag, he was alive. Bleeding, but alive.

"Well, he's lying dead in the kitchen. Looks like a piece of Swiss cheese, he's got so many bullet holes in him."

"Not my kill, I assure you."

170

"Lars Jensen."

"Who's that?"

"Helicopter ground crew dead guy. Yours?"

"Yep. I was trying to arrest Cane, he drew on me. So I shot and killed him. Anyone else?"

"Inez McShand? Yours?"

"Not mine! What about her? Didn't anyone else shoot any people here tonight besides me? Jesus Christ!"

"Calm down. Okay, Okay. Let me finish. She arrived here dead in the back of Cane's limousine. Some druggie parking attendant opened the trunk and found her body. Local police picked him up running down the street screaming."

"So who did it?"

"Don't know yet. She was shot in the head then gutted ala 'Jack the Ripper' style."

"Oh God." Mo rubbed his forehead. "Do you need me for anything else?"

"No. You can call it a night."

"Good."

"Just be back in the office at nine a.m."

"Shit. And how can I do that? I came here without a car remember?"

"Oh that's right. I'll have an agent take you home."

Mo felt like a baby. He was tired, wet and dirty, not to mention emotionally spent from punching out some poor unsuspecting sheriff's officer, killing his ex-partner and some poor slob named Lars Jensen. Eh. In a few days, he'd be over that. They tried to kill him. Fair is fair.

Getting over Claudette? Now *that* was going to take some doing.

Chapter 26

All he wanted to do was make a quiet entrance into his office. No fanfare, no noise, no fuss. Except when your face is plastered on the cover of a local Bergen County newspaper, you obtain celebrity status whether you like it or not. A secretary, Maggie Santa Maria, handed him a copy of the paper. The Headlines read 'Corruption Ring Busted by Joint Investigation between County and Federal Authorities.' There was a photo of Mo standing over Ronnie Fulchess' corpse.

"Here you go, hero." She said as she batted her eyes. "Oo-o-o-h look at the dead guy. Who is it?"

"Damn. I never even knew they took this picture."

"The camera loves you, baby."

"Yeah, but this office didn't love me a coupla months ago."

"Look, my honey, we all knew you were being set up by that beady eyed, bald-headed bastard. We just couldn't say nothing. But he got his right?"

"I hear he's in protective custody."

"That's right." Harper Grey stood in the doorway of Mo's office. "Welcome back, Detective."

"I guess. Long time, no see. So what do you want from me today, Harpo?"

"Just a few more questions and answers."

"Go. I got a lot of paper to fill out on all the stiffs."

172

"Lino DeSimone, the chauffeur."

"Dead and looked like Swiss cheese. That's what you said last night, right?"

"Yes. But killed by bullets that didn't come from a cop or one of the dead perps. I heard Hugo Scalisi's people were there. True?"

"Counselor, it was a zoo. I was dodging bullets. Mother Theresa could have shot him and I wouldn't have noticed. O'Hara and I were a little busy." Mo took a breath then asked the ultimate question. "Did he make it?"

"He's in Intensive Care. He pulled through the surgery but the prognosis is guarded. A bullet ripped through a lung. Nearly missed his heart."

"He didn't deserve that. He got ambushed. What about Cane? Is he alive?"

"He's in a Cardiac Care Unit, but yeah, he made it through his little heart attack."

"I hope he lives long." Mo said serenely. "Long enough to die in jail."

"Question."

"Go."

"What's happening with the Esel investigation?"

"Can't help you with that one. Talk to my partner, Tei." Mo looked over at the accumulation of paper on his desk. "Listen, this is my first day back. I haven't looked at my mail in weeks."

"Sure I'll get lost. No problem." Harper started to leave, but instead he turned to look at Mo, who hastily ripped open envelopes. "Mo, I just wanted to apologize."

The only thing his heart ached for was Claudette, the woman he felt betrayed him. "Nah, I'm cool." Once the prosecutor left, Mo continued pawing through papers. Then he realized something awful. Tei was probably on the street trying to collar a murder suspect by herself.

#

He opened his eyes to a smiling young nurse. The man lying on the hospital gurney had plastic tubing coming out of every bodily orifice but his ears. He was alive. Weak, but alive. That made the agony bearable. For the past seven hours he'd been living in the hazy world of the half dead.

"Frank Bradshaw, Mr. Frank Bradshaw? Time to wake up, okay? Do you know where you are? You're in the recovery room of Mercy General Hospital. You've just come out of surgery." The nurse shined a light in his eyes. In response, the man on the gurney winced and groaned slightly. "That's good Frank, your eyes are responding to the light. Nod if you understand me."

Smart enough to enter the hospital under an assumed name, once again Hugo Scalisi traveled safely beneath the radar. He had tentacles everywhere.

"Uh-huh." He grunted back at the nurse barely moving his head.

"Good. You have some people here to see you." The nurse gestured to a man and woman standing quietly in the corner to walk over. "Look, who's here. Your wife and nephew."

Lola Scalisi and her nephew G.P. walked over, and stood at the foot of the gurney. The nurse reminded them that Surgical Recovery patients have five minutes of visiting time. Lola Scalisi bent over and kissed her husband on the forehead. Under the oxygen mask, she saw the corners of his mouth try to turn upward into a smile.

"C'mon G.P., say hello to your uncle." She backed up giving G.P. enough room to squeeze around the medical equipment and get closer to his uncle's bedside.

"Hi, Uncle Frankie." He winked as he leaned over to his Uncle's ear. "Nice to see you. I just want to assure you that Mercy General uses strong disinfectants and has the lowest incidence of stapholoccus infections in the State. Hardly anyone has ever died of a staph infection here. Well, actually three people, but who's counting?" G.P. grinned. He took pride in assuring his uncle that he was in a near germ free environment.

First, the old man grunted as though he were straining his bowels. Then his face grew red like an over ripened tomato. The blood pressure monitoring system went haywire, signaling acute cardiovascular distress. A medical team ran over to his bedside. Hugo Scalisi started grunting loudly as though he were speaking some strange sub-Saharan dialect.

Despite the intravenous tubes in his arm, Hugo Scalisi summoned every ounce of strength. Raising his arm and index finger, he pointed back and forth between G.P. and the bright red Exit sign mounted over a doorway. He continued making noises which began to sound more like words in spite of the large tube shoved half way down his throat.

"G.P. what's he doing? Is he okay? My husband looks upset! What's he saying? What did you do?" His aunt bordered on complete hysteria.

"We better go, Aunt Lola," said G.P. "I think I understand what he's trying to say. He just told me to get the hell out of his sight."

"Oh G.P., not again? You've only been home a few days and you've pissed him off already." His aunt ran over to her husband. "So long, my honey. I'll be back tomorrow. *Without* him." She crooked her thumb in G.P.'s direction.

As the medical team tried to subdue old Mr. Bradshaw, an embarrassed G.P. and his aunt quietly left the hospital room.

#

Tei drove at her usual breakneck speed up to Sophiah Brinkworth's home in Ridgewood. She pulled across the street in front of the large house on Maple Avenue. Tei admired the house's gingerbread siding, with its dark eggplant colored turrets and mauve scalloped awnings. Sophiah's house could have fallen off a San Francisco post card, with its colorful yet elegant Victorian style.

The detective had more important concerns as she carefully studied the home's entrances and exits. If she intended on bringing Andrew Saunford in for questioning, and she cornered him like a rat, Tei needed to anticipate which way the rat would run. Or worse yet, if he attacked her, she needed to plot her way out.

Though she was a big strong girl, Tei figured that she probably shouldn't be doing this alone. As a beat cop on the Hackensack Streets, she dragged in many drug dealers or drunks by their shirt tails. It wasn't *that* hard. She only prayed that bringing in a man who killed his father in cold blood wouldn't be all that much harder.

She watched the house wishing she were somewhere else. The day, sunny and temperate, was great for outdoor oil painting or planting. On days like today, she'd be in her backyard, braless, in a Lakers tee shirt, wearing a big straw rice paddy hat, and cotton shorts gently melting colors together on a canvas board or tackling unruly dandelions. What the hell was she doing here? Nothing except chain smoking, and hoping her murder suspect would appear. She saw a large grey Pontiac sedan parked in front of the house.

One hour. No movement in the house. Only ten in the morning, she thought. *People are still sleeping.*

Two hours. No movement. "Bor-r-ing" she said out loud.

Suddenly, a large figure passed between windows. She heard a door slam. It sounded as though the noise came from the back of the house. For a split second she thought about radioing for help from the local police, but she was only here to talk to Andrew Saunford. That's right. She wouldn't bring him in for questioning. After all, innocent until proven guilty, right? All she wanted was a little information. Tei secured her gun, put on a baseball cap, and let her braids flow out from beneath the cap. She exited the car briskly.

The layout of the land was simple: long driveway, a garden in back of the house, and a small cottage nestled on 2.5 acres of woods. Tei made her way past the house, through the garden, until she finally reached a small, two room cedar shakes cottage. In front of it, a man dressed in blue jeans and a T-shirt knelt on the ground. Using a small hand held trowel, he carefully removed tiny pachysandra plants from plastic flats. His hair was dirty snow colored, just like Alfred Wicks described.

It was Andrew B. Saunford.

"Hi there," said Tei feigning friendliness. "I'm looking for Sophiah

Brinkworth."

"Mother isn't here right now."

"Okay, um, I see. Are you her son Andrew Saunford?"

As the kneeling man rose from the ground to greet her, he kept rising and rising like a giant who couldn't stop growing. This was no man. It was a six foot, six inch, oak tree that just happen to have legs and long grey hair tied back in a ponytail. Tei stood five ten easily, but the tree bypassed her several feet ago. He then crossed his muscular arms looking rather defensively at her.

"Yes, I am Andrew Saunford."

"Andrew, I'm a friend of you mother's. My name is "Detective Wheeler. Welcome. Yes, Mother spoke of you. She said that you were very bright." He smiled.

"Well, now, that was awfully nice of her. Can we talk for a minute?"

#

A sickening feeling hit Mo in the pit of his stomach. Bad news was on its way, he sensed it. It was the feeling he always got right before someone he knew was about to die. He sat in the backseat of the squad car wedged between Sylvano Lake and Alfred Wicks.

"Big Al, I'm going to show you a picture, okay?"

"Okay, Big Mo," Al replied, as he chomped on an Eskimo Pie. The melting ice cream dripped all over his hand. It didn't bother him. His long cow-like tongue came out and licked his hand clean.

Mo showed Al enlarged mugshots of Andrew Saunford. "Do you know this guy, Al?

"Oh sure. That's my new friend Marty, with dark hair. He's the nice man that offered to clean Judge Esel's chambers for me. Why did he make his hair white?"

"Al, if you saw Marty today, do you think you could recognize him?"

Sylvano interrupted. "Detective, Al doesn't have to leave this car to point out his friend Marty, right?"

"No problem, Sylvano. He can stay put."

Al cocked his head from side to side. "Big Mo, are you going to hurt my friend Marty?"

"Oh no, Big Al," said Mo sweetly. "We lost him and now that we found him we're going to put him in a nice safe place so we don't lose him again." Mo saw flashing lights. The traffic came to a dead stop.

"What the hell's goin on?" he yelled to the driver.

"Accident between a bus and Camaro. Looks nasty, Rodriguez."

"Godammit, take some back roads! Get us around this bullshit! Do it!"

#

"Do you mind if I plant this pachysandra, Detective? It's a shade plant and the flats are sitting in direct sunlight."

"No, go right ahead. I know how fragile they are. Bit of a gardener myself."

"Good. Pardon my back if you will." The large man knelt on the ground and started whistling. Tei thought he was remarkably poised for a murderer. With huge gentle hands, he systematically planted each pachysandra plant, one by one. When he finished whistling, he looked up at Tei.

"Recognize that song, Detective? Can I call you Tei? I think that's what Mother used to call you."

Where the hell is this conversation going? she thought. *I better go along with him.*

"No problem."

"The *song*, detective?"

"What song?"

"This one." He whistled a clear shrill tune.

"Sure. Bob Dylan. 'Blowin' in the wind.'"

"Very good. Now I want to test your factual knowledge, Tei. I'm going to give you some incidents and you tell me what they have in common. Marilyn Monroe. Adolph Eichmann." Saunford slashed his finger across his throat. "Dead. What's the common thread?" Saunford asked cheerfully.

Tei thought for a minute. "This all happened in the 1960's?"

Saunford looked disappointed. "An acceptable answer, but not quite what I was looking for. You know Tei, I went to a private school in Manhattan as a young man. We were taught how to think and analyze with precision. I presume you were a product of public school, correct?"

"Yes."

"Public schools take more a generalist approach. You are taught to memorize rather than think critically."

"Yeah, whatever. Are you done with your trivial pursuit game? I have some questions that I'd like to ask you."

"When I'm done Tei, I'll let you know," he snapped.

Psycho freak. She thought. *Gotta let him think he's in control.*

"Okay, so what's your next question?"

"Give me the common thread. Whose afraid of Virginia Wolf? Silent Spring? A Day in the Life of Ivan Denisovich? And of course, my personal favorite Happiness is a Warm Puppy?"

"Let me see. Edward Albee, Rachel Carson, Alexander Solzhenitsyn, and Charles Schultz. Books. All those authors published in the 1960's."

He turned around and smiled at her. "Excellent answer, but partially not totally correct. Can't blame you though. You have limited analytical skills."

"Can I ask you what your point is?"

He ignored her. "One last question. Willie McCovey, Bobby Richardson, and Marilyn Monroe."

The baseball question she knew immediately, the 1962 World Series. If her memory served her correctly, Marilyn Monroe overdosed in 1962. Bingo. All this stuff happened in 1962, the same year he was convicted.

"I know what you're hinting at Mr. Saunford. Or shall I call you Andy?"

He gritted his teeth. "My name is Andrew."

"All those books, the deaths of Eichmann and Marilyn, the Soviet missile crisis, all happened in 1962, the same year you went to jail for shooting your father."

"Exactly." Red-faced and angry, he stood up. "That's when my life stopped. I went to prison remembering the Soviet Missile Crisis, listening to Dylan singing 'Blowin' in the Wind.' Came out hearing about the Achille Loro Cruise ship, and listening to Def Leppard. For twenty six years, my life stopped. I don't really remember much between 1962 and 1988."

"So what are you trying to tell me?"

He reached for a shovel. "I'm not going back to jail Detective. Not now, not ever."

"You killed Judge Esel, Andrew."

He shrugged. "From everything I've heard, her death wasn't really a loss."

Tei pulled out a set of handcuffs. "C'mon Andrew, don't make this-"

Like a lion or a bear, he moved with one swift death stroke. Tei never saw the shovel come at her before he smashed her on the side of the head.

#

Her skin felt moist, and her vision finally went from blurry to clear. Her head pounded and blood dripped from her nose on the wooden floor. She moaned slightly. Her arms and legs were bound.

"Oh Tei, you're awake. Good."

"Why are you doing this? You-your mother is such a lovely person. She would never approve."

"Maybe not. But she did approve of me jamming two hat pins in the back of Judge Esel's neck." He smiled. "In fact, she did more than approve. Paid me two million dollars for it. Mother came through again. I spared her from getting more beatings from my father, the drunk. She paid me one million bucks in '62. I left it untouched, since I was otherwise engaged for the next twenty six years. And at five percent interest? That account is worth almost four million today. With the two million, Mother paid me to execute Judge Esel, I am worth nearly six million dollars now. Not bad after coming off a two decade stint in Rahway State Prison where I made seventeen cents a day."

"Andrew, your mother used you."

"And what of it?" He smiled. "But Mother always believed that children have different potentials. She knew what I was good at. I must tell you that she was a little disappointed that all the elite private school and a double major at Princeton didn't quite pay off the way she would have liked."

"Why? She didn't know what to do with an overqualified sociopath?" Tei muttered.

"She was embarrassed by my scrapes with the law. She had a particular hate for armed robbery."

"What are you going to do with me?"

Through a busted eyelid, Tei saw what looked like to two syringes lying on a small table. The cottage had one entrance and a few windows. But tied up to a chair, she wasn't going anyplace fast.

"Kill you the same way I killed the good judge. Except that I've filled the syringes with lidocaine so at least it will be quicker and less painful. I'm doing this out of respect for Mother, you know. You'll die a lot faster. Consider it a gift. I mean I really had to really wiggle the pins around in the old judge's neck while I held her by the hair. But then again, it wasn't intended to be a really pleasant execution. She offended Mother." He got up and walked over to her. "Sorry my dear, but I'm sitting on six million dollars, my freedom, and a plane ticket out of the country. I'm not letting you screw it up on me."

"People know I'm here."

"I don't think so." He started walking toward her armed with the syringe. "Even if they did, your people are a little slow. By the time anyone gets here, you shall be buried underneath one of those trees outside and I'll be long gone."

#

Mo pulled right behind Tei's car. She was nowhere insight. This wasn't good. "I'll go around the back." He directed the uniforms to look for Tei in the house. "You people go in through the house."

His stomach muscles tightened, and he felt sick. There went that bad feeling again, that cop sense, a heightened awareness when a situation isn't right.

He feared the worse. Tei was in danger, if she wasn't dead already.

Dashing into the woods, he saw a man moving inside of the cottage. He drew his weapon and kept walking. The man saw him and met him outside.

"Can I help you?"

"Yeah, Andrew. My partner Detective Wheeler was up here to speak to you. Where is she?" Mo's voice was controlled, but his stomach felt like the pistons of a Chevy engine in overdrive. He remembered that this was a cop's life: boredom, with moments of sheer terror. Right now, it was one of those terror moments.

"You know me? Good."

"Detective Wheeler is right inside." Mo watched as Saunford opened his arms and gestured like a waiter offering a patron the best seat at the Tavern on the Green.

Mo smirked and drew his weapon. "You first, big guy."

"As you wish."

Out of bloody eyes, Tei saw her partner. She panicked. "Mo! Stay out of here! Get the hell out!"

It was too late. Saunford grabbed two syringes and got behind Tei. "See what I have here, Detective?" Tei screamed as he jabbed the back of her neck with the lidocaine syringe. "See? One wrong move by you and she dies!"

Mo remained calm. "So what do you want me to do, Saunford? I ain't doin' shit until you untie my partner."

"You are not in charge, asshole!" He roared back. "I am! If I say so, the bitch dies!"

"Okay, you're in charge Andrew. I was wrong. You're in charge." He tried to talk to his partner. "You doing okay there, Tei?"

"I'm bleeding, I got a headache the size of the Grand Canyon and I'm about to get unnecessary acupuncture." She quipped nastily. "How the hell do you think I'm doing?" Tei didn't know what she enjoyed less, having her life snuffed out by a lunatic or being called a bitch. Either choice had no appeal.

Mo watched Saunford give a big smile. Obviously, he greatly enjoyed the exchange between the two. But back to business. "Here is what I require, Detective. First of all, have all your uniformed officers leave. Now."

"Deal." Mo picked up his walkie-talkie. "Yeah, it's me. Alright, I want everybody out there to stand down. I got a situation here. Let's all be cool about this. You read me?"

"And I also want you to drop your weapon. A simple request."

"Okay." Mo said.

Saunford was the scariest kind of killer because he was unpredictable. His use of language was almost schizophrenic. He copiously avoided the use of contractions yet jumped on words like "bitch" when he felt out of control. Mo's stomach burned on the inside. He had to think quick. What could he give Saunford without really giving him anything? If Mo dropped his weapon, they were both good as dead. He looked at his partner again.

"Hey Saunford."

"Yes."

"I just want to make sure my partner is okay. You know she's a mother with kids."

Saunford sighed, and kept the needle in her neck. "So was mine and look at me. Spawning infants does not a mother make. But if you want one final indulgence before she dies, go ahead. Drop your weapon *first*."

"Okay. I'm cool." Holding out his arm away from his body, he placed the gun on the floor beside him. Cocking his head side to side like the RCA Victor's dog listening for his master's voice, he looked at Tei.

"You sure you're okay? I mean you must feel awful right about now. Oh man. I feel like shit, myself. My neck is killing me." He began to crack his neck like an amateur chiropractor. Finally, he heard a nice crunching sound. "There. I feel better now. A nice right crunch. Oh yeah, that's it." He rolled his shoulders back and forth.

She just had the side of her head bashed in with a shovel. If she weren't tied to a chair with a syringe jammed into her neck by a homicidal maniac, she'd kick Mo in the balls. Where was he going with this bullshit? Then it dawned on her. The crazy bastard was trying to tell her something.

Saunford was left handed. She leaned hard right, forcing her chair to fall over on its side. Saunford looked down. His hand slipped, and the needle clumsily pulled out of her neck. Tei heard a blast, as she lay like a beached whale, still tied to a chair.

Hitting the ground with a loud "Thud," the body of Andrew Saunford lay alongside of her. His immense blue eyes were frozen open, as a tiny stream of blood trickled out of the side of his mouth. Andrew Saunford, the almost six million dollar man, joined the ranks of the dead with a lidocaine syringe in his hand.

Mo stood frozen in position with his gun pointed into empty air space. He'd just killed another man. Another body to add to his list.

Seconds later, uniforms rushed in. "Take my partner to a hospital. She might have a concussion." The uniforms untied Tei and placed her in a waiting ambulance outside of the cottage.

Since Baldwin's demise, Lieutenant Larry Miller was now Captain Miller. He walked in. "I saw the whole thing, Rodriguez. It was a clean shoot. Sharp shooters were supposed to do the deed if you couldn't. But I'm afraid-"

"Yeah, yeah you have to take my gun."

"Thanks, Mo. I'm sorry."

Mo rubbed his forehead. "This sucks."

"You did what you had to do to save your partner."

"It's not over." Mo looked up. "There's one more skell out there. Only this one's an octogenarian."

"Don't worry about her. She'll turn up," said Miller. "In the meantime, fill out your paperwork, and get the hell out of here for a few days."

"Look, there's a mentally handicapped man and his social worker in my car. He thought Saunford was his buddy. Do me a favor. Get them outta here before he sees Saunford's body."

"Will do."

As paramedics carried Tei away, Clarefield came in. He hovered over the body of Andrew Saunford, while his assistants fanned out. He looked around.

"Who the hell do you think you are, Rodriguez? Wyatt Earp? Doc Holliday? This isn't the Okay Corral, its goddamn suburban New Jersey. Every dead guy in the morgue has your name on it. You're wearing me out, pal. Why do you insist on shooting everybody? Be a lover not a fighter, like me."

"Shut up and sit down." He looked at Clarefield. "She's still out there, Tom. I think the old biddy set this whole thing up. She wanted Andrew dead. And she had me do it."

"The Brinkworth woman?"

"Yeah."

"Where is she?"

"Don't know. Saunford said that he planned on being long gone, just like his mother."

Clarefield shook his head. "I generally don't believe in this conspiracy theory crap, but with what's happened to you lately ..."

"Anything is possible," the two men chimed simultaneously.

Chapter 27

Mo finally settled down. It was his second day off, and life was good. Not a dead body in sight, no Claudette, or manipulative little old broads arranging to have people they don't like killed. As he lay in bed in the early morning hours, except for the occasional thought of a naked woman, his mind reached a wonderful, peaceful state.

Unfortunately the phone rang.

He answered it. "If you're not Cindy Crawford, then goodbye."

Through the static he heard a soft sweet voice. "Hello? Hello? Detective Rodriguez?"

"Holy shit!" He sat up in bed. "Sophiah, where are you?"

"About twenty thousand feet in the air and another hour to go."

"Sophiah, listen to me. You have to turn yourself in. I know you used Andrew to kill your husband. Then you bribed him to kill Judge Esel. You'll never get away with this." He was desperate. "You-you're too old!"

"Nonsense." The ancient bird laughed. "I never paid him a dime and I did say that I could never kill anyone *personally*. All I did was suggest that he take his trust money early. I'm a wealthy woman, you know. And the old drunken bastard who used to beat me and my children? *C'est la vie*. Sorry, I had to involve you and Tei with Andrew. He wasn't a very nice boy, was he? But you know what they say. The secret to success is to outlast your failures."

He tried to remain calm. He wanted to reach through the phone and strangle the old bitch. "Sophiah, this isn't *Arsenic and Old Lace*. You nearly got me and Tei killed. Where are you?"

"Headed for the fourth largest island in the world. Landing in a wonderful place called Antananarivo."

"Where the hell is that?"

"Madagascar. I've donated about two hundred thousand to a small Christian parish in Madagascar that teaches English and Christianity. Since I have none of my own anymore, I've decided to return to teaching children. Isn't that wonderful? I do so love kids."

"There weren't any kids in this country you could help? What gives Sophiah? The government doesn't have an extradition treaty for murder-for-hire in Madagascar?"

"Precisely." She giggled. "You figured it out."

"Sophiah, no matter where you are, I'll keep track of you. And if you set foot in the States, you're mine, babe. So sleep in your grass hut down there with one eye open."

"So sorry to have irritated you, Detective." She replied innocently. "I just called to say 'farewell'. I actually thought quite highly of you and Tei."

"That's a shame, Sophiah, 'cause I don't think much of murderers." He slammed the phone down. As truly pissed off as he was, he had to hand it to the old broad. She had her husband and a judge she hated, murdered. When she had no use for her son, she put things in motion to have him killed by the police. She cleverly watched her enemies, McShand and Cane, become victims of their own greed. Who knows if she wasn't the anonymous tip to Cane about McShand's secret life? Sophiah Brinkworth didn't care how the bodies dropped, so long as they dropped. She was good.

In a way, he envied her callousness.

He closed his eyes. He couldn't believe a killer woke him up. Now he wanted his euphoric slumber back. Not to be. His doorbell rang. Mo hopped out of bed, threw on a pair of gym shorts and ran downstairs. Cautiously, he looked out of the window. It was a bandaged, banged up, but very much alive Tei Wheeler.

He opened the door and greeted her with a kiss. "Hey girlfriend. How you feeling?"

"Better. At least my head's not pounding anymore."

"Good. Guess who I heard from?"

"Sophiah Brinkworth. The old hag called me this morning from an Air Phone. Do you believe this crap? I want that dried out little alligator ass in jail. She played us. She played us good."

184

"Forget it. Madagascar has no extradition treaties with the U.S. There's nothing we can do. I'm not worried about her, Tei. She'll be back. Want some coffee?"

Before he could put up some coffee, the doorbell rang again. Cautiously, he opened the door to Sheriff Fred Peters who chomped on the end of a stogie.

"Hey Peters, what's up?"

"Mo, your full name Moraimo Maximilliano Rodriguez?"

"Yup. M.M. Rodriguez .Who wants to know?"

The Sheriff handed him an envelope. "Sorry pal. Consider yourself served. It's a shitty world we live in, Rodriguez, a shitty world." He turned and left.

Mo opened the envelope and read the caption. "Hopmeyer v. the City of Hackensack, Bergen County Prosecutor's Office, Investigator Moraimo M. Rodriguez, Estate of Terence McShand, Esquire, et al." He skimmed over the contents of the complaint, then began cursing in Spanish. "I'm being sued."

Tei looked over his shoulder. "You being sued? What for? Killing all those people?"

"No! No! Remember that old fart playing Yosemite Sam when McShand's corpse was driving around in the Mercedes? This old codger is suing me, and the county for, get this, the vehicular destruction of property. His goddam grass! Claims McShand's car crushing his new patio grass was foreseeable and I didn't do enough to prevent it." He flung the document. "I shoulda shot the old bastard when I had the chance."

"He's suing you for squashing his grass?"

"Yeah."

Tei chuckled. Then she guffawed. By the time the conversation was over, the detectives' eyes were wet from tears of laughter. It was the first real laugh they'd had in months. When Mo gained his composure, he would call Clarefield and tell him about the lawsuit. The medical examiner would get a charge out of the wrongful murder of new grass. And knowing Clarefield, the crazy doctor would no doubt demand to autopsy the flattened seedlings to determine the cause of death.

Laughter is a good thing. Sometimes a man's just gotta laugh. It's all he can do to chase away the dead guy blues.

Theodore ("Ted") R. McCormick is a life long New Jersey resident. McCormick has worked in various law enforcement capacities. He enjoys baseball, deep sea fishing, and his stalwart companion, a dog named Fatboy.